CW01149785

CHASING SHADOWS

PETER W. ASHOOH

CHASING SHADOWS

Terrorist, Gangsters and Bankers and the Al Capone Method

THE FBI IN A POST 9/11 WORLD

CITI OF BOOKS

Copyright © 2024 by Peter W. Ashooh.

All rights reserved. No part of this publication may be reproduced, distributed, or transmitted in any form or by any means, including photocopying, recording, or other electronic or mechanical methods, without the prior written permission of the copyright owner and the publisher, except in the case of brief quotations embodied in critical reviews and certain other noncommercial uses permitted by copyright law. For permission requests, write to the publisher, addressed "Attention: Permissions Coordinator," at the address below.

CITIOFBOOKS, INC.
3736 Eubank NE Suite A1
Albuquerque, NM 87111-3579
www.citiofbooks.com
Hotline: 1 (877) 389-2759
Fax: 1 (505) 930-7244

Ordering Information:
Quantity sales. Special discounts are available on quantity purchases by corporations, associations, and others. For details, contact the publisher at the address above.

Printed in the United States of America.

ISBN-13:	Softcover	979-8-89391-450-4
	Hardcover	979-8-89391-452-8
	eBook	979-8-89391-451-1

Library of Congress Control Number: 2024923998

Table of Contents

Introduction vii
I. Worst Day Ever 1
II. The Five Thousand Arab Male Interviews 9
III. Investigating Dead Guys 13
IV. Reluctant Witness 25
V. Playing Whack-A-Mole 85
VI. All of the Above 89
VII. Gangsters or Terrorists? The Al Capone Method 103
VIII. The Terrorists Next Door 171
IX. All Others 221
X. Following the Money—Following the Cars 235
XI. A Week Blowing Up Cars 255
XII. From Baltimore to Beirut 267
XIII. I'm Here to Change Your Lightbulb… 273
XIV. Another Bite at the Apple 287
XV. The Bankers 301
XVI. Unfinished Business 309
XVII. A Parting Shot 313
Disclaimer 325
References 327
Index 331

Introduction

I joined the FBI in October 1979, shortly after graduating from the College of William and Mary in Williamsburg, Virginia. My intent was to work for the Bureau for a few years and then attend law school. After almost five years serving as an intelligence analyst at FBI Headquarters, I had by then taken and passed the entrance exam for the FBI Academy at Quantico, Virginia to begin New Agents training. No sense in law school now. In the long run, I had saved tens of thousands of dollars paying for law school and would embark on a lifelong career that I'm certain I would have still chosen to pursue with or without a law degree. I was also now a second-generation FBI agent; my father having served from 1953 until 1967. On the day of graduation, my father was there on the stage to present me with my credentials.

After graduating from Quantico in the summer of 1984, I was assigned, with my new wife Wini, to the New Orleans Field Office. I began with applicant investigations and civil rights violations but quickly fell into specializing in organized crime investigations, being initiated into the undercover world rather early on. Developing Confidential Human Sources, or

"CHSs" generally a requirement for all Special Agents, would also become something for which I found I had somewhat of a calling, and would prove to be the most productive, frustrating, risky and fascinating part of my 35 years in the FBI. As the story unfolds in the various chapters, I hope it will become clear how important the ethical development, handling, and operation of sources, while crupulously staying within the rules, is to the vast majority of federal investigations. The FBI is also well known for its use of undercover operations and sensitive investigative techniques such as wiretaps. Nothing covered in this book reveals any sources or methods not already known by the public. All cases detailed have been litigated in some fashion and are in the public domain, whether revealed in a press release, newspaper article, online discussion, or having been made public in open court, whether by trial, or hearings, or during a plea or sentencing in open court, available to family members and the general public. I submitted the original manuscript to the FBI for prepublication review. I will admit It was an 18-month ordeal that should have only taken three or four months at the most. In the end I feel confident I have done my due diligence. In the end, I believe this book will celebrate the real FBI and the true believer "street agent" in field offices across the country who are the backbone of the real FBI I used to know.

    I spent five years in New Orleans and was gifted with two new sons, Nick, and Ben. Then, right in the middle of a major organized crime investigation, where I had spent several years developing multiple significant CHSs and developing the probable cause for installing wiretaps on several high-ranking members, I received a routine transfer to my "top twelve office", Newark. I fought to stay until the case was concluded but I was refused. The case faded away in my absence only to be renewed a year or so later when the inspection team came in and pretty much asked "what the hell?". After landing in New Jersey, Griff, our third son was born. Three's a charm.

My eight years in the northern New Jersey satellite office known as the "Garret Mountain Resident Agency" in West Paterson, working again organized crime, resulted in over 90 convictions related to "traditional" organized crime, such as the "Mafia", or as the Bureau referred to it, the La Cosa Nostra, or LCN, ("This Thing of Ours") as well as a relatively new phenomenon, Middle Eastern criminal enterprises. Fortunately, I had found great partners in several other agencies, notably the Passaic County and Bergen County Prosecutor's Offices' investigators, the former Immigration and Naturalization Service or INS, the Paterson Police Department, and the IRS, who were all key to the success of these investigations. Many of the investigators from those agencies became close friends as well.

Agents are encouraged to take on collateral duties, such as joining the Evidence response Team, SWAT, or certify as a firearms or defensive tactics instructor, and often cross train in multiple complimentary disciplines. The undercover program is also very selective and demanding and very few are drawn to that life. I found myself heavily involved in the undercover world, along with serving as a SWAT operator for a short period, and as a firearms instructor and defensive tactics instructor for over 20 years.

I've spent over 50 years in the Martial Arts, and for the past 25 or so years, Okinawan style Isshin-Ryu Karate, which gave me an opportunity to provide after-hours training to my colleagues in every office in which I served, many of whom achieved Black Belts of their own. This I think also provided us with an hour or two to decompress and maybe a little camaraderie, and I found was a significant coping mechanism for the long hours, stress, and sometimes loneliness that came with the job.

But after 13 years away, I knew I needed to take the family back home to Virginia, so I applied, and I was accepted to a position and promotion as a Supervisory Tactical Instructor in the Practical Applications Unit "Hogan's Alley" at Quantico. I often reminded the New Agent Trainees that I planned to return to working cases in a few years and may end up as their squad mate or partner someday. That happily turned out to be truer than I ever expected. Over the years I had many chances to work cases with agents whom I had trained at Quantico. Several even eventually became my boss in later years. Go figure.

After three years at Quantico, it was time to return to "the street". I stepped down and landed on the Safe Streets and Cold Case squad at Washington Field in April 2000. After a year, I was transferred to an Organized Crime squad at the Northern Virginia Resident Agency in Tysons, Virginia to pursue a Middle Eastern drug trafficking network in Northern Virginia.

I only begin the book halfway into my career, on the day of September 11, 2001. The Title, "Chasing Shadows" has been used in other books as I have discovered, but it so clearly defines the effort and the struggle to investigate international terrorism in the US post 9/11, and it was a very common phrase many of us used to describe the struggles of working counter terrorism. The subtitle "Terrorists, Gangsters and Bankers" were those shadows I in particular found myself chasing.

After 9/11 the FBI switched gears and became focused on, and necessarily so, attempting to preempt future terrorist attacks. This effort proved to be a highly "damned if you and damned if you don't" dilemma. Some of us of like mind, over time, developed methods that were up to a point successful in navigating those dangerous waters. The subtitle also hopefully captures the collusive nature of the terrorist networks with criminal organizations and sadly even the financial sector. Over time, were able to at least neutralize and occasionally dismantle these networks. Most often, we found the most effective method was to find investigative means to "take them off of the playing field". We focused on their daily criminal activities raising, moving, and utilizing funds to traffic in arms, drugs, counterfeit currency, stolen vehicles, and the like. Human Source directed and undercover operations and electronic surveillance or "wiretaps" were key in identifying these conspiracies and in building a strong body of evidence, while avoiding the pitfalls of entrapment, circular intelligence collection, and confirmation bias.

The FBI has changed drastically over the one hundred-plus years of its existence. I was fortunate to serve during a period that I consider to be a "golden age" of the bureau, in the 1980s, 1990s and early 2000s, when we were trusted and universally regarded as the premier law enforcement agency in the world. We almost completely wiped out the mafia, solved massive financial criminal conspiracies, were catching significant spies, and taking down corrupt public officials. The FBI is at this writing, going through a rough period of its own making, and that concerns me greatly. Most major dramas within the bureau can historically be traced to FBI management mismanagement and self-serving insularity and careerism. But the vast majority of the roughly 13,000 FBI Special Agents and 35,000 or so employees, are simply going to work every day and pursuing complex and important investigations and operations that protect the American people.

I am very confident that the people of the FBI will eventually right the ship, probably after much internal and external turmoil, and return to its roots as a non-political, even-handed law enforcement organization. I spoke recently with a currently serving agent and a longtime friend whom I mention at length later in this book, who reminded me of the many significant cases and operations currently being conducted by agents across the country in cyber defense, child exploitation and rescues, and "safe streets" efforts. The vast majority of agents are doing what they always do, without regard to politics, and without expectation of reward or accolades.

I was and remain proud of my former agency and the people who were willing to put themselves at risk, work ridiculously long hours for weeks and months at a time, travel to far-off, dangerous countries, and defend and protect our country.

Retired Special Agents are provided with FBI credentials, the same as we carry when still on board, but stamped "retired". I carry those credentials with me everywhere.

I.

Worst Day Ever

September 11, 2001, just after 8:46 am; FBI Washington Field Office, "WFO", Northern Virginia Resident Agency, Tysons, Virginia:

The Squad Supervisors Office was crowded, everyone on the squad and a few from other squads were gathered in front of the TV set on the wall above his desk. We had all been called in to watch the news feed concerning a believed small plane that had crashed into the North Tower of the World Trade Center in Manhattan. We all stood around frozen as the damage was becoming evident and the smoke and flames belched from a gaping hole in the top third of the building. After a few minutes we instinctively felt the need to get back out to the squad area and get to work. We didn't get far. The second, now obviously commercial airliner slammed into the South tower at 9:03 am. Now we all knew what was happening as did the rest of the country.

Poor New York we thought, both the city, the people and of course the New York Field Office of the FBI whose members would now be absolutely overwhelmed as the tip of the spear investigating a major terrorist attack. We still hadn't witnessed the worst of it yet.

The rest of us had to address our own investigations so reluctantly we filed out of the office. I had to head into DC to conduct a meeting with a defense attorney who represented several cooperating defendants in a "yuppy" drug trafficking network that had been operating in the city nightclubs. I was assigned to an organized crime squad, so the whole terrorism thing was not my problem. Famous last words.

As I headed East on Route 66 into the city, I turned on the radio. Undoubtedly the news would be wall to wall coverage of the towers attack in New York. The worst of it was now happening. The towers were collapsing. People were jumping from their windows from floors engulfed in flames. The country watched in horror. The announcer on the radio was hysterically describing the collapse as the buildings disappeared in massive clouds of smoke and debris. We would not know the true carnage of civilians, police, firefighters and first responders until much later. This would extend to even years and decades later as police officers, firefighters and FBI agents succumbed to cancers caused by the extended inhalation of chemicals emitted from the wreckage during search efforts at the sites in New York, the Pentagon, and Shanksville, Pennsylvania. As I Approached Rosslyn, the dense, high-rise business district just across from DC and Georgetown and next to Arlington National Cemetery, in the upper corner of my windshield appeared a twin-engine commercial airliner angling downward at a crazy, steep angle but in the opposite direction from what would be a logical landing pattern at National Airport. My view quickly changed as the road curved away in the opposite direction. Route 66 tends to wind North and South as it approaches the city and is lined by trees interspersed with high rise apartments and businesses. As the road curved back toward the South-East, and I passed under a series of overpasses, the plane was again visible for a second as it continued its steep dive and disappeared behind the trees. The radio was still blaring with details of the Trade Center collapse. Again, the road curved away and then back towards the direction of the plane. What I saw now was a tall white mushroom cloud rising above the buildings and trees. I guess I initially hoped to convince myself it was just a smokestack emission from some power plant nearby. It was not. I was witnessing another terrorist plane attack now in here in DC. This was American Airlines Flight 77, a scheduled American Airlines flight originating at Dulles International Airport in Virginia and destined for Los Angeles International Airport carrying 58 passengers and six crewmembers. Less than 35 minutes into the flight the hijackers stormed the cockpit and assumed control of the flight, while the passengers called their relatives and friends to report on what was happening. And say goodbye.

Watching it on the news was one thing, it was now right in front of me, and I was driving right toward it. I was of course unaware of the trauma occurring on the flight itself until much later.

As I rounded the curve from 66 onto 110 South, the Pentagon came into view, engulfed in a massive white cloud of smoke and what appeared to be flames. It resembled a volcanic eruption. The cloud of smoke was turning dark. The FBI radio in my car erupted in panicked voices. Other agents from the Washington Field Office "WFO", were desperately trying to coordinate a response and additionally anticipate possibly more attacks. Various voices, some of whom I recognized, were simultaneously asking and answering rapid firing questions as to who should respond to the Pentagon and trying to determine the details of what had happened.

Strangely a minute or so later I observed a large boxy aircraft, directly overhead make what appeared to a "U-turn" in the air, and head back in the direction of the Pentagon. Only years later would I find out that it had been a National Guard C-130H cargo plane that had been called back from a flight to Minnesota to follow Flight 77 after its transponder had been turned off and lost to the FAA tracking it.

The road was now blocked off by two Virginia State Troopers, just past an entrance to National Cemetery. I took the entrance ramp up a small incline into the edge of the cemetery and pulled over to listen to the radio and figure out where I should be going. I was not a bomb tech or a designated first responder or evidence specialist, I was a proactive case agent tasked with investigating criminal enterprises and conspiracies.

The radio chatter was suddenly shattered by a frightened voice announcing that a car bomb had exploded outside of the State Department. This later turned out be false, but we never found out how this rumor was started. After several minutes of debate over the bogus State Department car bomb, it got worse. There was now a report that another plane was headed towards DC. I was still parked at the cemetery. Agents had begun arriving at the Pentagon. Multiple voices were shouting over the air to get out of the Pentagon and away from the area. This was real. But it never arrived. It crashed in Shanksville, Pennsylvania as the nation found out shortly thereafter.

I decided it was time for me to make a move, and head into the main office. I got past the troopers and made it onto Constitution Avenue. It was numbingly slow going. Traffic was at a standstill. Government and law enforcement vehicles were "going code" with lights and sirens in all directions, weaving through traffic and even jumping curbs to get around the jam. Confused and panicked people wandered around the Washington Mall and reflecting pool area in confusion, their cell phones clearly not working.

I finally made it to the intersection of Constitution and 3rd Street. The intersection was jammed. A man in a business suit was directing traffic. I recognized him as an agent from WFO and identified myself. I was not far from the office and guessed that was where he would direct me. Instead, he asked that I head to the home of US Attorney General John Ashcroft to provide security. I met several other agents on the front porch of the house. We stood there for several hours until someone was able to determine that Ashcroft was not even in town, and we were directed to get to WFO.

I arrived at WFO and was directed to a command post that had been activated. I was teamed up with another agent, Joe Palermo to head down to the Route 1 corridor just North of Mt. Vernon, Virginia to interview the manager of a motel who believed she had witnessed several motel guests gathered in the motel parking lot, cheering the terrorist attacks. The guests were described as appearing to be of Middle Eastern descent. Having grown up in the nearby Franconia area, I knew this Route 1 corridor well. The motels along this route were known to be cheap, low quality, and home to transients and drug dealers and sex workers. The manager was very cooperative and provided all the information she had identifying the guests who were now not in their room and appeared to have left in a hurry. We headed back to the office. It was now getting late, and we had been on the job for over fourteen hours. On the way back, the need for coffee struck. We pulled into the Krispy Kreme doughnut shop on Route 1. It struck me that this was the shop where my family got doughnuts and coffee after church on Sundays as a child. It had been many years since those days, and this would be the last time I would ever visit the shop.

The last stop would be the Pentagon. It was very dark by now and the massive building, built during World War II to house the then War Department, was lighted by spotlights, and we were awestruck by the damage. In front of us was a dark, gaping, massive, smoking hole in the western façade. The smell was overwhelming; black, acrid, chemical fumes, smoke and flames still bellowed from the hole. We picked our way among large pieces of debris scattered all around the ground in front of the hole. We then met up with another agent whom we recognized from WFO and were informed that rescue operations had been paused and there was not much we could contribute at that point so Joe and I returned to the office. Around 1am we were dismissed and instructed to return around 6am the next morning. We were all going to be functioning on little sleep or time off for the next few months.

II.

The Five Thousand Arab Male Interviews

The next few weeks meant 16-hour days, seven days a week, alternating between days at the Pentagon pulling security duty and being assigned interviews of suspected non-citizen Middle Eastern males who were believed to be residing in the country, and of various individuals whom to someone who called into the now operating tip line phone bank appeared to be Middle Eastern, many of whom turned out to Indian or Sikh. It was the turban and a foreign accent that apparently caused their confusion. Several interviews did produce some substantive information. The plane had circled over DC and flew at almost treetop level over Pentagon City, which is a commercial and residential area directly across Route 95 from the Pentagon. I spoke with a resident of an apartment complex in Pentagon City who had actually observed Flight 77 fly almost directly over his building on its final approach towards the Pentagon. A second interview on the same day involved a family visiting the US from Ethiopia and staying in a hotel in the same area. Again, the same observation; the plane had flown just over the height of the high-rise buildings and was visible through the windows of their hotel room. Multiple interviews of this type would certainly dispel any of the later silly claims that it had been a missile that had hit the Pentagon.

By this time, the wreckage of Flight 77 had relinquished the identities of the five Arab males who had hijacked the airliner and crashed it into the Pentagon, so therefore any Middle Eastern male living in the US on a visa or even a "green card" was deemed a suspect by FBI management. The WFO command center was located on the first floor of the building at 601 4th Street. At that time, it was a new, impressive facility lined with glass enclosed conference rooms and rows of desks equipped with the newest computers to which the FBI had access--of course never the newest computers available.

Upon entering the center in order to receive my day's assignment, I immediately noticed the disorganization and confusion going on. I had to ask around in order to determine who was in charge. It appeared that no one was. I looked around to identify who would be charged with managing the intelligence flow, the results of the days' interviews, and assigning new leads. It was clear certain agents had taken the reigns on their own initiative to try to coordinate and organize the effort without management direction. My previous assignment immediately prior to landing at WFO was as an instructor of new agents at the FBI Academy in Quantico, Virginia. Part of our delegated curriculum involved basic "command post operations". Clearly the basics were not at this point being employed. Agents were returning to the command center after having conducted interviews of individuals who had literally been previously interviewed as many as ten times. WFO executive management was noticeably absent from the scene. As it turned out they were ensconced in one of those glass enclosed conference rooms. Not sure doing what.

After several days I was then attached to an international terrorism squad along with other members of my criminal squad. Fortunately, the squad supervisor, Tom Frields was a reasonable and experienced agent, and we were given a specific investigative direction. The horrendous task of digging through the rubble of the Pentagon was the burden of the WFO Evidence Response Team along with of course the many firefighters from Arlington, Fairfax County, DC, and others who had to put out the massive fires engulfing the crash site. Bodies and related personal effects were being extracted from the wreckage. The consensus came about quickly as to the identities of the individuals who had hijacked not only Flight 77 but the other three flights. Among the items found were the non-driver's identification cards of Hani S. H. Hanjour, Khalid M. A. Almidhar, Nawaf Al-Hazmi, Majed M.GH. Moqed, and Salem Al Hazmi. The address noted on each card was the same; 5913 Leesburg Pike, Apartment #8, except for Salem Alhazmi whose address was listed as 3355 Row Street, Falls Church. How did they obtain these IDs?

The FBI by this time had initiated a massive nationwide investigation titled "PENTTBOMB", Major Case #182. PENTTBOMB, an acronym denoting the Pentagon and Trade Towers (although the "Bomb" part was quickly realized to be inaccurate, but it stuck) was considered a criminal case in that it was an investigation of a mass homicide. This was what is known as a "reactive case", meaning in general that the crime had already been committed and the investigation was focused on identifying and apprehending the perpetrators. This was the FBI's historical strength in terrorism matters. No agency was as talented and capable as the FBI at crime scene investigations as evidenced by the previous investigations of the terrorist bombings the World Trade Center in 1993, the Oklahoma City bombing in 1995, the two simultaneous embassy bombings in Kenya and Tanzania in 1998, and of the guided missile destroyer USS Cole in Yemen in 2008. The September 11 attacks would now instigate a sea change in how the FBI was expected to address terrorism. From that day forward we would be tasked with proactively preventing acts of terrorism. Intelligence collection was the emphasis rather than collecting evidence. The fear that there were more hijackers planning additional attacks drove us forward.

III.

Investigating Dead Guys

The team was partnered with Virginia State Department of Motor Vehicles "DMV" Agents in False Church, Virginia. DMV Special Agent Eduardo "Ed" Torre was our new partner. We quickly developed a great relationship with Ed. He had a good sense of humor, however, was also serious about not only solving this dilemma, but he and his fellow DMV agents had been gravely concerned for several years about the ease in which Virginia driver's licenses could be procured. Fraud was rampant.

Our concern was that although at this point, we were "investigating dead guys", there was a distinct possibility that there were other plots in the works. Because all five of the now "Flight 77 hijackers" had used the same address for their IDs, I wildly speculated if there were others still waiting to wage a second wave, could we possibly identify them by conducting a reverse look-up in the DMV database by searching addresses rather than names? Little would I expect that it led to not only a significant discovery but much conflict and actual competition among the many agents assigned to PENTTBOM teams. Fortunately, there were also many who cared more about the mission than themselves.

Further investigation relative to the address 5913 Leesburg Pike, Falls Church Virginia, determined the address was located in the Cullmore section of Falls Church-addresses used by the hijackers Khalid M A Almidhar and Hani S H Hanjour, Majed M GH Moqed. Salem M S Alhazmi, used 3355 Row Street, #3, Falls Church, which was determined to be a non-existent address. The address used by Abdul Aziz Al Omari was found to be 915 Buchanan, Apt. #27. He was later identified as one of the hijackers of American Airlines Flight 11 which had crashed into the North Tower of the World Trade Center.

ED Torre described to us how the current system for obtaining a Virginia driver's license had inadvertently encouraged widespread fraud whereby an individual could obtain a non-driver's license ID by appearing at a Virginia DMV office in the company of anyone who was willing to swear on a Virginia DL51 form that that applicant was a resident at the second individual's place of residence. The team began pouring through boxes of records to identify who had possibly "vouched" for the hijackers in order to obtain their ID cards. It turned out that someone named Luis Martinez-Flores had "vouched" for Almidhar and Hanjour, who then in turn "vouched" for Moqed.

Yes, we were looking for Middle Eastern names. Of approximately 150 names, only the names of the hijackers and two other Middle Eastern names were identified—unexpected new names that turned out to be the kick-off of a manhunt for another individual, possibly the first individual who had known and assisted the Flight 77 hijackers, whether witting or unwitting, however who eventually would certainly fill in many of the blanks as to the activities of the hijackers up until that horrible day. One of which was Abdel Rahman Omar Tawfiq Alfauru, listed as having an address of 127 South Fairfax Street Box 134, Alexandria, Virginia. Alfauru was also listed as having a second address of 5913 Leesburg Pike. Additional searching located a DL-51 form for Alfauru with a certifying person listed as Eyad Alrababah, also at 5913 Leesburg Pike, Falls Church, Virginia. Alfauru in turn certified on a DL-51 that another individual resided at the same address.

Alrababah's name stood out to Torre immediately. He now became the focus of the investigation. Torre recognized Alrababah as having been a subject of a past DMV prosecution for conducting an illicit business of "fraudulently obtaining Virginia ID card for non-Virginia residents for a fee". Alrababah had pled guilty to state misdemeanor charges related to his business. Torre produced a DMV Customer Primary Information printout listing Alrababah at the above address with a notation to the effect "Subject does not live in Virginia. Mr. Alrababah lives in New Jersey and was fraudulently affirming residency on Dl-51s. Alrababah's address was listed falsely as 127 Fairfax St., #134, Alexandria, Virginia, with a true address listed as 22 C Washington

Dr., West Patterson (sic), N.J." (It's actually Paterson). His singular piece of information launched a multi-state search for an individual who at that point had only the most tenuous connection to the events of September 11, but who would turn out to be the first identified, living individual, who had associated with and assisted the hijackers, however unwittingly.

My next step was of course, to document all these pieces of information, and begin to communicate with other field divisions, specifically the Newark Division, significantly the satellite office, or resident agency at West Paterson, NJ, (where I had served for eight years prior to instructing at Quantico, and then finally WFO). We still didn't know if Alrababah knew the hijackers, but this was the closest we had to a viable lead at this point and we were all desperate to determine if there were additional hijackers preparing for more attacks. We also needed to fill in the blanks as to how this could have happened, including identifying any living co-conspirators or anyone who had provided material support or assisted the hijackers in any way.

The focus on Alrababah concerned the possibility that that there were other terrorist plots in play and that he may have knowledge of association with individuals involved. His own involvement with the hijackers was still a question, but he was the one solid lead we had. So many agents were chasing so many diverse leads that we could afford to pursue this one. We also needed to identify who sponsored or "vouched" for the "dead guys". This was important because those individuals could possibly be part of a support network that was still in operation.

As I pursued the Alrababah thread, other teammates analyzed the DMV records to reveal who "vouched" for Hanjour, et al. For better or worse, it now appeared my DMV printouts had now become the holy grail. This also resulted in other agents and supervisors jockeying to claim ownership. A squad supervisor from a separate squad visited our squad area inquiring about the DMV printouts. At first, I was encouraged; the effort was being taken seriously. I had already served as a Special Agent for 16 years, had served in the New Orleans Office for five years investigating the local Mafia family (also known as "la Cosa Nostra", or the "LCN" in FBI parlance). I had served for eight years in the Newark Division, coincidentally in the Paterson, NJ Resident Agency (which became notable shortly), investigating the various Mafia families operating in Northern New Jersey (think "the Sopranos") along with, of all things, Middle Eastern criminal enterprises. I was fortunate to work closely with a team of Immigration agents, County Prosecutor's investigators, IRS agents, US Postal Inspectors, and other law enforcement officers, garnering over 90 convictions. For three years prior to landing at WFO, I served as a Supervisory Instructor at the FBI Academy at Quantico, Virginia, as I mentioned earlier. Yet I think no matter what an agent has accomplished in the past, it's never enough, both personally and usually in the eyes of FBI managementhence the expression "what have you done for me lately". We all wanted to have the "Big Case" and I was just as susceptible to this need as anyone else. But damn it, this was my work.

The squad supervisor who visited our squad was not there to give a pat on the back for my work or to offer assistance. She was there to snatch the DMV records. She then made copies of the records and provided them to the agents on her squad. This now caused a parallel investigation where my team would interview someone and then they would be re-interviewed by the other squad. Occasionally they would get there first. This conflict reached a crescendo when Alrababah emerged in the New Haven, Connecticut Division.

In the meantime, Special Agent (SA) Brian Weidner began looking into the individuals who co-signed for Hanjour and his crew of mass murderers. I had by this time partnered up with two other agents, Rick Cimakasky, and Dena P., both of whom were criminal agents, Dena being a squad mate of mine, and Rick being a close friend from another squad. We decided to head down to Cullmore and see if we could talk to some of the migrants who collected in the parking lots in the area trying to secure day labor employment. Fortunately, Dena is a fluent Spanish speaker. We walked up to the group of Hispanic males congregating in the parking lot of a Mobil gas station. We began asking around if anyone had encountered any unusual individuals several months ago who were looking for driver's licenses. The first guys we spoke with told us they had been approached by some "Pakistani guys" in a van who had picked them up, with the Hispanic males initially believing they were being driven to a day job. When the "Pakistanis" instead asked them to assist them at the DMV, they declined and were returned to the parking lot; however they then directed the van driver and passenger to speak with another Hispanic male wo would be willing to help them at the DMV.

As memorialized in an FBI reporting form "FD-302", or commonly referred to simply as a "302" dated October 2, 2001, on September 20, Weidner and Torre located and interviewed Victor Manual Lopez-Flores, based on the Mobil gas station lead. Weidner conducted the interview and Torre provided translation. It should be noted anyone interviewed under these circumstances were provided with an advice of rights form. Lopez stated his sole source of income consisted of assisting ineligible individuals in obtaining Virginia photo identification cards. After a few minutes of word games and equivocation Flores admitted he had assisted over 100 people, all of whom he assumed had been illegal aliens, to obtain Virginia IDs for a fee of $40 for each ID. Several weeks earlier Lopez was loitering at his usual place of business, in the area of the "Dollar Store and Mobil gas station" on Four Mile Run and DMV Drive, where he would loiter and wait to be approached by people seeking an ID. On one occasion, a minivan with out of state plates entered the parking lot. Lopez and a casual acquaintance known as "Herbert" approached the van assuming the two occupants were seeking someone to vouch for them in obtaining a DL-51 and offered their services. Lopez described the occupants of the van as being "Arabs". The "Arabs" agreed to pay seventy to eighty dollars for the service. Lopez and Herbert led the Arabs in their car while the Arabs followed in their minivan to an attorney's office nearby on Columbia Pike. All entered the building, went up the stairs, and entered the law office where they were met by a secretary, a "short, Hispanic female with long hair". As part of the process, the two customers provided their passports, which Lopez described as being red in color, while Lopez and "Herbert" provided their own identification. After a short wait, they were all called into the lawyer's office where the additional DL-6 form affidavit had already been signed by the attorney. The lawyer was paid between $35 and $40, and the group departed with forms in hand. Prior to departing the "Arabs" and the attorney spoke separately in "another language other than English or Spanish". At the conclusion of the interview of Lopez, he was displayed a photospread of the Flight 77 hijackers, along with photos of all the other now identified hijackers of the three other flights, where Lopez identified Hanjour, Al Hazmi, Moqed, and Ahmed Alghamdi. Once Lopez identified Hanjour, he added that Hanjour had told him that the attorney was "from our country".

The next day "Herbert", further identified as Herbert Villalobos, was located and interviewed by Weidner and SA Jesus "Jesse" Gomez at the parking lot location described by Lopez. As memorialized in a 302 dated September 26, he substantially confirmed the same events as having been described by Lopez, although he described the customers as being "Pakistani". Villalobos completed the process by accompanying the hijackers to the Arlington, Virginia DMV, which they completed on their own. In subsequent interview of Villalobos on January 15, 2002, memorialized in a 302 dated January 24, 2001, Villalobos also confirmed he had assisted two other Middle Eastern males in obtaining the DL-6 and DL-51 in August 2001. He identified photos of hijackers Abdulla Alomari and Ahmed Alghamdi. All of this answered some questions, and helped fill out the timeline some, but the key issue had not yet been solved because these men were clearly unaware and uninvolved in the hijacking scheme and were simply trying to make a buck.

Eyad Alrababah was now of course the center of attention. First, we needed to find him and interview him. I was able to coordinate with one member of the rival squad, SA Ed Cooper, whom I did not know personally, but who seemed to be an "old school", square shooter, and who was cognizant of the machinations of his supervisor and was willing to work with me, rather compete. Ed agreed to seek out the former landlord of Alrababah and interview her to possibly determine his current location. As memorialized in a 302 dated October 8, 2001, on October 8, Young Ja Morales was interviewed at her current address in Arlington, Virginia. She explained that in the spring of 2001, she was experiencing financial problems after having separated from her husband. Her close friend who lived next door agreed to assist her in finding roommates to share the rent. Shortly thereafter the friend brought two Middle Eastern men to her apartment. One man went by the name of "Dave", while the other was named "Eyad". Dave was a fifty-year old while Eyad was in his late twenties in age. Although her friend claimed he and the two men were all friends, Morales believed they were more likely acquaintances. Dave and Eyad agreed to pay $400 per month without signing a lease or providing any personal documentation. They had very few possessions, merely some clothes, some cooking utensils, and a propane burner for cooking. To the best of Morales's knowledge Dave did not seem to work but sent most of his time taking long walks. Dave told her that he frequently attended the "Moslem Church" on Route seven near Seven Corners in Falls Church. Eyad claimed to work, but never told her what he did for work or where he worked. Both men kept very irregular hours and often left the apartment in the late afternoon and not returning until the next morning. They would then take naps and go out again. Sometimes they would come home, make several phone calls and then go to bed, only to go back out again in the early morning hours.

Dave and Eyad only stayed at the apartment for between two and two and a half months, oftentimes bring friends to the apartment to visit, and on occasion stay the night. None of those friends appeared in the photo spread of the many September 11 hijackers, however Morales did recognize the photo of Alfauru as having been one of those friends. Eyad, who had no car of his own would frequently borrow either Dave's car or hers. The second time he borrowed her car he did not bring it back for a week but would call every few days and explain where he was at the time, most often in New Jersey, Connecticut or Pennsylvania. As roommates go, Dave and Eyad did not share the burden of food, the phone bill, and even rent. They never cooked their own food, rather relying on Morales to feed them. When they departed, in an apparent hurry, they left behind their cooking utensils, and a $1000 long distance phone bill.

Meanwhile, we continued to analyze the DMV records and police reports related to Alrababah. Individuals whom Alrababah attempted to certify were being identified. The names always seemed to correspond with addresses in Northern Virginia, such as Fairfax and of course Falls Church which seemed to the center of activity, and as it turned out, was the location for the largest mosque in the DC area, the Dar Al Hijra Mosque, which would itself turn out to be where Alrababah would meet two of the hijackers and provide proof that the Imam at the mosque was somehow colluding with the hijackers. Of all the names identified through these searches as having been sponsored by Alrababah, the name of Abdel Rahman Omar Tawfiq Alfauru would provide significant leads and a witness to an eventual prosecution of Alrababah even after his many lengthy interviews by bureau agents, and willing cooperation.

One of the addresses frequently used by Alrababah to obtain illicit Virginia IDs and licenses was 127 Fairfax St., Alexandria, Virginia. This address turned out to be a "maildrop" address which was a post office box in Alexandria. I eventually located the Mailbox facility and was provided with a lengthy list of individuals who used that same PO box, all of whom were Alrababah's customers, and all of whom possessed Middle Eastern names, including Alfauru. The Virginia ID records we were able to pull from DMV files would provide dozens of fraudulently obtained IDs sponsored by Alrababah and Alfauru, and which gave us the leverage we would need to secure their eventual cooperation.

Alrababah seemed to have frequent encounters with the Fairfax County Police. Alrababah had been stopped by FCPD on September 4, 2001, in the parking lot of the Fair Oaks Mall late at night. No official report was filed however notes maintained by the officer listed three Middle Eastern individuals as having been in the vehicle driven by Alrababah. IDs found in their possession include Virginia driver's licenses that matched records we found in the DMV searches. The number of fraudulent IDs and licenses were adding up.

Although we originally were simply trying to locate Alrababah as a potential material witness, we were inadvertently building a criminal case.

Those fraudulent IDs would provide ample evidence to be used in eventual prosecutions of the pair in Federal District Court in the Eastern District of Virginia. We would need that leverage in the future. In almost every case, we would need to use the threat of prosecution or deportation, or both, to convince potential witnesses to come forth. We were identifying individuals who had some peripheral contact with the terrorists who murdered close to 3000 Americans. The truth was, the common concern among them all was less that of prosecution, and more the fear of being associated with the hijackers in any way.

Continuing contact with the Newark Division and a short time later with New Haven Division also produced Alrababah and Alfauru themselves.

IV.

Reluctant Witness

Alrababah would prove to be one of the most significant material witnesses to the movements and activities of predominantly the Flight 77 hijackers. Everyone was trying find him. Instead, he found us.

No one ever really established whether it was just pure coincidence or Alrababah was tipped off by one of the many people we had contacted in trying to locate Alrababah. Various investigative and analytical teams had formed at WFO and I spent a good deal of time briefing WFO personnel and of course management in the progress of the Alrababah effort. On October 29, 2001, I received a call from Assistant Special Agent in Charge, or ASAC Keith Bolcar. It was the old "Pete are you sitting down?".

Alrababah had the day before walked into the US Marshals Service in New Haven Connecticut and claimed to have been watching the news and recognized two of the hijackers, Hani Hanjour and Nawaf Alhazmi. The Marshals quickly realized the significance of his claims and referred him to the FBI's Bridgeport Resident Agency (RA). Agents in the RA had already begun to interview Alrababah. I was encouraged to get on a plane ASAP and join in on the interviewing. Agents from the West Paterson RA out of Newark had already arrived. SA Robert Jacko had started the ball rolling and had begun an interview but was waiting for me to arrive. Alrababah was now a trophy to be grabbed by whatever office could get there first. Admittedly I certainly saw him as my trophy. I had identified him. I had determined his importance, even as much as it was considered a long shot. I had done my due diligence and got leads out to the rest of the Bureau. Now the rest of the Bureau it seemed was competing to claim the trophy. In my own defense, I also was doing my job and absolutely had to chase this shadow. We had found an individual who clearly and admittedly knew the hijackers for longer than just a short encounter as was the case of Villalobos or Lopez. I honestly cared more about solving the puzzle than getting the credit. After almost two decades in the Bureau I also knew not to expect any credit. Either way, I needed to get on a plane to Connecticut.

Before I could, I had another fire to put out. An agent on the rival squad as I described earlier, was creating a drama over who should go to Connecticut and conduct the interview. Because of the misdirected parallel effort, he was of the misguided belief that he was the rightful owner and deserved the trip. I sat down to discuss the issue and offer to work together. I reminded him that I had started the whole thing, and even more importantly, the ASAC had briefed me and assigned me to go. He did not take this well at all, to the point of almost becoming violent, in keeping with his reputation in the office. His fists clenched and face turned red. Very professional. It would not have ended well for him. Several years later he was fired for unrelated issues. Let's just leave it at that.

I headed to the airport. The airports were just reopening, and flights had been resumed after a nationwide lockdown for several days after September 11. A federal agent can and should fly while armed. FBI agents are required to fly armed if on duty because the FBI has jurisdiction over flights. To fly while armed, an agent must obtain certain forms at the ticket agent counter and fill them out in multiple copies, then go through a separate entrance to the gate and present identification to an officer. Another officer is called to also review the identification and the filled-out paperwork and observe credentials and badge-again. Lastly a ledger book is signed, including presenting other information I can't discuss here. I passed though the checkpoint with flying colors and arrived at the gate.

Once an agent enters the airliner he must then speak with the pilot and present a copy of the paperwork. l almost made it. My last name is of Lebanese descent. Apparently, this spooked the pilot. He looked at my credentials and then looked at me. He then looked again at the credentials and looked again at me. He then asked for additional identification. I dug into my wallet and presented my Virginia driver's license. He again scrutinized my license and at me. I was trying to be understanding considering what had just happened, but I had a right to be there, and this was becoming offensive. I was pretty sure he was not aware of the hijackers' use of Virginia DLs, so I asked him if he needed anything elsemaybe a credit card? My tone of voice I think let him know this was as far as it needed to go. I took my seat and headed to Connecticut.

The day before, on September 29, 2001, SA Jacko had conducted a very comprehensive, non-custodial preliminary interview of Alrababah. This would be the first of close to ten subsequent interviews by various FBI offices including myself at WFO, Newark agents from the West Paterson RA, and agents from New York. As memorialized in a 302 dated September 29, 2001, the Marshals Service had contacted Jacko who first met Alrababah at the Marshals Service office and then continued the interview at the FBI office. Alrababah had seen photos in the Connecticut Post and then on CNN.

Alrababah was born in 1971, in Jordan and considered himself Palestinian. He was raised in Saudi Arabia until he was 17 years of age. He then relocated to Egypt for seven years in order to study computer engineering at the Arab Academy of Science and technology in Alexandria, Egypt, however, did not receive a degree. At the present Alrababah was living in Bridgeport, Connecticut however he had friends in the Paterson, NJ area. Alrababah provided his previous address as 22 Washington Drive, in West Paterson, NJ. He was at the time working at computer store known as "the Computer Guy" in Bridgeport. Alrababah also worked at a sister store owned by the same owner, in Fairfield, Connecticut. It was Alrababah's boss who had encouraged him to contact the FBI after Alrababah had revealed he had recognized several of the terrorists as being people he had met in Virginia.

Alrababah had visited the US before, in 1997 in possession of a visitor's/ business visa. He had arrived from Cairo, Egypt and went to stay in Clifton, NJ, next door to Paterson, to stay with a friend for three months, then returning to Egypt in November. During this trip, He visited a girl in South Carolina with whom he had been corresponding on-line. A year later Alrababah traveled back to the US ending up in Bridgeport. He began his employment with several computer companies. In order to maintain the terms of his visa, Alrababah returned, again to Jordan for six months. Upon coming back again to Connecticut, he discovered the computer store had closed, forcing him to relocate a second time to Paterson, with a large Middle Eastern population, working at various gas stations. It was at this point he began his business involving transporting, translating for, and assisting Middle Eastern men obtain Virginia driver's licenses. Alrababah confirmed the ease at which one could obtain a Virginia licenses or ID cards. On one of his trips to Virginia he was able to open a post office box address at a "mailbox place" in Alexandria, Virginia. The address corresponded with the address I had identified earlier that was indeed a Mailbox Store and had been used on his Virginia Driver's ID card along with multiple fraudulent IDs and licenses arranged by Alrababah for Middle Eastern residents of

New Jersey. Alrababah began spending time "hanging out" in Alexandria.

In April 2000, Alrababah developed a relationship with professional figure skater Ardra Doherty, who he had met while working at a gas station. She was lost and needed directions. Alrababah kindly had her follow him to the location and ended up at a local bar for a drink. They became friends, which over time became a relationship. Eight to nine months ago he felt the need to leave, causing him to relocate to Falls Church, Virginia. He was able to rent a room, sharing the room with Daud Suleiman (later also later identified as Daoud Chehazeh, and "Dave"), an older Syrian man and an acquaintance from Paterson. While rooming with Suleiman/Chehazeh, Alrababah helped him obtain a Virginia's driver's license. Suleiman/Chehazeh would later prove to present one of the enduring enigmas of the Alrababah and the Flight 77 story. Later interviews with Chehazeh by both the FBI and even ten years later by Fox News in a documentary "The Secrets of 9/11", and a subsequent Fox documentary directly related to Chehazeh would raise far more questions than answers. We will cover that story in another chapter.

While in Virginia, Alrababah patronized the local 7/11 store "off of" Route 7 in Falls Church. While there he met a Middle Eastern man named Nawaf. They struck up a conversation, and Nawaf introduced his friend Hani. Alrababah at this point identified Nawaf as Nawaf Alhazmi and Hani as Hani Hanjour from photos of the hijackers, presented by Jacko. This encounter would present the beginning of the unending misery of Eyad Alrababah that would last several years, including incarceration, being moved from jail to jail in different states, prosecution, mental deterioration, and deportation. Such would be the travails of being a trophy.

Alrababah had assumed ownership of a leased vehicle before he left Virginia and he drove this vehicle back to Virginia. He left Connecticut around seven pm and arrived at his old apartment about six hours later. Alrababah now was to meet two more hijackers. Along with Nawaf and Hani were Majed Moqed and Ahmed Alghamdi, as pictured in the newspaper photos Alrababah had seen.

Nawaf appeared to be interested in Alrababah's travel history. Nawaf was clearly uninterested in elaborating on his own personal details. He then asked if Alrababah knew of a place where he and Hani could find a place to live in the area. Alrababah invited the two Saudis back to his apartment for tea where they met Daoud. Alrababah provided Nawaf and Hani with the phone number of an individual who he had met at a Virginia DMV office. Alrababah believed this individual had an apartment for rent somewhere "off of" Route 1 South, but he did not remember the exact address. Our successfully locating that apartment several months later would be a story in and of itself.

Alrababah unsuccessfully attempted to find employment, and without any financial support, was finding it difficult to live. In March of 2001 Alrababah returned to Connecticut and his employment at the two computer stores. About a month later, Daoud, or Suleiman or Chehazeh, take your pick, called Alrababah from Virginia. Daoud told him that Hani and Nawaf had stopped by the apartment accompanied by two other Middle Eastern men who had come to the US and "wanted to be shown around". Alrababah agreed to have Nawaf call him on his cell phone. They arranged for him to return to Virginia and show them around. The following day Alrababah traveled to Virginia after work.

Alrababah discovered that the Saudis had found and moved into the apartment near Route 1 South and met them there. The two new men spoke no English and were much younger than Nawaf and Hani, perhaps no older than 18 or 20 years old whereas Hani and Nawaf were in their late 20s. Alghamdi and Moqed had arrived in the US about two weeks earlier. Hani was from South Saudi Arabia. They all wanted to visit Six Flags in Maryland and Alrababah agreed to take them there the next day. The next day the four Saudi packed their belongings into a navy-blue Toyota bearing California license plates that Nawaf had driven all the way from California. They seemed to have no defined plan other than Six Flags. Hani drove with Alrababah while the others rode with Nawaf. Alrababah felt he more in common with the older members of the group. They never quite made it to Six Flags. Alrababah simply got lost after driving around for two hours. The plan changed and they all decided to head up to Connecticut. The sightseeing tour now was diverted to New Jersey and Connecticut and maybe even Niagara Falls.

The conversation with Hani on the way North was revealing. He was a rather quiet individual, but he mentioned having received flight training in Arizona and California and expressed an interest in resuming the flight training. They never discussed politics although Alrababah attempted to bring up the subject. Hani seemed only to be interested in being a tourist. The four Saudis did not present themselves as being particularly devout Muslims and seemed more interested in "girls and clubbing". They paid cash for everything, including tolls and gas.

The group arrived in Connecticut around noon. Alrababah had to go to work. The Saudis had to find a place to stay overnight. Alrababah dropped them off at the Fairfield Inn on the Post Road in Fairfield. They discussed going to Niagara Falls the next day along with other nebulous tentative plans that never came about. He dropped them off at a local restaurant, the Bombay Indian Kitchen. This would be the last time Alrababah saw the Saudis.

The next day he dropped by the Fairfield Inn, and they were nowhere to be found. They had checked out. The Saudis did not travel with cell phones or pagers so that would be his last contact.

Alrababah recalled the group had a lot of luggage consisting of suitcases, suit-bags and rolled up blankets, and one prayer rug that Alrababah had observed Nawaf use once. As for being strict Muslims, the younger members seemed more interested in going to strip joints and "hanging out with girls". Nawaf had a California driver's license and claimed to have been a student there obtaining the license through a student program.

Around August 21, Alrababah used a rental car, rented in the name of a friend to drive back down to the

Fairfax, Virginia DMV near Route 50, to translate for two Turkish men whom he knew from West Paterson, NJ. This was when he was stopped by the police. At the time he was transporting three Turkish men in his car. He was surprised the officer let him go even though he could not himself produce a driver's license. Alrababah did have to call the friend and have her assure the office she had allowed him to use the car and that it wasn't stolen. In a subsequent interview that day Alrababah admitted he had obtained an estimated 50 Virginia licenses for customers.

The Virginia DMV records we were able to pull from the many boxes of paper files corroborated the 50 or so licenses Alrababah had sponsored illegally and which eventually resulted in his indictment and prosecution in the Eastern District of Virginia. Approximately one third of those customers used Alrababah's post office box address for their license. I was later able to locate the PO Box store and secure a list of a dozen or so of the customers using the PO box. That information also served to corroborate the plethora of evidence we had already secured. Alfauru may have also used one of Alrababah's addresses for his own license and in turn to assist another customer in obtaining a license. It turned out Alfauru was much more involved in the illegal business, eventually also resulting in his prosecution shortly after Alrababah's, both in the Eastern District of Virginia.

During the interview with Jacko, Alrababah was shown a photo of Abdel Rahman Omar Tawfiq Alfauru. Alrababah confirmed he had assisted Alfauru in obtaining a Virginia driver's license a year ago. Alfauru would later prove to be a more important piece of the vast puzzle—more of a catalyst than a key player relative to the 9/11 investigation. At the conclusion of the interview Alrababah offered to continue his assistance but admitted he was afraid for his life or his family if the families of the hijackers ever found out. Let no good deed go un-punished.

Alrababah's good deed would over time would do him far more harm than good. His story would change in different ways upon each subsequent interview. His fear of being associated with the 9/11 hijackers and a growing guilt would prove to haunt him. His incarcerations in Connecticut with the then Immigration and Naturalization Service, or INS, and then having been snatched up by the Eastern District of New York strictly as a "material witness" with no articulated legal reasoning, would add to the eventual breakdown. He was again, a trophy to be traded among various law enforcement agencies and US Attorney's Offices.

Alrababah was interviewed twice more over the next day before I arrived. A second interview by Jacko on the 28th, including SA Ken Gray produced more of the same, with a few new details. Alrababah added that he and Suleiman-Chehazeh agreed they suspected the Saudis were "Mukhabarat" operatives, or Egyptian Intelligence because they were relatively "silent", they took more information than they gave, they did not talk politics unlike most people from the Middle East, and they "appeared smart".

Alrababah provided more detail regarding the Jordanian individual who eventually rented an apartment in Virginia. Alrababah had met the Jordanian at the DMV. He had called him twice on his pager to once visit the apartment with an interest in renting it for himself, and once more to retrieve a folder containing a driver's license of a client he had left in the apartment. In February 2001 he and Suleiman were driven to the apartment by the Jordanian in order to assess renting the apartment which proved to be too expensive. In a later interview Alrababah would recall the Jordanian's name as being an unusual Arabic name, "Derar" ("last name unknown" or LNU in FBI parlance).

After Alrababah had moved back to Connecticut, Suleiman called Alrababah from Falls Church several times. Suleiman informed him that he had seen the Saudis several times around town, including at the Route 7 Mosque in Falls Church—the Dar Al-Hijra Mosque whose Imam was later identified as being Anwar Al-Awlaki, who presented another enigma to be pursued separately. Alrababah also recalled he had offered to assist the Saudis in obtaining Virginia driver's licenses. They did not accept his offer, apparently choosing to use his information while approaching total strangers for their assistance— what we would assess as a method of tradecraft.

Alrababah filled in another detail about which we had wondered; why he had contacted the FBI. Alrababah had heard the FBI was looking for him and his girlfriend advised him to cooperate. We kind of thought that was the case.

Later that same day the Newark agents and two task force officers descended on the INS Office to where Alrababah had been delivered for a pending a status review. SA Bob Bukowski and Passaic County Prosecutor's Office Captain Jim Bush joined Jacko and Gray to continue the interview. Bush and I had known each other and worked together years before when I had been assigned to the West Paterson RA. In those days, coincidentally, we were investigating the rampant Middle Eastern criminal enterprises in Northern New Jersey of all things. Good man. Good investigator. Small world. The three of us would be joined at the hip for more than two years as the investigations unfolded and mutated in many different directions. We would have a few disagreements and divergent interests, but the common denominator was that we had the same sense of mission that felt overwhelming at times. The Newark-West Paterson agents were most interested in Alrababah's time living in Paterson and West Paterson and in Connecticut.

Alrababah had attempted to assist the Saudis in finding an apartment in Bridgeport, Connecticut. He had contacted a friend who had an apartment on Yale Avenue and brought them over to the apartment to meet him. The meeting did not go very well and ended with a dispute over money.

As for his time with the Saudis in Virginia, Alrababah added a few new details as would happen often over the course of his cooperation. He recalled the Saudis had lived in a basement apartment complex in Alexandria, Virginia. Two Jordanians also lived in the apartment and were present when Alrababah arrived there to pick up the Saudis. One of the Jordanians was a relative, possibly a nephew of the owner of the apartment, much later identified as "Derar", who owned a flower shop business.

As for Suleiman-Chehazeh, he was now living in Paterson.

His story as to what incentivized his approaching the FBI was now slightly different. He had seen the pictures of the 9/11 hijackers on the news and in the newspapers and realized he knew some of them. A week or so prior he had called a friend in Virginia who was employed at a driver's school where Alrababah obtained his paperwork for licenses. He was tipped off that the FBI had been looking for him because the tipper was aware the owner and Alrababah were friends. Alrababah asked that they give the FBI his phone number. Alrababah added that he had obtained his Virginia driver's license through the driver's school.

Upon being prompted Alrababah described his method of securing driver's licenses in Virginia. Alrababah would complete the application and swear that the applicant resided with him at a given address. One would have to obtain a "lawyer paper" from either a lawyer or the driving school to affirm one was residing at a particular address. Alrababah charged his customers $500 to obtain an ID first and then later the license. If he had been transporting customers from New Jersey, he would put them up in a motel on Route 50 and Route 7 in Falls Church. Customers were referred to Alrababah by several employees at a gas station on

Rifle Camp Road in West Paterson, New Jersey. This of course again corroborated the illegality of his operation.

Alrababah spent the night with the INS but was made available to me the next day.

The next day, September 30, 2001, I arrived at the Hartford Connecticut airport and was picked up by Jacko and SA Ken Gray. I will have to admit I was suffering from a terrible headache that lasted the entire time I was there. I had little time to arrange the trip and we had all been working 12 and 16hour days seven days a week. Not to mention the obvious stress and general disbelief at what we all were involved in. Pure adrenaline and the need to keep this line of investigation viable kept us going. It had amazingly turned out to be the real deal. The next interview with Alrababah lasted half the day. Every hour or so, I would receive a cell phone call from Keith Bolcar or other executive managers ensconced in the glass booth conference room in the command post, asking for a progress report. A lot of this was a sincere interest in staying informed as to the progress of what had turned out to be a significant lead. Always, though, was the need to "be in the loop" and in a position to "brief it up" to the executives above you in your chain of command—"face time with the Director" so to speak.

The first new detail Alrababah offered was the identity of Derar. Memory is a funny thing. We often conduct successive interviews of someone who we believe possesses extensive historical knowledge of a complicated issue. Additionally, Alrababah recalled he had used the cell phone of Derar's nephew when retrieving the Saudis from the apartment on the evening of May 7, 2001. He had made a personal call from that cell phone. Alrababah suggested we obtain that cell phone number and contact the nephew in order to locate the apartment. It was good suggestion however we would find that apartment on our own as a result of what we referred to as a "shotgun lead" and a lucky break that came about as a result of our own efforts.

Alrababah was still struggling with some of the finer details concerning the trip bringing the Saudis to Connecticut. He was not sure whether he had visited them at the Fairfield Inn on May 8th. We showed him a phone record sheet for room 73 registered in the name of Hani Hanjour for the period May 8 through 10, 2001. Alrababah recognized a number called from the room as being the number of his employer . He had given them the number so that they could call him at work. He had also called a friend from the room.

A follow-up investigation by the New Haven Agents at the hotel revealed that Hani Hanjour was listed on the registration record using the address of 22C Washington Drive, West Paterson, New Jersey, a prior address used by Alrababah. The arrival date listed on the registration form was May 8, 2001, with a departure date of May 10, 2001. The room listed was room 73. 75 phone calls made from the room included calls to flight schools and real estate agencies.

Alrababah further described the Saudis as being "Cheap, shady and scary". He avoided discussing politics with them because although he was an obsessive follower of politics of the Middle East, they were not interested in political discussions, and he felt it was not wise to try because of their overall demeanor. As for the attempted trip to Six Flags in Maryland, he admitted he had a season's pass, and had been at Six Flags with a group of others on May 6. Alrababah had recommended it to the Saudis because he was familiar with it, however he really didn't want to go to Six Flags again, so he did not try too hard to find it for them and was in a hurry to get back to Connecticut and go to work at the computer store. Alrababah recounted his friend's offer to rent his apartment to the Saudis. He added that the Saudis had nitpicked the friend over his insistence that they pay for furniture and telephone and had insisted he remove those charges. The Saudis upset him. He threw them out.

Alrababah explained how he obtained his own Virginia Driver's license. He had been living at Bellevue Street in Falls Church, Virginia. An acquaintance from Paterson had introduced Alrababah to an individual named "Jasser" in Falls Church, who in turn assisted Alrababah in obtaining a state ID, and then a driver's license along with "seven other guys from New Jersey". These may have been small details but he was unwittingly building a case against himself and later others. Alrababah further explained Jasser would provide the certificates, already having been signed by an attorney attesting to the address to be used on the ID or license. The address provided by Jasser was the address Alrababah used for his customers' licenses. Suleiman later assisted in the business.

Alrababah's recounting of how he met the hijackers took another subtle turn. He remembered patronizing the 7-11 on Belleview Street behind the Cullmore shopping center on Route 7 in Falls Church. He found himself standing next to Hanjour and Alhazmi and striking up a conversation. He exited the 7-11 with them and noticed they had a car bearing California tags. He walked with them to the gas station next door and offered to help them obtain Virginia licenses. Alrababah explained the process to them. Hanjour and Alhazmi remained silent other than Alhazmi explaining he had a California license. Hanjour's license was suspended, making him even more of potential customer, but it was eventually clearly evident they took the information and used it independently of Alrababah to obtain their licenses. As I mentioned earlier, this appeared to be a tradecraft move by separating themselves from Alrababah's business but using his advice to do it themselves. Hanjour had a suspended license, only admitting to that on the trip to Connecticut.

As for their visit to his and Chehazeh-Suleiman's apartment for tea, Alrababah remembered he must have called Derar while the Saudis were present. He now remembered Derar visiting the apartment after they had returned to their hotel. Alrababah recalled the Saudis returning to Alrababah's apartment where they met Derar, and then Derar's transporting them to his apartment to check it out. Alrababah remembered the Saudis being in a great hurry, remarking "we've got to go… we've got to go". In the end, Derar rented them space in his apartment lasting about a month.

Alrababah vaguely remembered Alhazmi calling him from Virginia to come down and pick them up. I showed Alrababah a parking ticket dated May 7, 2001.

That more than likely coincided with his arrangements with Alhazmi because Alrababah had a court date in Fairfax on that date. He believed he must have told Suleiman to contact Alhazmi in order to have Alhazmi call Alrababah. Alrababah was shown several photos of individuals we believed had been his customers, including Al Fauru, whose full name we had established as Abdel Rahman Omar Tawfiq Al Farou, among several other variations. The many different variations of the name would later create some minor confusion when discussing his involvement in the broader investigation. Alrababah confirmed again he had helped Alfauru obtain a license, but Alfuaru was not a friend. He identified several other customers, including the Turkish customers who had been in his car when Alrababah was stopped by the police.

Suleiman-Chehazeh was "an old man" with a "problem with one eye". He would occasionally assist Alrababah with his customers from New Jersey at the DMV. He was not a regular in the business however certainly knew enough about the system to help Hanjour and Alhazmi work the system if they requested it. This was potentially a key nugget because for a time Suleiman maintained in contact with them while Alrababah was back in Connecticut and may explain how they had turned down Alrababah's help yet were still able to secure IDs and licenses on their own.

Alrababah reiterated details placing the Saudis at the Fairfield Inn. We had the same phone records the Newark agents had from which Alrababah again identified several numbers, so that was redundant. He added one new detail about what he did immediately after the horrific day of 9/11. He now remembered he had called the owner of the driving school to "see how things were going". The driving school owner informed Alrababah he had been contacted and questioned by the FBI. Alrababah later called the owner's wife who also worked at the school to determine if there was any additional information. She was aware the FBI had specifically asked about Alrababah. The school owner had assured the FBI "Alrababah was a nice guy and not a problem". That confirmed again that Alrababah had an existing motivation to personally contact the FBI in Connecticut before we came for him first. Good move.

We returned to the subject of Derar. Could Alrababah provide any more details? Alrababah remembered he had originally met Derar at the DMV. Derar had a business selling flowers, and lived near Route 1 in Alexandria, Virginia. He repeated the detail about his contacting Derar about renting the apartment and then meeting him at the apartment to retrieve the Driver's license file for one of his customers. Not really new information, but Derar was now a key figure who could fill in a month-long gap in the hijackers' timeline prior to 9/11. We needed to locate the apartment and especially locate and interview Derar.

Upon returning to DC, I was asked to brief WFO Management. I entered the command center and was led over to the glass enclosed management sanctuary. The Assistant Special Agent in Charge "ASAC" of the Counterintelligence Division escorted the Special Agent in Charge "SAC" over to me. I gave what hopefully was a succinct overview of a rather complex interview and how it contributed to the overall PENTTBOM investigation. He stood there silently stroking his chin, nodded, and without a word, turned and strolled back into the safety of the sanctuary. That went well.

· · · · · · · ·

On October 1, Suleiman-Chehazeh, who we will from here on refer to as Chehazeh, was located and interviewed by Bukowski and Bush in Paterson. Detective Danyal Bachok, a colleague of Captain Bush's provided translation. Danny and I had worked together for several years when I had been assigned to the West Paterson RA working Middle Eastern criminal enterprises. We had formed a multi-agency ad hoc task force "coalition of the willing" including the then INS, with SA Mark McGraw, one of the best, most honorable agents with whom I have ever worked, along with Danny's mentor and legendary Passaic County Detective Jack Vervaet, and Paterson PD Captain of Detectives Jim Buckley, both of whom became valued partners and close friends. The task force's work resulted in over 90 convictions of mostly Middle Eastern subjects for money laundering, gun trafficking, drug conspiracies, a milliondollar bank fraud, insurance fraud, copyright violations and the like. What we all learned from pursuing Middle Eastern organized criminal enterprises gave me a useful perspective when investigating the financing schemes of suspected Middle Eastern terrorist networks.

Over the course of our investigations, Jack had noticed one perplexing common denominator among a majority of our defendants—they all had Virginia driver's licenses. Many years later we now had the answer.

Chehazeh had entered the US in July 2000, with a Syrian passport, on a now expired B1/B2 visa issued in Saudi Arabia. His driver's license address was 6095 Belleview Drive. #101, Falls Church, Virginia. He provided information regarding his prior business and family in Damascus, Syria. He came to the US because he was "in great debt". He had been involved in a business deal in Syria with Saudi Arabians attempting to secure work visas in Saudi Arabia. The visas were fraudulent and the "Syrian government was looking for him". He for a time lived in Pittsburg, Pennsylvania and then moved to Paterson, New Jersey, where he first met Eyad Alrababah. Years later Chehazeh would become the subject of a Fox News special and multiple online articles speculating as to his true identity and his actual role in the entire 9/11 story. Much of his personal history was discussed in both media venues.

During conversations with Alrababah, Chehazeh alluded to his ambition to obtain employment with the Saudi Islamic Academy in Alexandria, Virginia. Chehazeh claimed to have Saudi friends in Moscow, Russia. The Moscow contacts were to have contacted a Saudi associate DC for assistance. Chehazeh certainly seemed to be more than just an indigent old man.

In March 2001 Chehazeh moved in with Eyad Alrababah in Falls Church, with a woman who was the lease holder of the apartment. The residence was in a large apartment complex containing numerous buildings with approximately eight apartments to a building. While residing with Alrababah, Alrababah assisted Chehazeh in illegally obtaining a Virginia ID and then a Driver's license in May 2001.

During the last weeks of April 2001, Alrababah met two Saudi nationals at the Dar Al Hijra Mosque in Falls Church. Alrababah introduced them to Chehazeh at the mosque. Chehazeh reiterated the same information regarding Alrababah assisting the Hijackers in finding an apartment. He identified Hanjour and Alhazmi from the commonly used photo array. Alrababah and the two Saudis exchanged phone numbers and approximately one week later had located an apartment in the area for them. Hanjour and Alhazmi visited the apartment on at least two occasions. On the first visit the Saudis called the apartment before coming over. One subject of conversation involved the Saudis inquiring about the Arab communities in the New York area. They explained they were not interested in living in New York because it was just too expensive. Alrababah recommended they move to Paterson.

Chehazeh echoed Alrababah's suspicion the Saudis were "Secret Police" because they had no jobs, they were living in hotels for long periods of time and were inquiring about Arab communities in the area. Chehazeh asked if the men were students and they replied they were taking "civil aviation classes". Chehazeh recalled Alrababah helping the Saudis move from Virginia to Connecticut, but he did not seem aware of the details of the Audubon apartment. In June 2001 Chehazeh returned to Paterson.

We interviewed Chehazeh a second time a few months later in February 2002. As to be expected, his story changed a bit again and he made himself even more an object of suspicion as to his true involvement. The number of personnel joining the interviews was becoming a bit of a circus. Everyone wanted to be part of the spectacle. This interview included Bush, Bukowski, a headquarters agent, a translator, AUSA John Morton, and Chehazeh's defense attorney, who turned out to be from Paterson, and a relative of a rather wellknown community organizer for the Circassian Community of whom I was well aware from my time in Paterson. Again, small world.

At this point Chehazeh was in custody and his deportation was imminent. Prior to the initiation of the interview, he was provided with a letter of agreement explaining the ground rules of what was at this time a proffer session. He and his attorney both signed the letter.

Chehazeh proclaimed that without his cooperation and without his providing Alrababah's phone number the FBI would not have found Alrababah. We almost laughed at this one. Chehazeh was reminded the FBI had begun interviewing Alrababah several days before contacting Chehazeh. Nice try. Morton reminded Chehazeh he was formally in the custody of INS and would release him back to their physical custody in a few days. This was his last chance to come clean.

Chehazeh re-hashed much of what he had already recounted concerning his time in Virginia with Alrababah. He did reveal he had spent much of his time at the Dar Al-Hijra Mosque reading the Koran. He was not particularly religious but explained a lot of people spent time at the mosque for more social reasons. He generally did not trust the Imams' truthfulness. He had never personally spoken with the Imam. He and Alrababah attended services together at the mosque on two occasions and had met Hani and Nawaf on the second visit. He had been waiting for Alrababah outside of the mosque when they exited the mosque together and the Saudis introduced themselves to Chehazeh. Chehazeh expressed surprise at how quickly Alrababah and the hijackers had met. He did believe the meeting was spontaneous but curious in its timing. He insisted neither he nor Alrababah were terrorists and that Alrababah had simply been helping Hani and Nawaf because he was "committed" to the "Arab Community".

Chehazeh did recognize a photo of "Derar", who by this time we had identified as Derar Saleh. Saleh was now becoming more and more of a key character. Chehazeh believed Saleh and Alrababah had known each other for a while and that Saleh was also Jordanian as was Alrababah. He confirmed Saleh had been the owner of the Audubon apartment and Chehazeh's early interest in the apartment. He provided a detailed description of the apartment but could not recall the address or how to get there.

Chehazeh did not inform Alrababah that he had contacted the FBI and Chehazeh did not want anyone to know he had done so. He claimed to have not known that Hanjour and Alhazmi had been in Paterson until the FBI informed him of such during the first proffer session in January. He wished he could stay in the

United States but was afraid to go back to Paterson because people will think he was cooperating with the FBI and that he was responsible for Alrababah's arrest.

Chehazeh feared his family would suffer when he is released.

Chehazeh had been polygraphed in January. He insisted he did not fail the polygraph but had been thrown off by the question as to whether he had prior knowledge of the 9/11 attacks. He suggested that the FBI "read cups" as they do in Syria. Strange. I suppose we could read palms or tarot cards too. The unanswered question as to whether he had substantial prior knowledge would forever haunt the Chehazeh piece of the puzzle.

To date, Chehazeh unexplainably remains in the US.

So yes, we were at the redundant stage of the story telling. This was the dilemma of conducting multiple interviews, in a short period of time, by different interviewers with overlapping but somewhat divergent investigative priorities. This was still only the beginning. Alrababah's deterioration was clearly progressing each time he was interviewed by another group of investigators asking the same questions in another new location.

It was now The Southern District of New York US Attorney and the FBI's New York Office who wanted their turn. As of October 16, 2001, Alrababah was in custody resulting from a "material witness" warrant in New York in the Hell hole of Riker's Island. He had been transferred from INS custody in in Connecticut.

Alrababah was not being treated well by the jail guards. No one could ever really explain why he was snatched up by New York and incarcerated. His immigration status was in question, however he was cooperating fully and was providing valuable information, even though the story changed somewhat over time, it was certainly in part a function of time and memory. Some felt he was withholding key details, other felt he was filling in details over time as his memory recaptured those details. Everyone in federal law enforcement wanted to claim Alrababah for themselves it seemed.

On October 16, Alrababah was interviewed again by two agents from the New York Office "NYO". More of the same. By now we should have had a relatively clear picture of his involvement with the Saudis and what assistance he had provided. Most of the interview simply rehashed the same questions with the same answers. A few partial names were filled in. We now knew his friend from Paterson's full name, Zuhair Idris. Not that important, but that's what we were getting at this point. For the fifth time or so, he identified the hijackers from another photo spread.

One new detail emerged; Alrababah remembered having seen Alhazmi and Hanjour at the Dar Al Hijra Mosque on one occasion, and that Chehazeh had accompanied Alrababah to the mosque on that occasion. Alrababah provided one new insight. He believed something was troubling Hanjour. Hanjour knew he was facing death.

It wasn't until a later Interview that another agent and I conducted on April 24, 2002, that Alrababah admitted had been mistaken about his first meeting with Hanjour and Alhazmi, and that it had taken place at the local 711 but actually at the Dar Al Hijra Mosque. That was a significant detail that changed the complexion of the story. Alrababah had only attended the mosque perhaps twice. It was on the second occasion, possibly in March or April 2001, he met Hani and Nawaf. As the service was ending Alrababah began to walk out of the mosque with the two men and they struck up a conversation. This was at the point where they inquired about finding an apartment in the area. Upon exiting the mosque Alrababah was joined by his roommate Daoud Chehazeh, also known as Abu Suleiman, who joined the conversation. Their invitation to join them back to their apartment for tea followed.

Even later Alrababah would describe observing Hani and Nawaf in the office of the Imam, Anwar Al Awlaki, appearing to be engaged in an argument. Coincidentally, Awlaki had also been the Imam at the mosque in San Diego attended by the same two hijackers when they were living in that city. "Coincidence"? Sure.

Awlaki was a long-time person of interest to the Bureau but never having risen to the level of a successful investigation. Several years would pass and Awlaki would escape to Yemen and begin an Al-Qaeda cell "AL Qaeda in the Arabian Peninsula" that became the most dangerous and active one in the world. He would begin publishing an English language terrorist magazine "Inspire" on-line, accessed by numerous "lone-wolf", self-actualized terrorists. He would attempt to have bombs secreted in copier cartridges onto cargo planes that was surprisingly thwarted by assistance from the

Saudi government. Awlaki would die in a US directed drone strike in Yemen in 2011.

Alrababah revealed that he was depressed because he was "being treated like a prisoner" and was planning to sue the FBI. Alrababah warned the FBI to wait for his book because "someone in the government was tricking him". He added "go ahead and judge me for the driving licenses but everything will be in my book". Alrababah repeatedly stated he felt he needed to be protected because "this is a big case and there are so many people dead because of these motherfuckers". He knew the "Arabs would be blamed for 9/11 because the Arabs are always blamed and there are a lot of people in this country who hate Arabs".

Alrababah's legal troubles were only beginning. On October 4, I was contacted by Assistant US Attorney "AUSA" John Morton from the Eastern District of Virginia "EDVA". Morton was interested in prosecuting Alrababah "relative to his ongoing fraudulent activity in certifying individuals for Virginia identification". Alrababah would be charged with violation of Title 18, US Code 1028, use of false identification, and Title 18, US Code 1324, encouragement of illegal aliens (yes that's how it's phrased) to remain in the country. I informed my management at WFO and the PENTTBOMB team at FBI Headquarters of the plans to prosecute Alrababah in Virginia. He would of course have to be transferred from incarceration in New York City to incarceration in Virginia. Newark FBI had by this time determined Alfauru was in Custody in New Jersey in immigration custody.

On December 13, as a result of a detention hearing in the EDVA, Alrababah was detained until trial in Alexandria, Virginia. The process was such that a complaint had been filed on November 16, and a Federal Grand Jury would be convened on December 16 where an indictment would be sought.

In the meantime, the blue Honda sedan driven by Hanjour and Alhazmi, was subsequently located in the parking lot of the Dulles Airport in Virginia. The California license tag displayed on the car was run on a routine basis by a Fairfax County, Virginia police officer in April 2001 where it had been parked in the lot of the Hillwood Motor Inn on Arlington Boulevard in Falls Church.

We were still trying to find that apartment on Rouge 1 in Hybla Valley south of Alexandria. Fairfax County Police came through again. I was now partnered with one of our Task Force Officers, Detective Dick Cline. Right away Dick and I gelled as partners. That's a two-way street. We both made the effort. Often officers from other agencies are made to feel like "junior partners". Hopefully, I made sure Dick was not treated that way. I knew already he had a great reputation both with the FBI and with his own agency. It was well deserved. As had happened before, it was a "shotgun lead" bright idea that pushed us forward significantly. Dick suggested using a FCPD local data base that we don't use often because it holds mostly information such as speeding tickets or local complaints filed with police. In this case Dick ran the various names of the Hijackers who had lived in Virginia. We were blown away when it worked. A police report had been filed on

May 1, 2001, on behalf of Nawaf Alhazmi, date of birth August 9, 1976, alleging Alhazmi had been assaulted outside of his apartment at 7991 Auduban Avenue, Apartment #10, Alexandria, Virginia. This apartment was, coincidentally located off of Route 1 in the Hybla Valley area South of Alexandria, just as described by Alrababah. As documented in the police report now in our hands, Alhazmi informed the responding officer that he had been accosted by four or five youths who had attempted to grab his wallet from his hand. Alhazmi declined to pursue any further charges or investigation after filing the police report. The FCPD report was made a part of the overall PENTTBOMB case file. I was shocked. You don't get breaks like this very often. Dick was at first surprised at my excitement. He was not yet aware of the Derar situation, and the information concerning the use of the apartment by Hani and Nawaf and two others. Damn, we may actually have found that apartment and possibly located more people who had associated with the hijackers.

Dick and I headed down to Hybla Valley and found the apartment complex. It was an expansive complex of apartments and condominiums. We met with the office manager for the building designated as 7991 Audubon Ave. He was completely cooperative. The trauma of 9/11 was a great motivator in encouraging people to cooperate with us without their demanding a court order or some other additional legal incentive. We were fortunate to be able to take advantage of this because it would not last forever. After we explained the situation and its great significance to the worst terrorist attack in US history, the manager's look of astonishment gave way to one of motivation. We determined the apartment number given by Alhazmi was not a valid address. I began the slow process of reviewing the list of hundreds of residents. And there it was. The unusual name of "Derar". "Derar Saleh" was listed as the owner of an apartment in Building 7991. His personal information was also listed.

An employee who was also present in the office remembered Saleh. She described him as being "Middle Eastern", approximately 35 to 40 years old, and "heavy set". The apartment manager agreed with the description. NCIC records provided his actual physical description as being 6 feet tall and 240 pounds. A match. The employee also believed Saleh was a florist of some type based on her frequent observation of his disposing of "old" flowers in the trash dumpster behind the building. This also corroborated Alrababah's description of "Derar" as having "something to do with flowers". An open-source data base inquiry also listed Derar Saleh as having a business involving "flowers".

The employee recounted an incident where she had entered the apartment to perform maintenance on the air conditioner earlier that year during the period in question and there were several Middle Eastern males living in the apartment. She observed them standing in the middle of the floor counting "large wads of money".

A second contact number for Saleh was also listed in the apartment records. Saleh's current address was listed along with two other previous addresses, and two vehicles. Other residents of the previous address also matched one of Saleh's previous addresses. Saleh was steadily looking more suspicious as we delved into his background. SAs Rick Cimacasky and John N. were furthering the process. Rick determined Saleh's SSN was not an assigned number. That raised red flags as to his immigration status and maybe other questions regarding his identity. John identified seven additional aliases for Saleh via good old open-source inquiries.

On December 7 We ran by the older address and conducted a "spot check", noting several vehicles in the driveway. One of the vehicles was registered to a Ghazi Ghabayen, in Alexandria, Virginia at also one of Saleh's previous addresses. As before, FCPD came through again—they had arrested Ghabayen on December 9 pursuant to a warrant issued in North Carolina for robbery. A police report regarding the arrest indicated the vehicle in question was stopped by police in front of the address and the driver of the vehicle was registered to Derar Saleh. The police followed the car back to Bloomfield address where Ghabayen was arrested. Saleh had been also briefly interviewed by the arresting officers where he claimed to reside at the address. Follow up spot checks noted a white van and a large Buick sedan both displaying diplomatic license tags registered to the Jordanian embassy in DC. This would prove significant later.

Dick contacted his people and determined Ghabayen was willing to cooperate. Of course, cooperation takes many forms and has many motivations. Ghabayen acknowledged in his subsequent interview that Saleh and Saleh's brother Adel Shannag (he revealed Saleh's true name was Shannag) both lived with him at the current address.

Dick and I decided to talk to the current residents of the Audubon apartment. They had moved into the apartment in June of 2001 and were not familiar with any of the previous tenants. They did provide the name of the actual owner of the apartment/condo. Another lead. The owner was described as a Middle Eastern male and they provided his name. The management records for the complex listed him and another individual as the owners. More pieces of a puzzle we were still just starting to assemble. The new tenants mentioned the owner continued to come by the apartment to pick up mail for the previous tenant, and he had mentioned he was waiting for some "immigration papers".

We now really needed to locate the Jordanian roommates who had lived in the apartment with Hanjour, Alhazmi, Alghamdi and Moqed and uncle Derar. That could hopefully fill in a gaping one-month hole in the activities of the Saudis as they were preparing to hijack four airliners and murder almost 3000 Americans.

We had enough information now to locate Derar Saleh. On January 3, 2002, Dick and I interviewed Saleh at his apartment in Alexandria. Saleh informed us that he was a US citizen and had resided in the US since 1993. His six children still lived in Jordan. He used the other address in order to receive mail and for immigration purposes. He needed a permanent address since he moved around a lot. The address was the permanent address of his uncle. Saleh's family name was Shannag. His current roommate and lease holder for the apartment was Ghazi Ghabayen who had just been arrested. Saleh described himself as self-employed selling flowers in various nightclubs in the area.

The subject quickly turned to the Audubon address. Saleh claimed to be unaware that his name was still listed on the lease. He was at one time planning to move into the apartment but found it to be too far away from Alexandria where Saleh preferred to live. Around ten months ago Saleh had been planning to purchase the apartment and was in the process of renovating it. Saleh had traveled to Jordan to visit his family in April and attempted to return on September 11, but his flight was turned back to Paris. Four days later he was able to return to the US, landing at Dulles International Airport in Virginia. Upon his return Saleh relinquished control of the apartment. A friend of Saleh's cousin Rasmi Shannaq (another new spelling), known only as Ahmed, arranged with Saleh to share the Audubon apartment with Rasmi for a month or so. Saleh believed Rasmi was now living in Baltimore. He provided us with his phone number. Rasmi would eventually become a key figure, reluctantly, in filling in the details of the hijackers' month-long time in Virginia and while staying at the apartment.

Saleh was able to identify a photo of Alrababah as that of a Jordanian whose name he did not recall who he had met at the DMV about nine or ten months earlier. Alrababah had initially approached Saleh because they both were of Middle Eastern nationality and then in order to borrow Saleh's car to take a driver's test, to which Saleh did not agree. At the time Alrababah had been accompanied by two Syrian males, one of whom was older, perhaps in his 60s in age. Chehazeh again?

Saleh at the time was accompanied by his own roommate, Musa Qudisat. Saleh was assisting him in obtaining a driver's license. He gave Alrababah the cell phone number for the owner of the Audubon apartment after Alrababah expressed an interest in finding an apartment. Saleh initially did not actually assist Alrababah in obtaining the apartment and he claimed to never have met him at the apartment. His only face to face meeting he had was at the DMV. Saleh's story, just like everyone else's involved in the saga would change over time, not of his own volition but because he would be confronted with facts that clearly contradicted his initial statements. Almost a year later Saleh would be interviewed at the Offices of the US Attorney in Alexandria, in the presence of his attorney, where he would admit that the on the day he had met Alrababah at the DMV he was there assisting his nephew Rasmi Shannaq (illegally) obtain a Virginia driver's license.

By this time, we had connected Shannaq and numerous others in an illicit visa fraud scheme involving Jordanian nationals and a US State Department embassy employee in the Middle East. Those benefitting from the scheme were able to enter the US illegally. Saleh embroiled himself in the scheme by assisting several of those involved, to include Rasmi Shannaq and his roommates Mussa Qudisat and Ahmad Ahmad obtain Virginia IDs and licenses.

Saleh now admitted having given Alrababah his own cell phone number and that of Rasmi Shannaq's rather than apartment owner's. Saleh also gave Alrababah the address of the apartment. Shannaq was at that time was residing at the apartment. After a few days, Alrababah telephoned Rasmi, and informed him he had two people who needed an apartment. Rasmi in turn called Saleh and obtained his approval. Saleh also believed Shannaq contacted the apartment owner for his approval as well. Saleh admitted to being aware that the two individuals moved into the apartment two days prior to Saleh's departure to Jordan.

Sometime after the two individuals moved in, Shannaq visited Saleh at his other apartment in Alexandria and filled in some details about the newcomers. They were Saudis. They had their own car. They would only need to stay at the apartment for a few weeks until they found a school to attend and then they would move out. The Saudis were not very friendly, kept to themselves, ate by themselves, and Shannaq did not like them. Saleh emphasized he never met the Saudis and did not know about their roles in the September 11 attacks until Shannaq finally admitted their identities to Saleh after both had been contacted by the FBI in January 2002.

Saleh sure could have given us this information from the start. It would have helped. Saleh's initial equivocation would prove to unnecessarily extend the length of our investigation by several months. He would in the end pay a price.

Next, we needed to find Rasmi Shannaq. He should be the one to fill in the blank month. It would prove to be like pulling teeth. On January 22, 2001, SA Joe Sirenne from my current criminal squad and I interviewed Shannaq at Derar Saleh's home. Shannaq was barely cooperative. He did confirm his residence at an apartment near Route 1, Richmond Highway rented by his Uncle Derar Saleh in 2001. Yet he claimed not to recall the month or what time of year; he could only remember that he lived there for one or two months and was given access to the apartment by his uncle prior to Saleh's departure to Jordan. Shannaq lived in the apartment currently occupied by Saleh with his brother Akram Shannaq for five or six months after arriving from Jordan on a visa. Not surprisingly he could not recall the type of visa. Once the apartment became too crowded Shannaq moved to the apartment near Route 1, South of Alexandria, a garden style apartment. Shannaq had two roommates; his cousin Musa Qudisat, and Ahmed, whose last name Shannaq could not recall. All three sold flowers at nightclubs in the Northern Virginia area. He described the entrance to the apartment and drew a diagram that matched the plan of the apartment in question, #103. Shannaq never felt comfortable at the complex. He and his roommates were the only residents of Middle Eastern nationality, and he did not feel welcome. At the time his uncle was finishing up the renovations of the apartment. There was no "land line" installed at that time and all three used Shannaq's cell phone. He claimed he knew no one who lived in New Jersey.

Most significantly, Shannaq denied that any others had ever lived in the apartment, and he never spent the night away from the apartment. Obviously, this clearly contradicted every other person whom we interviewed, and every bit of evidence we had collected.

After living in the apartment for two months, Shannaq moved out and moved in with his father in Baltimore, Maryland, which was then his current address. Qudisat had moved to Nevada. Shannaq had no idea where Ahmed was living. Even more alarming was that Shannaq did not admit to recognizing any photos of either Alrababah or any of the Saudis. Clearly, he was displaying self-defeating behavior.

Rasmi's motivation for his evasion became more evident once we partnered up with the State Department's Diplomatic Security Service, "DSS".

It was not until we arrested him on June 24, 2002, at his father's house in Baltimore that he finally admitted to hosting the Saudis at the Audubon apartment.

Coincidentally, in another turn of luck I had been contacted by the US Attorney's Office and informed that DSS had been investigating a visa fraud investigation based on information from an FBI confidential informant that the father of Rasmi Al-Shannaq had paid $10,000 for two visas issued at the US Embassy in Doha, Qatar. Subsequent DSS investigation determined Shannaq and 69 other individuals received genuine US visas from the Doha embassy between July 2000 and May 2001. Consular records were searched and no records of these visas or payment records could be found. All the visa recipients were either Jordanian or Pakistani nationals, and all had entered the US and were still present. Many had been refused entry into the US in the past but had been able to enter the US with the fraudulently obtained visas in question. I had been in contact with the DSS case agent, Mike

Hudspeth. Eventually Mike and I developed a good working relationship, however it took some work on my part to overcome the common resistance by other law enforcement agencies towards working with the FBI—sometimes warranted but most often based on a misconception that the FBI was there to steal their case. I honestly gave away or shared far more than I ever took. Our various task forces were known to treat participating officers from other agencies very well. But Mike and I needed each other, and he realized I was not going to steal his case but would only make both our cases stronger.

DSS had a strong case that warranted an aggressive prosecution; however, it was having difficulty getting appropriate attention from the USAO. Our case was getting plenty of attention, but we were having trouble getting the full story from some of the same individuals involved in both investigations. We both needed pressure. Prosecuting individuals such as Rasmi Shannaq and Alrababah would hopefully force them to finally give an honest accounting of their knowledge of the terrorists. The 9/11 connection would hopefully motivate the USAO to prosecute the DSS subjects. The FBI's PENTTBOMB and DSS's "Operation Eagle Strike" were now joined at the hip. Shannaq's whole family as well as his roommates were all in the crosshairs. Qudisat and Ahmad would be next to be arrested based upon the visa fraud scheme and immigration charges.

At first, Shannaq was not at home at his father's row house in Baltimore. We had already interviewed his father, so he recognized us when we knocked on the door. At this point we were to use immigration charges to arrest Shannaq. The other charges would come later. Our arrest teams had arrived in the Baltimore area the night before, Sunday, and secured hotel rooms so that we could execute the arrest and a search warrant the next morning at "0 Dark thirty". The FBI team was a minimalist team of about six or seven agents from WFO and the Baltimore office. More than enough. DSS brought their entire DC contingent of close to 20 agents. Guess they didn't get out much. They also invited Baltimore PD and who knows else. When we determined Shannaq was not there, we set up a perimeter around the neighborhood. This was something DSS was good at. What we didn't know at the time was that CNN had also set up a perimeter and was filming everything we did. A suspicious truck was partially visible around the corner, down the street, however CNN was also good at surreptitious surveillance. Around 10:00 am, a small car appeared around the corner of the block. It clearly hesitated, not turning the corner. Several of us walked quickly in that direction. I recognized Rasmi Shannaq as the driver. He recognized me from previous interviews. He quickly turned around and drove away. Now what do we do?

I went back to speak with Rasmi's father and convinced him to call Rasmi and have him return. This time he arrived and parked directly in front of the house. A swarm of agents surrounded the car and took possession of the prize. He was led up the steps to the front door. I noticed he was not handcuffed. This was an arrest. He walked up to me and extended his hand to shake hands. I took his hand, placed handcuffs on him, and pulled him into the house. Now I felt better. It looked good on CNN that night.

National news later did an extensive news report on the arrest of Shannaq and Alrababah, and the DSS "Eagle Strike" investigation that detailed the connections between the massive visa fraud investigation and the now identified roommates and contacts of the 9/11 terrorists. Alrababah was described in the news report as being the most significant individual thus far identified as having been associated with the hijackers.

The one concern on my part was that I was also involved in an undercover operation in the Norfolk, Virginia area against a Chinese technology procurement effort and being shown on the news could have compromised my cover. Fortunately, a few days later I was down South in Virginia Beach meeting undercover with the subject of the case and did not face any scrutiny related to the news clip.

We sat Shannaq down and encouraged him to finally give us an honest accounting of his time living with the terrorists. Initially Shannaq reiterated his denial that any person connected with the 9/11 hijackers had ever resided with him at the Audubon apartment in the spring of 2001. At the urging of his father, Shannaq eventually capitulated and admitted that two of the hijackers, Hani Hanjour and Nawaf Alhazmi, had stayed at the apartment with him for one month in the spring of 2001. He then identified them from a photo spread. Finally.

Shannaq had lived with Musa Quidisat and Ahmed Ahmed for a period of two to three months prior to and after Hanjour and Alhazmi's having lived there. Shannaq insisted that the two simply "showed up" at his door and informed him that the apartment owner had said "we can stay here for one month". We had already identified and interviewed the actual owner of the apartment. Shannaq surmised he owed Shannaq's uncle Derar Saleh a large sum of money related to the renovations of the apartment, needed the money and wanted more people living in the apartment and paying him rent. Shannaq claimed he had very little contact with the Saudis because Shannaq worked at night and slept during the day while Hanjour and Alhazmi were out most of the day. Shannaq did not even eat meals with them. "Eyad", of course being Eyad Alrababah, was the individual who picked up Hanjour and Alhazmi from the apartment when they moved out. That was the only time Shannaq had met Alrababah. The interview had to be cut short because the INS agents were in a hurry to get Shannaq back to Virginia and before an immigration hearing.

Our last contact with Shannaq occurred much later in September 2002. He was incarcerated at the Worcester County Maryland Detention Center on the Eastern Shore. Mike Hudspeth and Assistant US Attorney, "AUSA" Neil Hammerstrom from the Eastern District of Virginia "EDVA" and I headed down to conduct one last interview before Shannaq was deported. It was a long trip. We got lost of course and ended up turning around in the muddy parking lot of a massive chicken processing plant and eventually found the detention center. Chicken feathers still stuck to the bumper of my bureau car. One bright spot was that

Neil and I had been fraternity brothers at the College of William and Mary in Virginia many years ago but had reconnected as a result of our two offices working so closely together. Over the years every one of my cases would be prosecuted by the EDVA rather than the USAO in the District of DC. Neil and I would maintain contact through several future prosecutions but also at Homecoming each year.

The Warden and several officers at the detention center greeted us with surprisingly tremendous hospitality. They even provided lunch. Wow. I guess having a celebrity prisoner connected to 9/11 was a thrill to them being in such a remote location. Never would you see something like that at any other jail or prison. Strictly business at the Alexandria jail in Virginia or any other jail where I have had to visit an inmate. The Alexandria jail would play a key part over the years in handling various subjects of my cases and was very professional and cooperative. They just never served lunch.

Shannaq filled in just a few more details but nothing earth shattering. He had entered the US in October of 2000 from Jordan. He reiterated he had lived with his Uncle Derar for a few months before moving into the Audubon apartment. The apartment owner had brought "Hani" and "Nawaf" to the apartment--a new fact. They would be staying for about a month. By this time Qudisat had moved out. Hani and Nawaf stayed in the room with the door closed most of the time. Shannaq recalled on one occasion he had given Hani and Nawaf directions to a store near George Mason Drive in Falls Church, Virginia for the purchase of food. This detail would prove to be much more important in a future investigation.

Again, a small fact would prove to be significant. The store would later be identified as the Skyline Butcher Shop. Credit card records for Alhazmi revealed he had patronized the Halal food store at least four times. Just as the 9/11 tragedy was unfolding, I had been preparing wiretap affidavits targeting the interstate drug distribution network of the Palestinian owners of the shop, Mohammed and Sami Said. Once I eventually completed my part of the PENTTBOMB investigation, I would return to pursuing Sami and Mohammed for several years more, eventually dismantling the network. That investigation would in turn spin off into several other Middle Eastern criminal and terrorism investigations-and chapters.

As of November 16, 2001, we had indicted Alrababah in the Eastern District of Virginia on identity fraud related charges specifically for operating an illicit business flagrantly violating the law and involving over 50 co-conspirators. However, we were still hoping to finally get the real story behind his association with Hani and Nawaf. We all believed he was withholding or lying about key facts. I sent a lead to the New York office to have Alrababah transferred from his incarceration in New York to the Alexandria jail. We were also preparing to indict Alrababah's sometime business partner, Omar Alfauru for being a co-conspirator in the fraudulent Virginia driver's license scheme.

Alrababah would eventually plead guilty to 50 counts of identity fraud and other charges. He would in turn testify against Alfauru who we had determined to be much more involved than originally thought. On February 11, 2002, we filed a complaint against Alfauru for violation of Title 18, US Code Section 1028 (a) (1) and Section 2, the same charges as were brought forth against Alrababah. Copies of the complaint, warrant and affidavit were sent to Newark. Alfauru was at that time in the custody of INS and was easy to find. Alfauru now joined Alrababah in the Alexandria jail.

The Headline in the Washington Post proclaimed:

"Man Charged in ID Scam to Aid Hijackers"

"Jordanian Man Living in Connecticut Accused of Helping Terrorists Use Va. Loophole"

A second and third subsequent Washington Post Headlines:

"Grand Jury Indicts Man on ID Fraud Charges"
"A Reluctant Witness"

The Newark Star Ledger:

"N.J Man Supplied Fake IDs to Hijackers"
"Affidavit Claims He was Unaware of September 11 Plot"

As often happens, incarcerated individuals confess secrets to their fellow inmates. One such inmate was in jail with Alrababah and Alfauru. In March 2002, while Alrababah and Alfauru were awaiting trial, that inmate, a fellow Middle Easterner, engaged in lengthy conversations with Alrababah. Over a two-day period, March 20 and 21, SA Charlie Price and I interviewed the inmate in the presence of his attorney at the Alexandria jail at his request via his attorney. The inmate was Price's defendant related to unrelated charges, hence his presence at the interview. The attorney had provided a letter to the Eastern District USAO summarizing a rather explosive series of admissions made by Alrababah concerning his former roommate, Daoud "Abu Suleiman" Chehazeh. The individual became acquainted with Alrababah as a fellow inmate about two months earlier. Alrababah was at that time "depressed" because he had been in "lockdown" 24 hours a day. A counselor had transferred Alrababah down to a "pod" which consisted of six single occupancy cells around a common area. That is where they first met. Alrababah discussed, among other subjects, his pending charges. He then was moved away from the pod for about three weeks and then returned with "full privileges". Their conversations resumed, and included the treatment of Arabs in the US, eventually touching upon his relationship with Hani Hanjour and the other individuals who were associated with the September 11, 2001, terrorist attacks. Alrababah explained he had first met Hanjour and one other hijacker at the "mosque".

Alrababah believed, in hindsight, that his roommate, Daoud Chehazeh, a Syrian who had lived in Saudi Arabia, had manipulated Alrababah's and Chehazeh's move from New Jersey to Virginia. His apparent ulterior motive was to maneuver a meeting between Alrababah and the hijackers. Strangely, neither Alrababah nor Chehazeh had had jobs or a prearranged place to live. Chehazeh had claimed to have lost "millions" in Saudi Arabia and was now broke and depressed over the loss.

Alrababah's suspicions were derived from Chehazeh's insistence that he and Alrababah visit the mosque, even though Chehazeh was admittedly not religious. This occurred about two weeks before Alrababah relocated to Connecticut. When Alrababah did attend the mosque, Chehazeh did not accompany him. Toward the end of the service, Alrababah turned to shake hands with the people next to him as is customary, which turned out to be Hani Hanjour and another Saudi, as they described themselves. As they all exited the mosque, Alrababah observed Chehazeh standing outside of the mosque. Alrababah introduced them, however he had the feeling they were already acquainted.

Alrababah's description of his return from Connecticut for a court hearing and his subsequent assistance to the Saudis to also move to Connecticut was consistent with what Alrababah had previously provided to the FBI. What was somewhat different or at least a significant new detail, was Hanjour's questioning of Alrababah's beliefs and attitudes toward the United States government. Hanjour described America as evil and opined that it should be punished for its assistance to Israel. Alrababah disagreed and replied America was an open country where one could spread Islam without a problem. Even more alarming was Hanjour's asking Alrababah his opinion regarding the hijacking of an airplane, to which Alrababah replied that he did not believe that would be a proper "battle" for "jihad". Hanjour inferred he wanted to arrange for a Saudi national "to do something to the United States to hurt the US-Saudi relationship" and eventually force all of the "Americanized" Saudi students in the US to leave the US. Hanjour believed that Saudi Arabia was helping the US to in turn assist Israel through the sales of oil.

Alrababah did not like Hanjour, but he did not feel it was "honorable" to break contact with him, which was consistent with Alrababah's prior statements. He did believe Chehazeh was encouraging him to continue to assist Hanjour, et. al., and to encouraging Alrababah to go to the mosque even though Chehazeh never went to the mosque himself and was not particularly religious. Alrababah even felt Chehazeh was trying to recruit him into Hanjour's "group", but Alrababah was "not qualified".

Alrababah's suspicions toward Chehazeh extended to Chehazeh's telephoning Alrababah while Alrababah was still in Connecticut and asking Alrababah whether he had heard of a pilot having been arrested, not specifying where that arrest had occurred. Chehazeh asked Alrababah to check the internet for him regarding this news event. Alrababah claimed to have simply ignored this request.

Even more bizarrely, approximately ten days prior to this call, Chehazeh called Alrababah to ask him if he wanted discounted airline tickers without specifying the destination. Alrababah refused the tickets. A wise move it would seem. Two days later Alrababah was visited by an unnamed "Syrian guy" who was a friend of Chehazeh's who put a knife to his throat. Alrababah responded by praying aloud, causing the knife wielder to desist, and claim he "was only joking". Alrababah speculated Chehazeh felt Alrababah "knew too much to left alone if he was not going to cooperate. Chehazeh once admonished Alrababah that although Chehazeh "had only one eye he was not to be underestimated". The online article concerning Chehazeh covered this very weird situation in Chehazeh's own words.

Another tale concerning Chehazeh related to the time Chehazeh and Alrababah were rooming together in Falls Church. Chehazeh had discussed the bombing of the USS Cole Naval vessel during a news broadcast concerning the event. Information from Israeli news alleged that an attack by Osama Bin Laden was imminent. To Alrababah's shock, Chehazeh jumped up and exclaimed "shit! they know about us". Chehazeh then ran out to make a phone call and left the apartment. Alrababah shortly thereafter received a call from overseas that was cut short. The caller appeared to have an Iraqi accent. If these tales were true, it would be understandable Chehazeh would certainly not admit any of this to us. Why would Alrababah conceal these rather significant details about Chehazeh's behavior if he had been so concerned about it all?

Upon relating these events to the inmate, Alrababah explained he "didn't know that they were important until now". Until Alrababah was arrested he would never have thought Chehazeh was connected in any way, and he had never indicated he was "part of anything" and that he was "always behind the scenes". However, Chehazeh did "get excited" when discussing the subject of "martyrs", and it now led Alrababah to believe, in conjunction with all of his strange and suspect behavior, that Chehazeh was more than he seemed.

Chehazehs' professed, in his own words to us, connections to several Saudi embassies in places such as Moscow and his ambition to gain employment at what was eventually discovered to be a radical Islamist and anti-Western and anti-American school in Northern Virginia, tended to support Alrababah's suspicions.

One last tale Alrababah told was that when he was incarcerated in New York, he had also met Hussein Attas who turned out to be convicted Islamist terrorist Zacarias Moussaoui's roommate. Attas made the statement prior to 9/11 to Alrababah that Moussaoui had told Attas that he would take him on a "jihad" trip by the end of the year.

It's still a mystery as to why Alrababah had included this tale in his many interviews with us.

Alrababah's last interview took place on June 6, 2002, at the Alexandria Detention Center. This interview took place in the presence of Alrababah's attorney. The subject of the interview concerned his future testimony regarding his involvement with the driver's license scheme, the methodology used to obtain the licenses and to identifying the many individuals who benefited from this scheme, most significantly Omar Alfauru whose trial was impending. Alfauru, as it turned out was a part-time partner with Alrababah and not just a one-time customer. Alrababah had by now pleaded guilty, while Alfauru insisted on a trial in Alexandria. Alrababah would testify against Alfauru as part of his plea agreement. The details were pretty much what we had already extensively documented. A few new details involved the owner of the driver's school. He was intimately involved in the scheme and notably possessed a "lawyers stamp" that would be used on the forms. Alfauru used the owner's services to assist several other illegal immigrants to obtain Virginia licenses. Alrababah specifically reminded Alfauru that the whole scheme, most importantly falsely using an address in Virginia was illegal.

Alrababah by this time had deteriorated drastically. He claimed to be so depressed he could not separate what was real from what was imagined. Ardra Doherty echoed this worrisome turn.

The Washington Post Headline on May 5, 2002:

"A Willing Witness, A Painful Price"

"Man who Went to FBI to Detail His Trip With Hijackers Faces   Deportation"

"Second Hijacker Wasn't in on Plan Man Says"

Alfauru was convicted at trial in Federal Court in Alexandria in June 2002. Alrababah pleaded guilty in the same US District court in the Eastern District in the same month. Both were convicted of conspiring to and having produced false Virginia driver's licenses and non-driver's identification for illegal immigrants who were transported interstate for that purpose. Both were sentenced later in August. Rasmi Shannaq and his roommates Musa Qudisat and Ahmad Ahmad were also indicted and pleaded guilty in the Eastern District of Virginia for violation Title 18, US Code Section 1546, visa fraud, ID fraud, and Section 1001, providing false statements. All were eventually deported.

Ahmad Adeeb Ahmad was now incarcerated along with the rest at the Alexandria lock-up. He proved to be rather cooperative. On October 4, 2001, Mike Hudspeth, Neil Hammerstrom and I interviewed Ahmad at the jail. His defense attorney was also present. Ahmad admitted Derar Saleh was the individual who had assisted him in obtaining a Virginia driver's license, including providing an address and filling out the initial forms for him for the ID card and then during Ahmad's stay at the Audubon apartment, assisting him in obtaining a driver's license.

This clearly implicated Saleh in the broader conspiracy and explained why he was so reticent to admit his knowledge of the presence of the hijackers.

"Hani" and "Nawaf" lived with Ahmed and Rasmi Shannaq at the Audubon apartment for a period of one month. Ahmad explained that in May of 2001, Saleh informed him that "he had two guys who were living in the hotel" who were going to live in the apartment with them, and they "had come here to study". A few days later Saleh brought Hani and Nawaf by the apartment.

To add to that narrative, when Hani and Nawaf first moved into the apartment, upon arrival, they asked "where is Derar?". This again significantly, unnecessarily, contradicted Saleh's early statements.

During their stay, neither made any phone calls from the apartment. That could be explained by the fact there was no hard-line phone installed in the apartment. Their only visitor was "Eyad" who came to pick them up when they moved out. Ahmad emphasized Saleh had been the one to show Hani and Nawaf the apartment. This clearly contradicted Saleh's initial story as told to us. Saleh was still in Jordan when Eyad came to pick up the Saudis.

Ahmad found out later that Eyad had helped them obtain their Virginia licenses. Hani and Nawaf notably asked Ahmad if he had ever attended the Dar Al Hijra Mosque. Ahmad replied he had attended in a sporadic fashion. Hani appeared to be displeased at Nawaf's mentioning the name and gestured as though he wanted Nawaf to change the subject. This exchange seemed to fit a pattern between Hani and Nawaf that echoed Alrababah's description of their relationship as though Nawaf was somewhat naïve and not careful of his conversations, and Hani had to occasionally reign him in. The only other detail Ahmad could recall was that Hani and Nawaf had met in college, possibly in Arizona.

Hani and Nawaf were known to pray five times a day as do devout Muslims. Significantly they had also discussed going to Afghanistan to engage "in jihad". Nawaf Had gone to Saudi Arabia instead. During a rare dinner together, Hani and Nawaf brought up the subject of Osama Bin Laden on one occasion, to which Ahmad replied he had seen him on TV. The two Saudis referred to Bin Laden as "Sheikh" and as a "good guy, the best in Islam" and one who "loves Islam". Hani did mention he had attended classes at the Dar Al Hijra Mosque but did not mention the Imam there.

As to the subject of flight lessons, the two had not taken lessons in Virginia, but only in Florida and Arizona, prior places Hani and Nawaf had lived. The day Hani and Nawaf moved out, Eyad came to pick them up. This was the third or fourth time Eyad had visited the apartment. At the time, Eyad had a car but no driver's license. A few days later Hani and Nawaf were gone, and Ahmed never saw them again.

Last in line was Derar Saleh. We would arrest him a few weeks later for the same charges. If he had been forthcoming from the start about the apartment and his knowledge of the hijackers' time living in the Audubon apartment, we would have saved possibly six months of investigative time answering the key questions about the activities of the Flight 77 terrorist hijackers. I made that very point to him as I put the handcuffs on.

On July 8, 2002, I was requested to head over to FBI Headquarters at the J. Edgar Hoover Building to brief then Deputy Assistant Director John Pistole. According to an email from my Assistant Special Agent in Charge to my criminal Squad Supervisor Rich Klein, the FBI Director, Robert Mueller III "wanted to be briefed/updated regarding he 9/11 hijackers and their nexus to Northern Virginia". It was assumed DAD

Pistole would in turn brief the Director. Supervisor Tom Frields accompanied me there for moral support and make sure I didn't say anything stupid.

I found Pistole to be approachable, and respectful towards a regular "street agent's" work. He asked reasonable questions intended to elicit information and to understand the facts of the briefing rather than the typical "gotcha" questions typical of Bureau management. Reportedly Mueller was notorious and greatly feared for doing just that. Initially the briefing involved just Pistole, Frields, and me. We briefed the details of Alrababah's entire time with the hijackers and clarify the circumstances surrounding the confluence of events connecting our investigation with the DSS Operation Eagle Strike.

Halfway through the briefing, a small army of Headquarters PENTTBOMB supervisors invaded the room. It was clear even Pistole had not been expecting any other participants-since he asked them a collective "who are you guys?". "Oh, we're the PENTTBOMB team". I had been bombarded throughout the Alrababah investigation with requests from PENTTBOMB HQ supervisors for updates and briefings on an almost daily basis. They were certainly kept "in the loop". Everybody wanted their own personal email update they could "brief up" the chain of command even though I had sent an update to the unit the day before.

Fortunately, we had already established a rhythm in the Pistole briefing because the "PENTTBOMB team" had nothing to offer other than repeating everything Frields and I would say. Guess they just needed face time with the DAD. It apparently worked to some extent. They got all the awards. I got none.

Several years later I was interviewed by two members of the 09/11 commission. It was a cordial interview, focused upon the many 302's we had generated, all of which had by then been declassified, provided to the 9/11 Commission, included in their report, and made available to the public. They seemed appreciative of what we had accomplished bringing light to the activities of the Flight 77, hijackers. Later, feedback from FBI management seemed to confirm this.

Of this entire two-year long investigation into Flight 77, the 9/11 Commission Report gave it one and a half pages out of several thousand pages. See page 523. According to the authors of the report, the FBI provided over 1000 documents related to PENTTBOM to the commission.

Ten years later, on the anniversary of 9/11, I was interviewed by FOX news investigative reporter Catherine Herridge for a special called "The Secrets of 9/11". I was interviewed for about an hour and a half. My piece on the show lasted about a minute and a half. I tried to explain the most important or significant or successful elements of our work and give credit to my various partners. She seemed far more interested in whatever conspiracy theories she could dig up about the FBI's interest in Anwar Awlaki and whether we had dropped the ball in some way. I had tried to connect with the case agent on the Awlaki case as soon as we had connected Awlaki to Hani and Nawaf, however he was still stuck in the "wall" mentality and literally turned and walked away from me. I do believe we lost something in his refusal to coordinate with me. I also believe Awlaki was knowledgeable of the Al-Qaeda affiliation of the hijackers and was supporting them in some manner, although perhaps not the actual hijacking plan. The fact that he was the Imam at the San Diego mosque attended by Hani and Nawaf, and then at the Dar Al Hijra Mosque in Falls Church when they showed up in Virginia, was just too coincidental.

My return to my criminal squad was imminent. My Middle Eastern criminal enterprise case was begging to be addressed. My "Title III" (Title III of the Crime Control and Safe Streets act of 1968) criminal wiretap affidavits were almost ready to go. The Skyline Butcher shop and the Skyline Grill next door figured as the center of the criminal activity, predominantly drug distribution. This was the same shop Nawaf Alhazmi had patronized four times.

One significant interview during the Flight 77 investigation would prove to be a diamond in the rough and would prove to be one of the most valuable long-term investments in the new war on terrorism going forward. During the preparations for trial against Alrababah and Alfauru, I was contacted by The US Attorney's Office in the EDVA that an inmate incarcerated with Alfauru had witnessed Alfauru admitting to his involvement in the DMV fraud with Alrababah. The inmate was willing to be interviewed and possibly testify on behalf of the government. He had also apparently met Alfauru at the DMV in Fairfax, Virginia and believed that an employee there was the contact for Driver's licenses. We arranged for his transfer to the Alexandria detention center and via the US Marshalls, brought to the US Attorney's office.

A very large Middle Eastern man entered the room dressed in a prison jump suit. My being of Lebanese descent always helped build rapport with Middle Eastern interviewees as would be expected. We actually hit it off pretty quickly. This individual provided the information relative to Alfauru, but his dates were a little bit off and we decided since Alrababah was going to testify to first-hand knowledge on the government's behalf we decided we did not need his testimony.

Aside from the subject of Alfauru, this individual, an Arab American, who I will refer to as Yusuf, not his real name, was anxious to redeem himself for the legal transgression that landed him in jail. He wished to assist the FBI in investigating the criminal and possible terrorist activities in the Middle Eastern community in the Northern Virginia and DC area upon his release in about ten months. Yusuf did not ask for early release or any favors. I took his personal identifiers and figured that maybe it might pay off sometime down the road. Ten months later, to my surprise, I got a call from Yusuf. That call would begin a decades long relationship with the most dedicated, productive, and successful Confidential Human Source "CHS" of my 30-year career. It's very rare that someone who claims to "want to go straight" or make up for something troublesome in their past actually means it and then proves it definitively. In his case, time showed that it can happen. Our work together would years later be highlighted in a 2009 article by Harry Jaffe in the Washingtonian Magazine. We will get to that in a much later chapter.

V.

Playing Whack-A-Mole

My return to my criminal squad was short lived. A new intelligence/counterintelligence squad dedicated to the Saudi Arabian Peninsula was being formed. My reward for all my work was to be transferred to a squad I had no desire to be a part of. To add insult to injury, my new supervisor was Brian Weidner, with whom I had worked on the DMV fraud aspect of the Flight 77 investigation. Not that I didn't like Brian. I think he had a good heart. He was not a malicious or particularly ambitious guy. But he played favorites to the point of damaging the morale of the squad. The mission of the squad deteriorated to playing "whack-a mole" as we all called it, chasing targets and opening a multitude of cases with minimal reasonable suspicion of any connection to a terrorist organization or cell. The focus was not there.

To his credit at least initially, I was able to lobby to keep the Skyline Butcher case. The hijackers had patronized the store multiple times. All of this gave me the ammunition I needed to work the case as a terrorism finance case. My "Title-III" wire-tap affidavit, started when I was assigned to the organized crime squad, was already almost complete. I had an Assistant US Attorney over at EDVA assigned to the effort.

The FBI has been described sometimes (actually, by a DEA Agent with whom I had been working) as a high-end sports car that can go 100 miles an hour so long as the road is straight and flat, but if it had to go off-road and go around obstacles it gets stuck in the mud. This case was clearly an off-road adventure.

A Title-III, to clarify, is a criminal investigative wiretap designed to collect evidentiary conversations between suspected criminals and has strict rules as to the nature of calls that are allowable to be monitored and recorded. This is in contrast to a "FISA" (Foreign Intelligence Surveillance Act) wiretap, the current subject of much controversy and criticism, which is designed to only collect intelligence against foreign nationals engaged in spying or terrorism and is not designed for prosecution. In this case, I had identified criminal activity, specifically drug trafficking, by individuals who were possibly involved in terrorist activity.

The overall case didn't exactly fit the accepted template at the time. At one point my new ASAC asked me whether the case was a criminal case or an intelligence case. My answer was "yes". It didn't quite fit the established administrative method for categorizing a case and met with some consternation. I had to spend the next ten years or so constantly defending "thinking outside the box".

My new squad was formed out of thin air. As a reaction to the perceived intelligence failures leading to 9/11 the Bureau completely changed gears and effectively abandoned the war on drugs to place a massive focus on counterterrorism. Prior to 9/11, Counterterrorism investigations were somewhat a backwater. The Bureau focused on organized crime, white collar crime, and counterintelligence. Now we were mandated to open any case that had even the most tenuous connections to a mosque or a local Middle Eastern subject— with only the most distant "six degrees of separation" with an individual in a foreign country —who was connected to another individual in a foreign country—that was suspected of ties to another individual who might seem to be a member of a terrorist organization. Once a case was opened it was extremely difficult to close. All of this was driven by the new Director Robert Mueller III, who had seemingly abandoned the Bureau's historic emphasis on criminal investigation and prosecution and was creating a domestic intelligence agency. Collecting and developing intelligence has always been essential in successful complex investigations, especially in regard to large conspiracies such as in organized crime or terrorism, however we were in effect now emphasizing endless collection of intelligence with no end game.

Organized Crime had developed into my specialty, having spent my first five years as an agent in New Orleans investigating the Marcello Mafia Family (also referred to as the "La Cosa Nostra" or "LCN" in FBI parlance), and Colombian cocaine trafficking networks, among other more local criminal conspiracies. I served eight years in my second office in Northern New Jersey assigned to a squad investigating the LCN (the "wise-guys" upon which the Sopranos were based) along with various Middle Eastern and Central Asian drug trafficking conspiracies.

As it turned out, the investigative tools and strategies we applied to investigating organized crime could be applied effectively to investigations targeting the various terrorist funding and money laundering networks. We discovered that those groups employed the same criminal, racketeering activity as did the traditional mafia or drug cartels to finance themselves. Those criminal schemes eventually proved to be their Achilles heel, and much easier to prove in court than a connection to a terrorist organization.

VI.

All of the Above

The roots of my particular investigations into Middle Eastern criminal enterprises began a decade earlier. In the early 1990s, the "coalition of the willing" task force we had formed identified a surprising criminal network of Lebanese, Palestinian, Syrian and Egyptian criminals operating in the Paterson, NJ area and surrounding counties of Bergen and Passaic. As I mentioned earlier, my closest partners were Passaic County Prosecutor's Detectives Jack Vervaet and Danny Bachok, INS Special Agent Mark McGraw, and Paterson Police Department Captain of Detectives Jim Buckley among many others. My squad supervisor was Bob Lenehan, a timid, risk averse and disinterested supervisor. Sadly, the supervisor I would suffer under for five years at the Washington Field Office would be even worse. See a pattern here?

The criminal activity we discovered provided targets of opportunity while other counterterrorism squads struggled to identify a terrorism connection. Each law enforcement member of our "coalition of the willing" would at some point identify a violation within their agency's wheelhouse we could conceivably add to the mix of eventual prosecutions. As to be expected, our cases frequently bumped into other existing counterterrorism investigations.

The number one tool in our toolbox was the recruitment and operation of confidential human sources, referred to by the bureau currently as "CHSs". The recruitment and operation of CHSs would throughout my career prove to be the most effective investigative tool in taking down criminal enterprises and conspiracies, as well as to expand and corroborate intelligence collection even outside the continental US ("OCONUS" in government cliché). There are many types of sources, and many different motivations to cooperate with the FBI. Most often a criminal defendant would agree to cooperate in exchange for sentencing consideration. I was fortunate to stumble upon quite a few "volunteer" sources who were not in any legal danger but were motivated by patriotism, or perhaps a less noble motivation such as a desire for help with an immigration problem. Some were looking for vengeance against someone who had wronged them or committed a crime against them.

Early on we categorized them as "confidential informants" ("CI") or "cooperative witnesses" ("CW") on the criminal side, or "Assets" on the national security side of the house. An Informant provided information and as a rule had his or her identity protected for long term effectiveness. If the individual we recruited was willing to be operational and "wear a wire", purchase evidence or engage in other authorized criminal transactions with criminal subjects and eventually agree to testify, we designated that individual as a "CW". The term "CHS" came in vogue around the mid-2000s and is currently acceptable term. I will agree that consolidating all sources as "CHSs" did simplify things, however under Director Robert Mueller, the reporting requirements, headquarters oversight, and rules and regulations became so overwhelming it discouraged many agents from putting any real effort into "working" sources. I was stubborn and kept at it. My obsessive efforts would certainly serve to prove the adage "let no good deed go unpunished".

In the Early 1990s, a large Pakistani heroin trafficking network was operating in the Boonton and Parsippany areas of Northern New Jersey, extending into New York City. The CW/CHS in the case was a volunteer. He was himself an immigrant whose immigration status was a bit murky, but we did in the end work that out for him based upon his extensive operational assistance. The source was key to identifying how a Dominican dominated distribution conspiracy in the Washington Heights section of New York City was being supplied large shipments of Pakistani brown heroin by Pakistani national Fahim Sabr and his Dominican wife in Parsippany. A second competing Pakistani drug smuggling group was identified by the source and we were able to play the two Pakistani groups and the Dominican group off against each other.

The source was clever and had the ability to work his way into a group of "bad guys". He was excellent when wearing a wire. He eventually connected with Sabr, his wife, and was in the middle of the second Pakistani trafficking group in Parsippany. Sabr trusted the CHS so much he asked him to help arrange a heroin deal with the lead Dominican dealer from Washington Heights. As to be expected, I had to handle monitoring the deal myself at midnight. The CHS was at the time working the night shift at a local hotel where the dealer was to meet him and provide the cash for the heroin purchase to be passed on to Sabr. Sabr would then obtain the heroin with that cash and then meet the dealer in New York.

Once again I just plain got lucky. I was ensconced in an empty room waiting for the money transfer and monitoring the CHS's transmitter. At the conclusion of the transfer, I would meet the CHS in the room and take possession of the cash, count and document the bills and hold the cash at the FBI office until we would then have the source meet Sabr and give him the money. I was alone. My supervisor did not care enough to assign anyone to partner with me. But every success of mine was claimed by him as his success with upperlevel management.

The CHS let me know the dealer was arriving. I just happened to look out the window of the hotel room and at that moment a black Nissan Maxima bearing New York plates backed into the parking spot directly in front of the window. Bingo. After completion of the deal the CHS walked with the subject out to the same car. Now I would be able to identify a key subject. My wife found me at the kitchen table around 2:00 am counting a pile of tens of thousands of dollars.

The next morning, I found another agent to confirm the count in the office and the money was turned in as evidence.

We were even able to use Sabr's group's money to purchase drugs from the other group. We didn't have to use and essentially give away government funds for an undercover transaction. The actual heroin deal as we found out a short time later happened in New York and out of our control. We were able to confirm the deal had occurred through a consensually recorded phone conversation between the CHS and Sabr and then a subsequently a recorded call between the CHS and the Dominican dealer.

The source was able to work himself into the middle of everything that happened within the conspiracy. Over time he engaged in almost 300 recorded phone calls and body recordings. Probably the most pertinent call between the Source and Sabr proved to be the most amusing as well. Sabr called the source to provide instructions as to how to talk on the phone when discussing the multi-kilo heroin negotiations. Sabr instructed the source "from now on don't say heroin—say rugs". We could not have asked for better evidence. Thanks, Fahim for that little gift.

I was by now working closely with the Parsippany Police Department Detectives. We began to conduct joint surveillances at the homes of several of the co-conspirators who lived in the Parsippany area. One evening the main detective with whom I had developed a good working relationship called me at home and informed me They had been observing activity at the home of the key member of the other faction, such as several people carrying large containers into the residence. He was certain this was it.

We partnered with the Parsippany Police to conduct search warrants at that location and at the residences of the other identified subjects and execute arrest warrants for a total of seven subjects from all three groups. Sabr, unknowing of the arrests of his co-conspirators had left for Pakistan. We had by that time arrested the ringleader of the Dominican group, who had conducted the transaction with the CHS at the hotel.

Another new CHS agreed to help us locate Sabr, who was also included in the arrest warrants. The CHS was eventually contacted by Sabr from Pakistan, who was interested in beginning shipments of heroin to the US from Pakistan. I was introduced over the phone to Sabr as a potential distributor for Sabr. Over a period of several months, we attempted to negotiate shipments from Pakistan to the US. The shipments never materialized. Sabr also wished to return to the US but was having trouble obtaining a visa. We lost track of Sabr for a while until a year later he entered the United Kingdom to ostensibly visit relatives and attempted to obtain a visa back to the US at the US Embassy in London. Out of the blue I received a call from the DEA attaché in London, asking me if I was interested in a Fahim Sabr. Hell yes. Sabr's arrest warrant was in the system and popped up when applying for the visa.

With the assistance of Scotland Yard, we had him arrested and extradited back to the US and eventual trial and conviction for conspiracy to distribute seven kilograms of heroin. The CHS continued to assist the FBI for years, including identifying several terrorism subjects in Jersey City, New Jersey, the home of the first World Trade Center bombers.

• • • • • • • •

Moving on to other matters, I was contacted by Jack Vervaet who wanted to meet to discuss an arson case he was working in Paterson. Yes, Paterson, the sometime home of Hani Hanjour and Nawaf Alhazmi. The large Middle Eastern community in Paterson was suffering from arsons, frauds, drug trafficking and other criminal activity. We met at our office in West Paterson, designated as the Garret Mountain Resident Agency, or "RA".

Haidar Rabah was a Lebanese store owner in Paterson who was suspected of torching both of his stores to defraud his insurance company and importing heroin into the US secreted inside large containers of olives. Over time Jack and I would become close friends. We would recruit many other investigators into our ad hoc task force targeting visa and "green card" fraud, gun trafficking, vast copyright violations, bank fraud, money laundering, and other crimes. As expected, we would constantly bump up against counterterrorism agents from the Newark FBI office. We made a great effort to coordinate with the CT agents but the "wall" between criminal agents and CT agents would constantly get in the way. We would always research the background of our subjects to determine whether they were already CT subjects so that we could support their ongoing cases with whatever intelligence we could provide, but also to offer to build criminal cases against them in order to bring pressure to cooperate. Since the CT agents were so reticent to share information with us, on several occasions we would end up building a criminal case and arrest one of their assets. Oops.

The concept of a criminal case seemed to baffle the CT agents who were geared towards intelligence gathering and at most clean up after a terrorist bombing. Again, all of this was occurring prior to September 11, 2001, and the rules were much different in those days. Of course, after 9/11 the rules and the priorities changed frequently as well. Over a period of six or so years, our task force racked up over 80 convictions of members associated with various groups from the Middle East.

In July of 1994 Mark McGraw contacted me, hoping I could help him investigate a group of Palestinians who were involved in producing counterfeit permanent resident cards, more commonly known as "green cards". Mark had recruited a CHS close to that group. I was quite familiar with the CHS, who Jack and I had been targeting as well as a subject. The CHS, for whom I will use the alias Harry, and his brother whom I will call Izzy, owned a small store in Paterson that we always suspected was a front for criminal activity. It was. In the past, they had been convicted of passport and food stamp fraud. They had served as sources off and on over the years, usually when they had gotten into trouble, which is why I am using alias for their names.

Mark brought Harry to a neutral location where he was introduced to me, and subsequently I "opened" him as an FBI joint source with INS. The "green card" fraud was also of concern to our CT agents, but we were concerned with the related racketeering activity.

Harry had been approached by Mahmoud, his son Mohammed, and a friend Alaa who were interested in obtaining green cards for re-sale to illegal immigrants, an INS violation. They were also attempting to engage in a large bank fraud, which would be within the FBI's jurisdiction. Harry introduced me undercover to Mahmoud, who was looking for counterfeit checks that he planned to deposit into multiple bank accounts in New Jersey and New York. He would then send co-conspirators to the banks several days later to withdraw whatever the banks would allow. The checks would eventually be discovered to be counterfeit by the banks, but in the meantime the banks habitually would allow an account holder to be credited with a percentage of the deposit, allowing a certain amount of the bogus funds to be available for withdrawal. Luckily a separate case I had been working provided us with two sets of fake checks to offer to Mahmoud.

In the meantime, another CHS had informed us that the group was shopping for a better deal with another individual with whom we were well acquainted, because he had also served occasionally as a source when in trouble. He was also offering stolen checks for sale. We had a dilemma— we did not want our subjects to complete the deal with anyone else and successfully defraud several banks outside of our control. We had information that our competitor, had offered $300,000 worth of checks to Mahmoud. We had to offer a better deal. We had enough fake checks to offer a million dollars. Mahmoud took our deal.

A few days later I met with Mahmoud and his son and Harry in my car, which was "wired up". Coincidentally, this was the vehicle we ended up seizing from Fahim's distributor, and later converted to undercover use. Jack and Mark and members of my squad were scattered around the area maintaining "the eye". I could see Jack across the parking lot. It gave me a sense of security. Jack and the others were listening via a transmitter I had hidden in my jacket. The most memorable line from the whole conversation came when Mahmoud accepted the deal. He exclaimed "only in America" can you get away with something like this. This really set Jack off. I could see his expression from across the parking lot. The phrase would become a source of amusement for years. We would cite "Only in America" whenever we identified another criminal scheme.

A week later I met again with Mahmoud and Mohammed in my "wired up" car. We had agreed to deposit fake checks worth $250,000 at each of four separate banks. Mahmoud had requested I have someone endorse the checks. Another agent on my squad had a short, simple name and he volunteered to spend some time endorsing the checks. That worked for Mahmoud. He and his son and I then spent the day driving around to the banks, where Mohammed would take the checks into the bank to be deposited. A surveillance team followed us everywhere. Fortunately, I was the driver, so I could tailor my driving so as not to lose the surveillance teams at traffic lights and intersections. As we departed each bank, an agent would enter the bank and approach the teller, explain the situation, and retrieve the checks to prevent their actual deposit and credit to Mahmoud's accounts. I had already contacted the security officer at each targeted bank to inform them of the operation so hopefully any teller involved would not be surprised when the agent showed up to retrieve the checks.

Seven days passed. Enough time for the checks to be credited to Mahmoud's account. We again contacted the security managers at each bank to coordinate the anticipated attempts to withdraw cash from their banks. There of course, were no actual funds in the banks, but we needed the conspirators to believe there were, and attempt to withdraw funds in order to complete the bank fraud and money laundering violations. We agreed to meet in a hotel, where Mahmoud would bring "smurfs" to collect checks from Mahmoud, and who would then go to the various banks and cash out as much as the banks would allow, bringing the cash back to us at the hotel. I would split the proceeds with the group. At least that was the agreed upon plan.

We had the room set up. I had arranged with the hotel to supply us with coffee, tea, and a large basket of baked goods. Hospitality is important in the Middle Eastern culture I thought. Fortunately, I got to the room early to get set up. The basket of muffins I had delivered to the room and the beverages looked good. I went next door to watch the tech agents set up the remote cameras that would be monitored by the rest of our team. That team would also "crash" the room when it was time to make the arrests. As I returned to my room, I noticed the basket of muffins seemed to have shrunk. As I turned around, I caught several team members sheepishly walking out with muffins stuffed into their bags. They reluctantly returned the muffins to the basket. It was good source of ribbing for a few days thereafter. They got to finish them off once the operation was over.

Mahmoud and Mohammed the room. Negotiations ensued as to how we would split the proceeds and how the "smurfs" would cash the checks and return the cash to us. One thing that we needed to verify was that the banks had credited the accounts. The accounts up to that time contained minimal funds. We had contacted the bank security people again the day before to emphasize that if called about the account to advise the caller that the checks had been credited to the account.

Fortunately, Mahmoud asked me to call the banks because his English was sparse. Funny how that worked out. Two of the banks apparently did not get the message because when I called, the employee on the other side of the call stammered that there was a "problem with the account". I turned to Mahmoud and informed him "yes, the money is in the account". I'm allowed a little white lie when undercover.

It was over after about 30 minutes of negotiations. Each co-conspirator was vying to pull me aside and work a side deal. I was wearing an individual body recorder rather than having the entire room wired for sound for this very reason. These side conversations were whispered and away from the rest of the people in the room and might not be picked up by the hidden camera set up. I will not reveal where the camera was hidden. I will say the tech agents were excited to be utilizing what was at that time some new technology, where the camera could pan and zoom. Separate conversations to which I was not a party elsewhere in the room could not be legally recorded without my presence because that would constitute a Title-III interception for which we did not have authority.

I realized Mahmoud and his co-conspirators were trying to scam me out of my share and were trying to escape the room once they believed the money was in the bank. They did not escape. My squad mate, Rick Southerton realized the same thing and called the room. Rick suggested the team crash the room. I agreed.

This was the fun part everyone was waiting for. I had enough fun for the day. Mark, Jack, Danny and Rick burst through the door and swarmed the room. Mark of course felt the need to jump on me, jam his knee in my back, and handcuff me just to make it look good. His gleeful grin was caught on the video just before the tech agents turned off the recorder.

The last bit of amusement for me came when I walked into the interview room where Mahmoud was being held. This time I was wearing my holstered sidearm and badge on my belt. Clearly Mahmoud now knew who I really was. Strangely he still spoke to me as though I was his friend and began claiming his innocence. Eventually, he concluded that he was screwed. He and his coconspirators pled guilty, spent time in federal prison for engaging in a $1 million bank fraud and money laundering. Eventually all were deported back to Jordan. The local papers carried a short article about the case, naming all of the guilty parties.

As would happen so often, our CHS, Harry, who started as a defendant, became a source, and eventually became a defendant again. In 1998 we partnered with IRS and convicted Harry and Izzy of bank fraud—$150,000 of fraudulent checks stolen from a mail facility in Jersey City by a co-defendant. Leopards don't often change their spots.

We constantly bumped into radical or terrorist elements or individuals while rooting out the racketeering activity, and vice versa. Were our Middle Eastern subjects terrorists or criminals? Did they infer terrorist connections to enhance their negotiating positions or as a method of intimidation? Very often it was "all of the above". This would influence how I approached Middle Eastern-based terrorism cases after 9/11. The racketeering activity was much easier to prove. We could attack the criminal activity as a means of addressing the national security concerns by taking the players off the field. Unfortunately this methodology often clashed with the changing and competing priorities and policies in addressing counterterrorism cases.

VII.

Gangsters or Terrorists? The Al Capone Method

Over the years we would find that the majority of successful CT cases would indeed be prosecuted for the underlying criminal activity. We could at least remove the means by which suspected terrorist supporters used to finance themselves here in the US and their terrorist groups overseas.

Developing intelligence identifying the group or organization was not the most difficult part. But intelligence is not evidence. Intelligence provided by CHSs and gained by other methods may convince us or even substantiate the target's connection to a particular group. Proving that an individual provided "Material Support" to that terrorist group at trial is the tough part. Illegally raised funds intended for a terrorist group are usually transferred overseas via complex money laundering schemes, obfuscating the end recipient. The domestic criminal activity used to raise those funds is within reach. I came to refer to this investigative methodology as the "Al Capone method". Capone, the Mafia boss of Chicago in the 1930s was a horrifically violent and powerful criminal mastermind who engaged in murder, corruption of government officials, bootlegging, and a plethora of other criminal acts virtually with impunity. Federal authorities tried in vain for years to develop prosecutable charges against Capone but were finally able to convict Capone on tax evasion charges and send him to Alcatraz prison where he died while incarcerated.

Just because a subject is of Palestinian extraction does not automatically mean he would be a member of or supporter of a Palestinian terrorist organization such as HAMAS, the largest and most powerful designated Palestinian terrorist organization. There are several other Palestinian groups such as Islamic Jihad or the secular, nationalist, Marxist PFLP (Popular Front for the Liberation of Palestine). The Wahabi fundamentalist Al Qaeda has members from all the various Islamic countries as well as non-Muslim and European countries.

Members of a criminal enterprise comprised of fellow Palestinians or other Arabs may merely express a favorable opinion about a group to a CHS. It takes time to figure that out. Over the years we would receive targeting packages from the Counterterrorism Division directing us to initiate cases into suspected individuals or conspiracies whose affiliations were uncertain and very often without an underlying articulated investigative goal.

But once a case was opened, it was virtually impossible to close, no matter how thorough the investigation, and despite the complete lack of any definable terrorist activity.

The apparent connection of the butcher shop to Hani Hanjour and Nawaf Alhazmi somewhat confused the situation—did they just patronize the shop to purchase halal food or were they attempting to utilize the Saids in some manner, as they had done with Alrababah and the Shannaqs? Were the Saids and Khatib just drug dealers for their own personal profit or were they also involved in raising funds for terrorist goals?

We, the agents, typically do the grunt work writing affidavits, whether for a search warrant, an arrest or a wiretap. A Title-III affidavit entails developing a lengthy and detailed historical document, frequently a 60-page-plus dissertation. Policy, on paper, dictates that the agent provides the investigative documentation to be included in the affidavit to the AUSA. The AUSA should then write the affidavit—because of the AUSA's legal expertise. The reality is that the agent always writes the affidavit and the AUSA mostly just edits the document, usually just to put their imprimatur on the document to make it look like they did the work. As we would joke, "changing 'happy' to 'glad'", and "paragraph one to paragraph three". Unlike on cop shows on TV, obtaining authority for a wiretap installation does not happen in an hour. It is an excruciatingly long process. Once the AUSA finishes his or her review and editing, the affidavit is then reviewed by FBI management and legal counsel and is signed off by the FBI director or Deputy Director. It is at the same time being reviewed by the Justice Department and is reviewed and eventually approved by the Attorney General or Deputy. Then the affidavit is finally reviewed by a US District Court Judge who will authorize and then monitor the progress of the actual wiretap proceeds over the several months while it is in operation.

The Title-III case targeting the owners of the Skyline Grille and Skyline Butcher was submitted to the US Attorney's Office in Alexandria for review. AUSA Larry Leiser was the assigned prosecutor. Larry was an old-school prosecutor. A bit of a curmudgeon, but a good, aggressive prosecutor. Although this case was officially a counterterrorism case, the US Attorney's Office in EDVA assigned it to their criminal division because the anticipated prosecutable violations involved drug trafficking and money laundering.

I had more support from EDVA than I did from my own squad. Unfortunately, the squad was formed by mostly pulling agents from drug squads. Most did not want to be reassigned and were rather bitter. Immediately after 9/11, Director Mueller decided to virtually abandon the "war on drugs" and disband entire drug and violent crime squads and convert them into CT and intelligence squads. This made for a lot of very unhappy criminal and drug agents who had spent sometimes years developing an expertise and a base of knowledge. That was my new squad.

Strangely, though, I found that several squad members objected to using a drug case to pursue a CT or counterintelligence case. The only blessing turned out to be the few new agents now assigned to our squad as their first assignment, Jeff "JD" Taylor, Mike P., Shawn Devroude and Jeff H (for agents who are still active, and I cannot contact, I am simply using their first names. JD has given his permission and Shawn has recently retired). I was assigned as Shawn's training agent. We actually made a pretty good team. The guys were new and what they lacked in experience, they made up for in enthusiasm. Being the old salt, I still tried to maintain my enthusiasm too. They would be the only squad-mates who Brian would ever even assign to monitor the wiretap and therefore when the case concluded would be the only squad mates I would include in the arrests and search warrants, the part most agents looked forward to.

We had been conducting surveillance for weeks at the Skyline Grill and the Skyline Butcher shop prior to 9/11 and then beginning again afterwards. We had initially partnered up with the Fairfax County Police Narcotics Unit and they had introduced a CHS to us who was very familiar with Sami and Mohammed Said in their drug distribution business. This CHS was the eventual key to development of the probable cause, or "PC" that would be included in the affidavit. I was partnered with a young narcotics detective. Unfortunately, the detective was severely injured during a drug arrest and FCPD never assigned another detective.

While I was still assigned to the drug squad, we had been lent a remote camera with recording capability. The location was an extremely difficult place to conduct surveillance. It was located at the back of a strip mall on George Mason Drive in Alexandria. It had a narrow parking lot that was bordered by a chain link fence covered by green plastic strips separating a Coca Cola plant from the strip mall. My partner at the time, Glen Mai and I decided to secrete the camera (I can't describe that any further) in the vicinity of the Skyline Grill. The grille was owned by Mohammed and Sami's cousin, Issam Khatib, also a co-conspirator in the drug network. The Dar Al Hijra Mosque was only about a mile away. This was to be a dry run and we had activated the camera so that we could watch the front door from a distance. We had the ability to monitor the camera remotely. Almost immediately Issam exited the restaurant and retrieved a plastic bag containing white powder from a bush in front of the restaurant. We kicked ourselves because we had not yet installed a tape in the camera, so we did not have a recording. This time luck was not on our side. At the time it was a frustrating disappointment but in the end we would have more than enough PC for a Title-III, and then a massive amount of evidence to prosecute eighteen defendants.

As stated in the introduction of the affidavit, (generally standard language in any wiretap affidavit):

The facts and circumstances of the investigation as set forth below show that:

> a. There is probable cause to believe that the Suspects have committed, are committing and conspiring to commit offenses involving the distribution and possession with intent to distribute cocaine (a Schedule II controlled substance) , marijuana (a Schedule I

controlled substance), and ecstasy (C3,4-Methylenedioxymethamphetamine, a Schedule I controlled substance) and other illegal drugs in violation of 21 USC Section 842 (a) (1), the unlawful use of a communication facility, that is, a cellular telephone in committing, causing, or facilitating the commission of drug felonies…

b. There is probable cause to believe the Suspects have used, are using, and will continue to use communication facilities… 1) cellular telephone facility utilized by Sami Said, subscribed to by Mohammed Said 5452 Colfax St., Alexandria, Virginia 2) cellular telephone facility (phone number redacted) utilized by Mohammed Said, 5452 Colfax St., Alexandria, Virginia and 3) cellular telephone facility utilized by Issam Khatib, at 4205 Sandhurst Court, Annandale, Virginia, all in furtherance of and to facilitate the commission of the specified drug offense.

c. There is probable cause to believe that the interception of certain wire communications of the Suspects occurring over cellular telephone facilities…

- will reveal the identities of the persons from whom the Suspects receive cocaine, ecstasy and marijuana and to whom the drugs are distributed;
- the methods for the disposition of the drugs and drug proceeds;
- the dates, times, and manner of the transportation,

receipt, storage, disposition, and delivery of both drugs and drug proceeds;

- the nature and scope of the conspiracy;
- and the identities and roles of other co-conspirators;

(The affidavit continues to list possible co-conspirators, including both suppliers and customers, to include, Misum Said, Sami and Mohammed's sister, but not limited to a suspect who is allegedly responsible for the storage of their drug supply; various limousine drivers, one of whom, Jamal Kweis was described by confidential sources as a driver for Khatib and a drug distributor for Khatib; other suspects, Ayoush Abutaa and Armon Keyablian, who are frequent callers to the Saids, involved with calls that are made between suspects and Mohammed Said; calls between suspects and Sami Said, and those who have been identified in other, unrelated drug or other criminal investigations;

One suspect, Salman Abuelhawa was described by confidential sources as a significant customer of Khatib's, a frequent caller to Khatib's cellular phone, as well as making frequent calls to Mohammed Said and who has been described by confidential sources as also a significant customer of Mohammed Said.

Other suspects, Nabil Hamad and Nasser Aburish, Dean Smalls, Clint Asmar and George Torres, AKA "Shorty", were also described by confidential sources as a supplier to Mohammed Said and a frequent caller to Mohammed Said's cellular phone; one described by a confidential source as either a supplier or customer to Mohammed Said and one believed to be described by a confidential source as a drug associate of Sami Said and a frequent caller to Sami Said...and others as yet unknown)

> d. There is probable cause to believe that these wire interceptions will produce admissible evidence of the specified federal drug offenses by the Suspects, that is, the tapes of the intercepted communications themselves; and
>
> e. Normal investigative techniques have failed or reasonably appear unlikely to succeed if continued or tried or appear too dangerous to pursue in developing the quantum of evidence necessary for prosecution of the above-described offenses.

Investigation leading up to the installation of wiretaps included the use of dialed number recorders ("pen registers") intercepts. A pen register intercepts the phone numbers called by the subjects and received by the subjects without intercepting actual conversations. Other crucial investigation would include surveillance, CHS development, and coordination with other law enforcement agencies, notably Fairfax County Narcotics.

9/11 had significantly stalled the investigation for almost six months. One real glitch occurred when the WFO Criminal ASAC, who had no experience in investigating terrorist matters, was desperate to be involved in the PENTTBOMB investigations. Careers could be made (except for mine, apparently). She sent her criminal agents to flood the high-rise apartments and shops in the overlapping areas of Falls Church and Alexandria around George Mason Drive, Seminary Road, and Route 7, and conduct interviews of Middle Eastern residents. Not sure what they were asking.

One person whose door was knocked on was an associate of Issam Khatib. At the time she was the true subscriber of Khatib's cell phone--the cell phone on which I was developing PC. The cell phone was immediately shut off. I lost six months of phone records. Eventually we identified the new phone used by Khatib and got back on-line.

We determined that since 1996, Sami Said and his brother Mohammed Said had been distributing illegal drugs in the Northern Virginia metropolitan area and were significant suppliers to a university in Virginia. Their base of operation had always been the Skyline Butcher Shop located in Falls Church. Mohammed worked sporadically at the shop, owned by his father Asad Said. Mohammed's primary source of income was illegal drug trafficking. Source information and surveillance determined Sami was not employed at the shop and his sole source of income was from drug trafficking.

Both brothers distributed both cocaine and marijuana, with Sami mostly dealing marijuana in up to 800-pound amounts. At the time, this was a significant amount of pot to rise to the level of federal scrutiny at that time. Mohammed distributed mostly cocaine in multiple kilogram amounts. A CHS provided by another agency described the brothers as "24-7 drug dealers", relying almost exclusively on their cell phones to conduct business. The CHS noted the brothers are Palestinian and the overwhelming number of their customers are of Arab extraction. The overall circumstances legally made it necessary to initiate telephone interception.

Issam Khatib was a cousin of the Saids. His clientele was also predominantly Arabic. He and Asad Said had jointly owned the Butcher shop and the Skyline Grill next door, but eventually separated. The Grill was almost exclusively used as a front for Khatib's drug distribution business, while the butcher shop did conduct legitimate business. Since 1995 Khatib had been selling drugs out of the grille, nightclubs, hotels, restaurants, and bars in the Northern Virginia area.

By the time I was authorizing the Title -III affidavit, I had developed five CHSs, all of whom had observed Khatib and, or the Saids selling drugs, and using their cell phones to arrange drug deals. These two factors; a source's personal observations of the suspected criminal conduct coupled with the subjects' use of the targeted personal cell phones to facilitate that same conduct were the necessary elements of probable cause needed to convince a Federal District Court Judge to authorize the electronic monitoring of a subject's personal conversations. Phone records obtained for the three subjects' phones disclosed a pattern of phone calls between their cell phones and phones subscribed to by known drug dealers and customers—a total of over 9,000 calls. Surveillances we had conducted at the grille and the shop confirmed much of the source reporting. All this information became the basis of the probable cause underpinning the affidavit.

The affidavits would be provided to the court in order to obtain the wiretaps and the subsequent renewal of the wiretaps, and much later to the defense during the pre-trial proceedings known as "discovery". The affidavits and resulting transcripts of conversations would even, years later, be provided to the US Supreme Court relative to an appeal by one of the convicted co-conspirators, Salman Abuelhawa, who negotiated drug purchases with Mohammed Said. The case was even studied by Georgetown law students, whom I met when we were all attending the hearings at the Supreme Court, which really surprised me.

Notably, source information alleged "Khatib maintained the practice of secreting some of his supply of cocaine in the bushes in front of his restaurant the Skyline Grille". Our observation during that early surveillance using the hidden camera corroborated the source. Sources also reported the three subjects used countersurveillance techniques in order to "detect the presence of law enforcement in the area of their drug distribution activities". Surveillance agents consistently were scrutinized by individuals who appeared to have been directed by Khatib and the Saids to post outside on the sidewalk in front of the butcher shop and grille. Surveillance was so difficult that we had to innovate. We also had to be wary of the other stores and their owners and patrons if we were set up in their vicinity.

My affidavit included a passage stating, "surveillance established a frequent and consistent pattern of what appeared to be drug customers entering the grille and the shop in a manner which would not be consistent with the innocent purchase of groceries or a meal;

commonly entering the one of two locations furtively and exiting quickly so as to avoid detection".

All of the below described probable cause was included in the initial affidavit and provided to the US District Court in the Eastern District of Virginia, "EDVA". All of this information would eventually be provided to the defense at discovery, including transcripts of the intercepted conversations between the Saids and their co-conspirators, and made it all the way to the Supreme Court (See FINDLAW publication concerning United States v. Abuelhawa).

The initial CHS, referred to in the affidavit as "CS-1", probably had the most first-hand information, as well as the most to gain or lose in his cooperation. I spent two years in the run up to the wiretap installations debriefing the source and then following up on the information, trying to corroborate it. The source had charges pending but had proved reliable to another agency, providing information leading to search warrant affidavits, arrests and indictments. This history would also give the source credibility to the court. The source was also afraid of testifying against the Saids, having observed them in possession of firearms during drug deals, and overhearing them in conversations alluding to having engaged in acts of violence against some of their drug associates.

CS-1 described Sami's business model. Sami would receive a call on his cell phone from a drug customer and would usually reply to the customer to effect that he "had to go pick it up". Sami's next step would be to visit his sister Misum's apartment to retrieve a supply of marijuana. If Sami needed a supply of coke, it was Mohammed who would provide it to him at the butcher shop. Sami and Mohammed handled the distribution and Misum would handle the storage.

Sami had a vast multi-state supply network traveling with his cousin Yusuf Abutaa, (not to be confused with our CHS Yusuf) to retrieve drug loads on trips to Florida to purchase the cocaine supply, to New York for pills of various kinds, and to Texas for marijuana, and into Washington, DC and as far as Canada for a little bit of everything. CS-1 was present when Sami and Abutaa returned from a trip to Florida flush with new supply. Abutaa hauled in several suitcases and a duffel bag filled with plastic bags of yellowish-white powder. CS-1 described Sami as "one step" from the direct importer of high quality "kind bud" marijuana from Canada. Mohammed was capable of pound quantity sales of coke to someone he trusted. The Saids' had another storage location in the home of another co-conspirator, Mike Marone. Marone's car was observed by surveillance at the Saids' house in Alexandria and even more significantly, his phone was called 779 times from Sami's phone.

Sami and Mohammed both still lived in the family home with Asad and his wife. Mohammed stored, weighed, and "cut" the cocaine at the house. On one occasion the Saids stored 800 pounds of marijuana in the shed behind the house that shed would eventually be searched, and lead to an embarrassing moment for one of my squad mates. Some shipments of marijuana arrived in packages of tens of pounds, coated in petroleum jelly and covered with an unknown spice meant to fool a drug dog. The supplier in this case was a Somali cab driver in DC, Mohamud Abdifatah. Said, Abdifatah, and George Hall had previously been arrested and convicted in DC for sales of drugs to an undercover Metro Police officer. Abdifatah's taxi was observed by surveillance at the grille. More PC for the Title-III.

Sami and Mohammed always spoke in Arabic on the phone when negotiating drug deals believing if their calls were monitored by law enforcement it could not be understood. This was fortunately for us a mistake on their part. We had an entire squad of linguists. According to CS-1, the phones were busy "24-7".

Sami was known to force a drug customer to ingest drugs in front of him before selling him any cocaine, apparently to flush out any undercover agents. Mohammed frequently would send Sami back to their home address to retrieve drugs.

CS-1 proceeded to identify most of the drug distribution co-conspirators cited in the Title-III affidavit. A Vehicle registered to another co-conspirator was observed by surveillance teams parked in the Said's driveway on several occasions. More corroboration of the CHS. PC was building.

An FBI CHS of three years added to the story. This source, referred to as "CS-2" had previously identified several members of a Middle Eastern crime families and had provided information that had led to the arrest of a fugitive and an arrest of a drug subject in a separate investigation, and the seizure of $13,000. This source was not compelled to cooperate although he did have a prior arrest for drug distribution. The CHS was not willing or able to make an undercover drug purchase from the Saids or Khatib because his fear of reprisal. CS-2 was acquainted with the Saids and Khatib and had been a regular patron of the grille over a five-year period, also having purchased cocaine a few times but he claimed it had been several years since those purchases. CS-2 was aware Khatib and Asad Said were at one time business partners but separated because of Khatib's perceived lack of a work ethic. CS2 confirmed from personal observation Khatib had been selling cocaine for at least five years. Unbeknownst to the CHS, we had already observed him patronizing the grille.

In the late 1990s Khatib began working together with Sami and Mohammed in a drug distribution business, with Mohammed known to "cut", or dilute for resale cocaine shipments for Khatib. Khatib himself was a heavy user of cocaine, displaying common "jittery" behavior and a constant runny nose. The CHS identified two suppliers to the Khatib-Said network, "Mustapha", and Aubrey Pierson, known as "Smiley", who were both neighbors of the Saids. We were able to confirm Smiley's address through the usual investigative methods such as public records checks, surveillance of vehicles in his driveway. CS-2 identified Smiley's photo from a photo array. Surveillance confirmed Smiley exiting his house and entering the vehicle and meeting with Khatib at the grille and engaging in what appeared to be a drug deal.

CS-2 had also observed Mustapha distributing cocaine to Khatib and Pierson, however Mustapha eventually was arrested, and Pierson located a new supplier named "Kenny", the driver of a distinctive old yellow Cadillac with Maryland license tags. On one occasion, Khatib admitted he was "dry". He was shortly thereafter visited by Kenny, who met Khatib in the back of the grille and clearly delivered coke to Khatib judging from Khatib's sudden possession of the drug after he departed. The pen registers showed over 240 calls between Khatib and Kenny. CS-2 described Khatib's business model as commonly meeting a customer inside of the grille to discuss the deal, and then complete the deal outside on the sidewalk.

Khatib and the Saids eventually became competitors in the drug business. Kenny would not meet Khatib at the grille because Khatib was known to have been arrested in the past. Therefore, a cocaine customer of Khatib's, a limousine driver named Jamal Khweis, would be recruited to drive Khatib to his supplier Kenny. CS-2 was able to identify Khweis the limo driver's vehicle, a black Lincoln Town Car, and the license tag, and his cell phone number. The sign of a good source. We ran the tag and the phone number. The Town Car was registered to Khweis. The cell phone connected to Mohammed Said's and Khatib's over 700 times. The phone was subscribed to—the Embassy of a significant foreign embassy.

CS-2 echoed much of what CS-1 had reported to us. Khatib sold cocaine at various nightclubs and hotels in the Washington, DC area. The CHS also provided the cell phone numbers for Said and Khatib. The numbers matched what CS-1 had given us. He additionally identified another employee of Khatib at both the restaurant and in the drug business, known as "Maachi" whose vehicle had already been observed at the grille and was registered to an Elmaachi Chatib. A third CHS would also confirm the employee's role at both the restaurant and as a distributor of coke for Khatib. CS-2 described several cell phone conversations he had overheard between Khatib and apparent drug customers, immediately followed by a trip outside to the bushes.

Several other drug customers were identified by the CHS, predominantly Middle Eastern males, specifically Abuelhawa. CS-2 had observed a drug transaction involving Issam Khatib, Abuelhawa and Mohammed Said in front of the butcher shop. Of significance was a new player who was also present would later prove to be the lynchpin of the next phase of investigations into international terrorist financing. Those investigations would last for years and involve multiple agencies and countries and take me and other partners to Jordan, Lebanon, Cyprus, Benin, Turkey, the UK, Netherlands, Germany and France. Back to Mohammed Said, CS-2 had been informed by Said that Said had been traveling to New York City to pick up loads of cocaine. Mohammed boasted to others in front of the source hat he had been purchasing up to a kilogram (1000 grams) at a time. Each kilo would be sold in less than two weeks. Mohammed arranged his drug deals by cell phone but was careful not to discuss the deals in front of his father. We learned later on that Asad simply chose to turn a blind eye to his two sons' drug dealing, and in the end was happy to benefit from the lucrative proceeds. Mohammed spent most of his time at the butcher shop running out to brief "meetings" at various locations in the area that had no connection to shop business, including the Coca Cola plant immediately behind the Butcher shop's shopping center, and in the parking lot of the Alexandria campus Northern Virginia Community College. Dad had to know what was going on.

Mohammed's "best customers" included the owner of a car dealership and a drug dealer in his own right, "Modar", and of course, Jamal Khweis, the embassy driver. Fifteen of the nineteen 9/11 hijackers were Saudis. Any connection? Osama Bin Laden came from a fabulously wealthy Saudi family who owned a large construction company. Many members of his family, who allegedly had disowned him, were living and working in the DC area and elsewhere and were spirited back to Saudi Arabia by the Bush administration just days after 9/11.

Mohammed also had a significant customer in the owner of a shoe repair shop in Springfield Virginia named George. Mohammed had made hundreds of calls to the shoe repair shop and over 250 calls to the car dealer. George Sherman Hall, the employee at the butcher shop had been arrested with Mohammed in DC several years before for drug distribution by the Metropolitan Police Department. He was still Mohammed's and Sami's partner in the drug business with over 500 hundred calls between him and Mohammed and dozens of calls with Sami. Sherman helped Mohammed sell ecstasy pills as well as cocaine and confirmed Mohammed had been "ripped off" by someone in New York for $6000 and 2000 pills.

"Mohammed's man" for marijuana, Dean Smalls, would deliver loads directly to Mohammed and

Sami's house in Alexandria. A CHS identified Small's car which the source had observed in the driveway as he delivered a load. We identified 180 calls between Smalls and Mohammed. Mohammed certainly spent a lot of his time on the phone with his suppliers and customers. Smalls had previous convictions for "selling dangerous drugs", possession with intent to distribute heroin, and various frauds and other crimes. Clearly a careerist. The inmate, eventually identified as Salman Abuelhawa, and several others, George Torres, Nabil Hamad, and Nasser Aburish were all identified by CS-2 as being additional customers and frequently "hanging out" with Mohammed in front of the butcher shop. All of whom were captured on phone records. One drove a black Cadillac and two others both drove Lincoln Towne Cars. All three appeared to fit the pattern of limo drivers being involved in the re-distribution of the Saids' cocaine. Again, hundreds of calls between Mohammed and the limo drivers on the phone records. On one occasion a driver co-conspirator attempted to make a purchase from Mohammed who was in his Mercedes Benz in the parking lot of the grille. The deal fell through to his dismay because Mohammed had observed multiple police vehicles in the area.

Khatib eventually moved his drug sales away from the grille and set up shop at the Hilton Hotel in Alexandria, where he met on a regular basis with Smiley to pick up coke from him.

A third CHS, CS-3, corroborated most of the details provided by CS-1 and CS-2. CS-3 had already located a federal fugitive and provided information that led to the arrest of a subject for cocaine distribution and the seizure of a small load of cocaine. The CHS was closest to Maachi in the Said's drug distribution network. During the source's cooperation with us, Khatib called the source and offered to sell him cocaine. Mohammed would "take care" of the source. The source and I decided I should accompany him to visit the grille and have lunch. CS-3 introduced me to Khatib. Fortunately, my Lebanese heritage always worked well in these circumstances, and I clearly looked the part. The CHS met Khatib in the rear of the grill where Khatib quoted a price of $250 for an "eight ball" or one eighth of an ounce of coke, which was a stupidly high price for an eight ball. We later speculated that Khatib was testing the source to see if he could be working for law enforcement and would be willing to pay any price to make the deal. Khatib instructed the CHS to go home and he would call him later. Khatib never called him back. No worries, this was still additional good PC for the Title-III.

• • • • • • • •

As for my undercover bona fides, during this time I was also serving as the undercover agent in two separate cases at WFO, and the one I mentioned earlier down in the Norfolk-Virginia Beach area. The Norfolk case also overlapped the PENTTBOM investigation as I detailed earlier, and involved my working with a CHS, who was a patriot, and a former military officer who owned a tech company. The tech company had been approached by Chinese intelligence officers to purchase a contract on some non-transferable tech. I posed as the middleman trying to broker the transfer to a Middle Eastern country. Can't say more than that, other than I got to drive a very cool undercover vehicle. One of the WFO cases involved an Iranian opium distribution network, and the other was a completely different stolen property case against a group of Northern Virginia "boosters" or shoplifters who then sold the "swag" to a group of DC gangsters in Southeast DC. I won't go into the details of the cases, not because of any confidentiality but more so as not to divert too much from the story line. I will say that very few agents are willing to work undercover. Even those who made it through the meat grinder undercover school, often decided not to continue in the UC program, so there were only a few of us at WFO who were constantly being asked to do the undercover in multiple cases. Think unrelenting stress. Especially if one was also a busy case agent trying to juggle multiple cases of one's own along with handling CHSs. And of course, the epic, overwhelming paperwork.

Rarely did the case agent for an undercover operation really appreciate the work an undercover agent did for their case, even when the case was successful specifically because of the UC's work. Undercovers go through training as to how to function in an undercover situation, case agents running an undercover operation do not receive training as to how manage such an operation and often do not have a workable investigative plan or a defined end goal. Nor do they know how to treat the UC who is helping to make their case. I will say I did work with a few agents with whom I would do a return engagement because they had an instinctive feel for how to treat colleagues and cooperative witnesses or CHSs. I ended up serving as the undercover agent in about 15 different cases at both WFO and other divisions over the years. That doesn't include the cases I worked in New Jersey and New Orleans. Very often management pushes UC operations in order to cite their having "supervised" a complex investigative technique in their promotion packets. I will save all of that for maybe another book (although after what I had to go through to have the bureau approve this one, I'm not sure I would have the energy for another one).

• • • • • • • •

CS-4 confirmed Khatib's use of the bushes in front of the grille and added that he would use magnetic boxes placed underneath the tables in the grille containing cocaine for retrieval by his customers. The CHS also further identified the car dealer with a dealership on Columbia Pike in Arlington, Virginia as a cousin of Khatib's and a drug customer of Khatib's. Notably, the source had observed the car dealer secreting two ounces of cocaine inside the roof lining of a vehicle he was shipping to Saudi Arabia. He was heavily involved in the shipment of used cars to Saudi Arabia as well as shipping household goods on behalf of Saudi embassy employees. He also functioned as a freight forwarder, arranging for the shipments at the port of Baltimore for other auto exporters. Over time we would identify other used car dealers and freight forwarders involved in the shipment of cars to Middle Eastern countries, with business relationships with individuals with whom we identified as Hizballah and Hamas financial supporters and money launderers which would serve to identify a world-wide network of terrorist finance extending to Lebanon, West Africa, South America and as far away as China.

Again, CS-4 confirmed the identity of Aubrey "Smiley" Pierson as a major supplier to Issam Khatib, and two other suppliers to the Saids, Mustapha and Kenny, and identified their photos from a photo spread. A new co-conspirator, Said Abdelreheem was added to the list of subjects. Smiley would travel to New York to pick up kilo loads of cocaine and was the financier of the loads. Smiley was described as directing the entire drug network around the DC area from his barber shop located towards South Capitol Street near the Maryland border. CS-4 had witnessed Smiley in possession of 25 kilos of cocaine, and estimated Smiley had trafficked over 250 kilos using coded language when discussing deals over the phone.

The CHS added Mohammed was receiving multi-hundred-pound shipments of marijuana via UPS from Texas. The drugs were processed at the family home in Alexandria with Misum's assistance. Mohammed was the "main supplier" of weed to Virginia Tech University in Blacksburg, Virginia. Mohammed and Sherman were known to have traveled to New York ove 100 times to retrieve cocaine shipments.

Mohammed and his crew were very surveillance conscious and engaged in counter-surveillance methods around the butcher shop when conducting drug deals.

Lookouts would be posted at key locations around the shopping center with cell phones and they would call Mohammed if they observed any vehicle that appeared to them to be law enforcement. We observed this behavior on almost every surveillance. It was tough going. On one occasion a CHS observed a twelve-year-old boy who was used to deliver an "eight ball" to a customer for Mohammed on his bicycle. Nice guy. A real pillar of the community.

A fifth and final source, CS-5 in the affidavit, claimed to have developed a coke habit because of his association with Issam Khatib. The CHS observed that Khatib frequently weighed out and packaged his coke in his office at the rear of the grille. He would store the packages in his desk and conduct deals in the office. The restaurant did little legitimate food service and was mostly used as front for drug distribution. Khatib never seemed to run out of cocaine, always had it on hand, and never had a problem obtaining it.

All this sordid history was woven into the Title-III affidavit and presented to the army of officials within the FBI, US Attorney and "Main Justice". We were ready to turn on the recorders.

On June 5, 2003, US District Court Judge in the Eastern District of Virginia, James Cacheris signed the court orders. The wiretaps on the phones of Issam, Mohammed and Sami were initiated. A criminal "T-III" is specifically intended for the gathering of evidence. That evidence is generally the contemporaneous statements made by the intercepted parties, including the specified targets and those with whom they communicate. The conversations often stand alone, however it is incumbent upon the investigators to attempt to corroborate possible criminal acts alluded to in those conversations. As an example, if we were to intercept a discussion of a pending meeting between subjects for the purpose of engaging in a criminal act, in this case predominantly drug deals, a surveillance team would be deployed to "cover" that meeting. Code words used by the intercepted parties could be corroborated by the eventual testimony of a cooperative witness or an undercover agent who had been privy to in person conversations regarding the use of those code words. Unlike a national security FISA (National Security Surveillance Act), a T-III must be monitored at all times by law enforcement personnel.

In this case, we anticipated the targets would be speaking in Arabic a good portion of the time. Therefore, we would have to have agents and linguists teamed to "sit the wire". There are strict rules regarding what conversations may be monitored and those that are considered "privileged", such as those between the intercepted party and his clergy, lawyer, spouse, or physician. Those conversations may be listened to for a minute or so and then must be turned off for two minutes once one of the participants is identified as privileged. The exceptions arise when it can be construed the participant is also engaged in criminal conduct with the target. Spouses and lawyers are most often the ones who turn out to be co-conspirators in my experience.

The phones of Sami and Mohammed were crazy busy. "24-7" as the CHS described, was accurate. Issam seemed to have gone dark. Strange. We found eventually that Issam had been arrested by Fairfax County PD for an alleged rape charge and he had ceased dealing just as we finally got up on his phone. After all that work.

Mohammed and Sami clearly did not quit and seemed to be the energizer bunnies. They never took a rest. The phones were going non-stop and the calls identified more than sixteen co-conspirators. We were interested in suppliers and re-distributers, not just users. Some callers were definitely on the large supplier side. Sometimes it was not completely clear whether a caller was either. Some were calling to obtain amounts that could be a user quantity or a small re-sale amount.

In those days, the "push to talk" function was new and quite popular. Monitoring these broken conversations was tricky and tedious because a monitor is required to keep a contemporaneous written log of each intercepted call and each call is numbered. The push-to-talk function created a separate call each time a participant pushed the button. Often the calls were a mix of English and Arabic.

Of the more than sixteen co-conspirators intercepted, the most significant co-conspirators included Said Abdelreheem, George Torres, their cousin Shadi Ghabayen, whose house turned out to be a location where drug loads were processed, George Tenkerian, the shoe repair store owner in Springfield, Abuelhawa, Jeff Nguyen, who was Mohammed's key transporter of weed to colleges, and one of the many limo drivers involved in the re-sale of coke to limo customers and elsewhere.

The lack of support from my own squad at first presented a problem in staffing the wire. I had fortunately developed a good relationship with the Linguist squad and was able to secure enough linguists. The only agents from my squad who volunteered were the four new agents, JD, Jeff, Shawn, and Mike. They were required to "check the box" for their probationary checklist which included monitoring a T-III at least on three occasions. Also, fortunately because WFO was heavy with New Agents, who were all trying to complete their checklist, I was able to staff the wire on my own. Brian never really stepped up to support me, but he did know I had already handled prior wires and could do it regardless of his support. I had already written a dozen T-III affidavits as the case agent, managing the interceptions of organized crime Title-IIIs in my first office, New Orleans, and a four-month T-III targeting a major organized crime and corruption case in Lodi, New Jersey which received a great deal of publicity, maybe more than it deserved. Brian also knew as the squad supervisor he would take credit for all my work. And he did.

During the monitoring period of Sami and Mohammed's phones, we intercepted hundreds of drug distribution related calls with various co-conspirators. Calls involving Sami served to incriminate Mohammed and calls involving Mohammed implicated Sami. We noted a common pattern during Sami's calls with drug customers; frequently Sami would express the need to consult with "Mo" as to the availability of drugs. Sami would then immediately call Mohammed and inquire whether the drugs in question were available in various, specific hiding spots such as the attic of their house where they lived with their

parents or at Shadi's house. During calls with drug associates, Sami and Mohammed would often identify their location as being at their residence or at their cousin Shadi's house nearby, or other places when arranging locations for a drug deal. Our surveillances often succeeded in corroborating these meetings. Sami's phones netted thousands of completed calls. hundreds of intercepted calls were judged to be "pertinent", meaning related to criminal activity, that is, some portion of the call included a reference to some aspect of the criminal activities of the Saids' drug trafficking activities. It was required by the court that all of this information be included in timely reports to the court.

Mohammed's phones were even more prolific.

Our Special Operations Group, or "SOG" was assigned to cover meetings between Sami, Mohammed and their co-conspirators. One element of proof to support the eventual indictments was the observation of and documentation of the targets' use of their cell phones matching the times of the intercepted calls. Sami and Mohammed seemed to prefer talking on the phone while walking around outside. Easy to surveille. Great evidence.

As noted earlier, the Saids and their underlings employed counter-surveillance techniques, such as posting sentries at the butcher shop and at their homes. Our SOG was well aware of this. I found the SOG agents to be very professional and easy to work with. Many of their agents were folks I had worked with in the past on other matters. A complex case such as this was well within their skill set and they seemed to enjoy the challenge.

As documented in the arrest warrants at the conclusion of the wiretaps:

"The frequent and consistent pattern of what appeared to be drug customers entering the home of Mohammed and Sami Said and at the home of Shadi Ghabayen in a manner which would not be consistent with individuals who were innocently entering the home for social activities, but rather for the express purpose of entering furtively and purchasing illegal drugs, and then departing quickly in order to avoid detection.

"Surveillance has also confirmed the presence of various individuals at the residences who have been identified by confidential sources and corroborated through pen register interception and current Title-III monitoring as being drug customers or suppliers to the targeted individuals. Impending meetings which were to occur at various locations, between Sami Said and his customers and suppliers, and between Mohammed Said and his customers and suppliers and which were discussed over the monitored phones have been corroborated through surveillance of those meetings".

A few days after monitoring began, on June 20, 2003, Sami called Mohammed in the direct connect mode and asked him to bring "a big brick". Mohammed responds, "three and a half", to which Sami replies "when I get in the house". This call already gave us early PC for a search warrant at their house in Alexandria. That same day, Sami calls Mohammed and confirms that Mohammed is "still in the house". Sami instructs Mohammed to leave him "a half" on the shelf inside the "Snap-on" tool-box; the code to open the box is three zeros". Clever.

On July 2, Sami calls Mohmmed via the direct connect function. Sami asks Mohammed to get him "a one", and "three and a half 'white'". Mohammed replies he is "coming right now". Sami additionally asked Mohammed to get $600 from beneath his pillow.

During the first day of monitoring, Sami, and cousin Shadi Ghabayen traveled to Pennsylvania and Delaware to pick up a load of drugs. Sami and Mohammed maintained constant contact by phone. At one point Sami informs Mohammed that he will put the car in the garage when he gets back. The garage turned out to be that at Shadi's house. This was certainly a test of the monitoring of the "push to talk" feature. At first it drove the monitors a bit crazy because this created ten times more numbered calls than what were usual, but our targets also felt more comfortable using the "walky-talky" method and were a bit less careful in their code talk. Another search warrant in the making.

A few days later, a series of calls ensued between various customers and the Saids. They discuss the drugs that another supplier has. When Sami returned to the house from the trip to Delaware he had left the drugs he had purchased in the trunk of his car. Mohammed had clearly removed the drugs and hidden them in his room.

On June 9, Sami engaged in a series of calls. Sami acknowledged he had put "it" next to Sami's bed and later acknowledging he had put "the bag" in Mike's car.

On June 26, a new co-conspirator appeared, Said Abdelreheem. Abdelreheem was an Egyptian with a lengthy background of criminal conduct according to multiple sources and criminal records. He eventually was revealed to be a significant partner in the Saids' network with possible Islamist ties. Abdelreheem and Mohammed discuss what was clearly loads of both marijuana and cocaine.

Abdelreheem again called a few days after. Abdelreheem wanted to see Mohammed "right now". Over series of calls, they engage in a price debate, and the weight of a recently obtained "load".

Doreen Bettius showed up on the wire. She would turn out to be most tragic figure in the whole conspiracy. Doreen was mostly involved in the marijuana business, and small amounts of cocaine. Her calls mostly involved discussing drug prices and later getting price quotes from Sami for a "quarter-pound". Doubtful she was talking about hamburgers. Doreen as we later found out was addicted to several hard drugs. She would be an early casualty of the now rampant fentanyl crisis. Mohammed had begun daily sales to Doreen. Mohammed confirmed he was processing the drugs for sale at his home. We would later discover a "white box" filled with pre-wrapped tin-foil balls of cocaine in their hall closet.

Additional calls demonstrate Sami is interested in whatever he can supply. Several more calls involve discussions of coke shipments and the poor condition of the coke. They refer to cocaine in this instance and future calls as "white girl", a common code name for cocaine.

Shadi Ghabayen appeared to serve as the warehouseman for the Saids. Seemed like every spot in the house was a hiding place for drugs.

A series of calls with Sami appear to be related to be heroin.

Subsequent calls involving Sami involve prices and large amounts of drugs, clearly fitting the premise of using the phones to facilitate a drug transaction. The relationship between Sami and some co-conspirators appeared to be of both supplier and customer, depending on who was flush.

The earlier mentioned shoe repair shop owner, George, now identified as George Tenkerian engages in a series of calls with Mohammed. A later call brings Mohammed to the shoe repair shop to make delivery .

Salman Abuelhawa clearly deals exclusively with Mohammed. During one call, he asks Mohammed for "one from the small, the one from the 177, like that that time when I saw you last, but please fix it well". We were thinking this referred to the bad batch about which an earlier customer had been complaining. Abuelhawa calls for "a half", and then later for "a full, big sized one"; he would pick this one "at the store". Amazingly, these calls would be quoted, along with dozens of other related conversations, in the final affidavits submitted to the court and to the defense, and years later be at issue before the US Supreme Court.

One regular customer who had had shown up many times at the Saids' residence called Mohammed and they discuss what appears to be either heroin or hashish, "the brown", both of which the Saids were reported to distribute. Further discussion confirms Mohammed and Sami are conducting business at their residence, and at Shadi's house.

Toward the end of the interception periods Jeff Nguyen calls Sami, telling Sami he is five minutes away. They agree to meet at Shadi's house rather than at Sami's. We were in time to observe the meeting and see Sami drive up and transfer a package. Successful day.

Later on Nguyen calls Sami and asks about Sami's customers. At that time Sami acknowledged he was only getting from two people but lately just from Nguyen.

Again, it was evident Sami did business with many types of people, but Mohammed's customers all seemed to be Arabs. The majority of the customers turn out to be limo drivers connected to various embassies.

Unfortunately, the one significant character we did not catch was Smiley. Smiley would be caught later, but it took more effort than was really warranted. A this point, Larry and I agreed that we had pretty much what was necessary to put together indictments and arrest and search warrants. The decision was ours to make. Often squad supervisors like to keep wires going indefinitely because it makes them look good to have a T-III going on their squad and it keeps the squad busy and the supervisor less busy managing other cases or issues. My undercover assignments had also ended--all three of them, and I was waiting to hear from the various case agents to see if I would have to testify. As it turned out I had to contact each one on my own. Guess they didn't need me anymore so out of sight out of mind.

Search warrants were planned for the homes of the Saids and Shadi Ghabayen. As for arrest warrants, we had at least sixteen to execute. Sami, Mohammed and Shadi would come first. We would round up the rest one at a time over the next few weeks. It is common that in a case such as this, with numerous arrests to make and searches to conduct, that the whole office would be recruited to conduct one large round up all on the same day. I had a different idea. We would arrest each subject individually with the same small arrest teams formed from the agents who actually supported the T-IIIs; that would leave out most of the squad. Maybe I was being a bit vindictive, however despite Brian's request to include the other members of the squad, to "repair the relationship", I certainly had not damaged that relationship. Several members of the squad had actually been rather snarky about the whole endeavor behind my back, to say the least, and I wasn't going to reward them for that. I guess I'm just human. But if you didn't help make the bread, you don't get to eat the toast. The new agents from my squad and agents from other squads who assisted on the wires did deserve the reward of going out and having some fun. Yes, that was the fun part for most of us. I would also share the stats with them, because it would look good for a new agent to have credit for an arrest or later an indictment or conviction. At this point in my career, I really didn't care about stats. I wasn't seeking another promotion. Being a senior, old school GS-13 "street agent" was the best job in the bureau as far as I was concerned. Unlike in the military, there was no "up or out" requirement, and many agents went into management and then "stepped down" after seeing what sitting behind a desk and grading papers so to speak was really like. I had done just that, having instructed at the FBI Academy at Quantico, Virginia for three years as a GS-14, but then going back to "the street" where I felt I belonged.

So, the search and arrest warrants were signed, and we planned out the date and time. Sami and Mohammed were still living at home, and that house was a key location for their storage of drugs and cash. Same for Shadi. The search and arrest teams formed up about a mile away at around five am to be ready to execute at 6:00 am, also known as "0-dark thirty". The Saids' house was an older rambler style house that had several ramshackle additions attached to it. Mohmmed's room was at the far-left corner of the house so we would have to enter the front door and move quickly through a very narrow corridor to his room and wake his ass up.

Sami, on the other hand had a room in the converted garage on the farright side of the house. Sami as we found out through one of the many CHSs, had recently been in very bad car accident and had broken his leg. He was in full leg cast and was using a walker. We hit his door first since it was closest to the street. We did not have to breach the doorSami very slowly exited the house and rather pathetically hobbled outside and down a small ramp to the waiting agents. It was new experience to handcuff someone in a walker. He was placed in car--very gingerly.

We moved to the front door. Another team was stationed at the back door. There were lots of doors in that house. Only one team is designated to enter the house. If the team at the back door and the team at the front door would enter simultaneously, there could be at worst, a crossfire situation, or at best, just a traffic jam and a lot of confusion. We maintained radio contact, but Brian had insisted on being included in the arrest team-at the back door. We were able to enter first, as planned, but Brian was anxious, and we ended up meeting in the narrow hallway off the kitchen on the way to Mohammed's room. It took me by surprise. I saw his gun before I saw him. Despite the crowded conditions, we moved quickly to Mohammed's room, got to the door, pushed it open, and woke Mohammed up. We had intelligence he possessed an illegal handgun, so we posted at the doorframe, and I yelled for Mohammed to take his hand out from under the covers and show them. He was still groggy but cooperative and we had him walk toward us until we could put the handcuffs on. I took him into the kitchen, sat him down and started chatting. Mohammed and his family were from the Palestinian territories. I know no matter how I phrase that someone will sure to be offended. My grandparents immigrated from Lebanon. That often gives me some form of connection. We both were born here.

As I was building rapport with Mohammed, one of the Immigration and Customs Enforcement, or "ICE" (the new Post 9/11 name for the former INS) agents who had been included in the operation, entered the room. He had just come from Shadi's house. Shadi was not a US citizen, while Mohammed was. The ICE

Agent was an immigrant from Nigeria, and still had a strong Nigerian accent. He swaggered into the room, and waved leg irons at Mohammed and threatened him with deportation. I was not sure even why he was there since he was assigned to the Shadi arrest, and I was clearly in the middle of an interrogation. Shadi was in the US on a "green card", which fell into ICE's jurisdiction. Mohammed responded in a clearly Northern Virginia accent, as expected, to the effect "hey dude I'm a US citizen…how about you?" That took the wind out of his sails. I explained, just to be sure, that Mohammed was US born and could not be deported, and it would be a good idea if he left, since Mohammed and I were bonding.

At that point I think Mohammed had had enough and our conversation ended. The search of the house began. We went straight to the closet where we believed the "white box" was hidden. It was there, and filled with round, tinfoil wrapped balls of cocaine, just as we expected. Wrapped in paper in the same closet was about $60,000 in cash. Who keeps that much cash in their closet? Maybe the type of person who stores it on the same shelf next to a load of cocaine?

In the back yard, two agents were assigned to search the storage shed, which at one time allegedly held 800 pounds of marijuana. Unfortunately, there was a rather large, loud dog in the back yard that kind of got in the way. Plus, as it turned out, one of those agents was not very fond of large dogs. Nothing was found in the shed. For lack of trying. It takes some experience to conduct a drug search and to know where to look. My fault,

I should have brought along some other experienced drug agents to help with the search.

We found out much later that there had been a kilo of cocaine secreted in the rafters of the shed and we missed it. But we do expect all agents to be capable of conducting a thorough search of any place for any type of contraband. Nobody's perfect.

As we were shutting things down, I walked out to the front yard to check on the transport of Sami and Mohammed. Another agent came up to me and informed me as we were conducting the search, a vehicle showed up in front of the house and its occupants were an older adult Middle Eastern Male and a younger Middle Eastern male perhaps in his 20s, both apparently watching the festivities. A FCPD officer staged out front for security approached the car and asked them for identification. As it turned out, the older driver was a limo driver and the younger passenger was his son, who we had been told earlier had been a member of the Saids' drug crew. This could have been an opportunity. Unfortunately, (I use that word a lot it seems), they both got on a plane back home the next day. Not really a surprise there.

Nevertheless, we had succeeded in the first part of the last phase of the investigation. We had Sami, Mohammed, and Shadi solid. Time to move on the rest of the arrests. Each arrest would present a different and unique scenario. Some of the arrests would go down without a hitch. We customarily knock on the door at 6:00 am and hook them up at the doorway. A few were located at their place of employment. Transport to the office for fingerprinting, then to the US Marshals for their identical version of processing, and then an initial appearance before a US District Court Judge or Magistrate by 9:00 am. Then back to the office for a day of paperwork.

Then there were the chases, on foot and in cars. Jeff Nguyen was arrested at his house in Falls Church. The house was somewhat ramshackle, and the yard was muddy and overgrown. We got to the front door and were met by a family member. Despite their assurances that he was not home, we entered the house and made our way through the hoarder's paradise. No luck. We had a hunch he had ghosted. We decided to take a chance and sit down the street for a while and keep an eye on the house from a distance. It didn't take long. He had scooted out the back door when we arrived and must have hidden down the street because we saw him sneak in the back door shortly after we had left. We got to the house within five minutes. He flew out the back door, again. This time we had agents waiting for him. It was muddy. The back yard was sloped and unkempt and slippery. We approached him as he turned around and ran up the sloping side yard toward the front of the house. The front yard team slammed into him just as we hit him from behind. Kind of a rugby scrum, or a football blitz on the quarterback. I finally got the cuffs on him as we slid around in the mud. We actually think that sort of thing is kind of fun.

A year or so later, after Nguyen was released from a short time in prison, we ran into each other at a Panera Bread in Springfield. Surprisingly, he smiled sheepishly and said a quiet "hi". That happens more than one would think.

George Tenkerian happened at night. We knew his work schedule and figured we would get him as he left the shoe repair store. Funny being there because at one time I had lived just down the street. The parking lot was dark, and we placed our cars around the perimeter. The team consisted of all new agents and me. They were getting a lot of tactical and operational experience very quickly. This would be all that most of them would get for years after this case was done, partially because of the growing emphasis on intelligence collection to the detriment of the prosecution of "bad guys", particularly within that squad's division.

George finally closed his shop. He began to walk across the parking lot towards his car. He was a little faster than we were and got into his car before we got there, and he started to move. Our only choice was to close in with our vehicles and box him in. This was the chance for one of the new agents to take the reins and do the call out, meaning using the car's public address system to call Tenkerian out of his car and give him the commands to kneel, and put his hands up. A good way to end the evening.

Abuelhawa was arrested at his home in Vienna, Virginia. Abuelhawa was an easy arrest tactically. However, he was quite difficult to talk to. Not so much a language problem, but he seemed a bit nutty and had trouble thinking logically. He was somewhat cooperative, and we eventually worked out a deal where he would plead to misdemeanor possession charges based on six evidentiary calls with Mohammed. We gave him almost a year to provide something of value to our investigations, but he continually stalled and equivocated, and eventually we had to indict him along with everyone else.

Strangely, of all of the defendants in the case, Abuelhawa would be the only one to go to trial. Instead of a few misdemeanors, we had to try him on six felony counts related to the use of a communication facility to facilitate drug trafficking. His recorded conversations with Mohammed Said, detailed in the massive wiretap renewal and arrest affidavits, coupled with corroborative surveillance logs were more than enough for a conviction. Jumping ahead, he was tried in federal court in the Eastern District of Virginia, in a very short, half-day trial. The jury returned with a conviction in 26 minutes, the shortest I had ever experienced. Abuelhawa now should be deported after serving a minimum time in prison. He certainly did not want to be deported to Israel.

Not sure how Abuelhawa could afford it, but his attorneys appealed over and over and lost each time until his case actually made it up to the US Supreme Court. Larry and I were allowed to sit in the courtroom and watch the government attorney and the defense attorney argue the case before the nine Justices. The six conversations between Abuelhawa and Mohammed Said detailed in the affidavits were the issue debated. Did Abuelhawa's requests for cocaine from Mohammed over the phone constitute the facilitation of a drug conspiracy? We lost. The Justices determined the government's use of the charge of the use of the phone was unconstitutional because they believed the charge was not suitable to a felony. In thirty years as a case agent, and over 120 convictions, I never lost a single trial. This was the only loss ever, but really was a unique situation. Nevertheless, this was once in a lifetime experience to attend a hearing at the Supreme Court, so it was worth the loss. While there, we met a group of law students from Georgetown University who had studied the case in class. As stated earlier, the case of the US v. Abuelhawa, and the defense petition, citing the affidavits and recorded conversations from the wiretaps can be found online. That came as quite a surprise.

Abdelreheem clearly presented the greatest challenge in first just locating him. We had information that he hung out in Georgetown. One evening Shawn and I and the rest of the team decided to check out that location. There he was, walking down the sidewalk. Then he wasn't. As we approached him, he disappeared down an alleyway and into the darkness. Abdelreheem was an older guy, but he sure moved fast. After days went by, a CHS located Abdelreheem again, this time at a small restaurant in McLean, Virginia. This day got more and more messy. We got the word that Abdelreheem was there at the restaurant. I knew the area rather well. My wife grew up in McLean.

Shawn and I jumped in my car. JD and Jeff jumped in their car, and Mike went solo. Five agents. Should be enough for an arrest at that location. We headed out from WFO. We had a bit of a drive to get to McLean. We all stayed on the radio to make sure we stayed together. Suddenly JD and Jeff peeled off and headed back to the office. What the Hell? As it turned out, Brian had called them back to the office for a meeting. Yes, Brian knew we were on the way to make an arrest that had been planned and approved. It didn't seem to matter. Unfortunately, again, Poor Mike was behind them, and he also peeled off thinking there was a change of plans. It was down to two of us. I wasn't going to lose this opportunity to get this arrest done after chasing Abdelreheem around the DC area for weeks. It took a while to figure out what had happened and get Mike back in the game.

Shawn and I found ourselves in the area of the restaurant. We arrived Just as Abdelreem was leaving the restaurant and was in the parking lot heading for his car. It was just down to Shawn and me. We pulled up and jumped out on Abdelreheem. I was, I admit pretty pissed off at the guy because we had been chasing him around for several weeks, and half my team had been called off, leaving a two-man arrest team, and I got a little testy with him. It included a few F-bombs. With only two of us and one of him, we both had guns drawn. We got him to kneel on the pavement and I came around behind him and we put the cuffs on him. Just then I looked up as Mike arrived in the parking lot. Better late than never.

As for Doreen, we had a little trouble finding her. Her registered address turned out to be a house in Northern Virginia. Amy and I were beginning to work together on several matters, so we teamed up on looking for Doreen. We located and interviewed a relative of Doreen's at home. She lamented that Doreen was a drug addict and had become physically abusive and she had been kicked out of the house where she had been living.

She gave us Doreen's new address which turned out to be a large high rise apartment building. That would be a tough place in which to find her actual apartment for an arrest. We determined Doreen's vehicle, an older SUV, was in danger of being repossessed. That gave us an opportunity. A few days later, Amy and I and another agent had to double up arrests. Amy had to meet with Fairfax PD to arrest a subject of hers. We got that one done quickly. We decided to at least check out the apartment building and get a lay of the land.

We headed over to the complex. Doreen's relative had also given us some information identifying Doreen's roommate. In the parking lot, parked next to each other were Doreen's vehicle and her roommate's vehicle. Doreen's SUV was filled with clothing and luggage as though prepared for a quick getaway. We stood off to the side trying to come up with a workable plan. The plan worked itself out for us as it turned out. Doreen's roommate showed up at his car. I walked up to him and asked if he knew the owner of the SUV. He admitted it was his roommate's. Amy and I exchanged smiles. I informed him we were here to repossess the vehicle, and that I would give her a chance to clean out the vehicle of her personal belongings before we snatched the SUV away. He appreciated our kind offer and returned into the building. A few minutes later, the roommate returned with Doreen in tow. I gestured her over to the car and identified myself as an FBI agent. We placed her under arrest. Doreen quickly agreed to cooperate against Sami and Mohammed. That cooperation was never completed. A week or so later I received a call to inform me Doreen had been found dead of a drug overdose in a motel. She had somehow secured a fentanyl patch from a local hospital and had extracted the fentanyl and injected it. She died.

As mentioned before, we just missed Smiley. My complaint to the Linguist squad supervisor went nowhere. We still believed Smiley was a major player. He was a member of the Moorish Temple, a Black Muslim sect, which may have explained his relationship with the Arab members of the crew. Fortunately, a new CHS happened to be acquainted with Smiley and admitted to having purchased small amounts of coke from Smiley in the past.

By this time, I was handling eighteen CHSs. I was accused by more than one person of being insane for that. The paperwork alone was overwhelming, thanks in part to Robert Mueller's massive new administrative requirements for everything, but often a lot of those sources are short term cooperators who are "working off a beef".

The voluntary, long-term CHS are generally the most valuable. The CHS in this case, we will call Rami (an alias to protect the CHS), made a phone call to Smiley and began attempts to meet up with Smiley. Smiley was strangely illusive. He was rather rude and a bit nutty. Several times he would agree to make a sale to Rami and then change his mind, yelling at Rami in a string of expletives. He would tell Rami to call back or make excuses such as he was going to be out of town. It took many frustrating recorded calls between Rami and Smiley over several months to get Smiley to commit to a meeting.

Eventually Rami was able to arrange for the purchase of an "eight-ball". Rami set up a meeting in the parking lot of a gas station near the shopping center where the butcher shop and grille were located near George Mason Drive. Rami and Smiley met in the lot and spoke car to car. Rami was provided with a body recorder and transmitter. Smiley was as irascible as ever and made the negotiation painful, but finally agreed to the eight-ball for the next week. All the source reporting was that Smiley was a multi-kilo dealer, however he also was known to sell smaller amounts to less well-known customers. This was all we expect between Rami and Smiley since Rami had not in the past purchased large amounts, and we did not have any other cooperators who could make a purchase.

Rami and Smiley met the next week at a Walmart parking lot in Fairfax. Rami backed his van into parking spot and waited for Smiley. Smiley was late of course. We almost called it for the day. Smiley finally showed up and pulled in next to Rami's van. They spoke through the driver's side windows. Rami was again wearing a wire. We had provided him with several hundred dollars of government cash for the purchase. The deal went down through the windows and Smiley left the scene. We decided to do one more transaction and make the arrest. We planned this one out, deciding to arrange the final exchange at the same location with Rami placing his van in the same spot as before, that way we could stage our cars in a predictable position to block Smiley in and call him out of his car for the arrest. Having taught this type of arrest tactic at the academy, I was a big believer in actually taking the team out and practicing the tactics so there would no confusion as to who did what when it was time to move in. Using cars to effect an arrest provides a modicum of safety but can also be more complex than just banging on the front door. Once the transaction is completed, the drivers of the cars must move in in a coordinated fashion, close enough to block the subject's car but not so close that it results in an accident. Something to keep in mind as this story unfolds.

I tried to anticipate where Smiley would be positioned at the conclusion of the deal so that we could in turn position our cars to be able to move in quickly and block him in and be able to safely approach him. It made sense to anticipate several scenarios, including Smiley parking next to Rami and maybe park a few spots away and walking over to Rami's car. The day came for the deal. We had a quick briefing since we had already gone out and practiced the possible arrest scenarios. Three cars were assigned to execute the "car block" (I had come up with the term, for lack of a better term, after developing the curriculum while teaching at Quantico). Four cars were assigned to the perimeter in case Smiley got away from us. One of the new agents from another squad had dressed a bit too much like she was planning to go out to dinner. Tight jeans and high heeled shoes are not tactically sound attire in case you must jump out of your car and possibly chase someone across a hard pavement. I tried to gently suggest she at least put on more appropriate and tactically sound foot ware. I was a little surprised at the resentful attitude but at least she put on some running shoes.

We set up around the parking lot of the Walmart. Rami backed into the exact same spot as before. He was equipped with a body recorder, transmitter, and we had a surveillance van nearby to videotape the proceedings. I gave Rami a paper bag from Starbucks with the purchase cash inside, and we placed it on the dashboard of the van. The plan was that when Rami removed the bag from the dashboard to give the cash to Smiley, that would serve as the signal to come in for the arrest. Rami would not give the money to Smiley until Smiley gave him the coke. We waited.

Smiley showed up, more, or less on time. Of course, he did the only thing we did not anticipate or practice. Smiley drove up and pulled in front of Rami's van and called him over to Smiley's car. We could not see the bag or the exchange. It went down very quickly, and Smiley started to drive away. He was now mobile, and we had to assume the deal went down. The radio traffic among the arrest team was a bit panicked. A decision just had to be made. We had already completed one transaction, so we had probable cause for an arrest either way.

I called out to move in. Smiley was already on the move and headed towards the exit. One of the arrest vehicles headed straight towards Smiley's car-head on. My car headed toward the passenger side and a third car came up towards the left rear bumper in a proper "triangulation". This configuration is designed so that there is a clear line of fire and avoids a crossfire situation. At least we did that correctly. Smiley did not seem to appreciate our professional tactics. Nor did he appreciate that the vehicle that blocked him front bumper to front bumper was blocking his exit. I could tell the two agents in the front seats had not identified themselves but had guns drawn and pointed at him. Smiley slammed into them head on, and then backed up and slammed into us and tore off our front bumper. We referred to this as playing "bumper cars".

Then he tried to back into the third car and stopped. I was sitting in the passenger side of the car, positioned to address the subject, while remaining in the car behind cover. I did not use the PA system, I just yelled at Smiley to put his hands out the window. He did not comply. Smiley reached down inside his car, and then popped up, looking out the windshield. He did this several times. I was becoming concerned because Smiley was known to be armed during drug deals. What was on the floor he kept checking on? I kept yelling and he kept bobbing up and down. On the third or fourth time he popped up I had my finger on the trigger. I had been able to go over twenty years with having to shoot anyone. I was certainly hoping this was not the time.

The standoff finally ended. He slowly put his hands out the window. I realized I had been holding my breath. I let my breath out. I took my fingers off the trigger. I called Smiley out of his car and over to me. I got out, and always reliable Amy exited her car to provide back-up. She and her partner Bobby Wells, had done a perfect job in positioning their car. Arrest completed.

What was on the floor of Smiley's car? Smiley was taken away by the transport team. I went over to the van where Rami was still seated waiting for permission to go home. I still had to debrief him and retrieve the cocaine he had purchased and the recorder, and get all of that into evidence, which in and of itself is a true pain in the ass. Amy and Bobby were charged with searching Smiley's car and transport it to a storage facility in DC. Another question was where was the "buy money"? I was initially concerned when we couldn't find it anywhere. I expected to find it on Smiley's person. Did Rami keep the money or part of it? Smiley had of course been searched after arrest and it was not on his person. I questioned Rami. He was actually a little hurt I would suspect him of keeping the money or some of it. It had happened with other sources in the past, but Rami had been working for me for several years and had been reliable and easy to get along with, so I did feel a little bad to even ask. Bobby and Amy completed their search of the car. Underneath the floor mat on the driver's side was the cash. I told Rami we had found it. He was relieved and understood I had to at least ask. He had done a great job.

The trial preparation for Smiley should have been a simple matter. We had finished the prosecutions of Sami and Mohammed and a total of seventeen defendants caught on the Title-IIIs, all who had pled guilty, just waiting in vain to resolve the Abuelhawa situation. We had two drug purchases from Smiley and loads of consensually recorded calls with him. I met with Larry, and we discussed our prosecution strategy. Several days later Larry informed me the case had been reassigned to another AUSA because Larry had another unrelated trial to prepare for and this was considered an easy case to prosecute.

I met with the new AUSA. He seemed satisfied with the case. I was headed to Virginia Beach with my family on Saturday. Boy did I need a vacation. It was Friday evening, and I was headed South and starting to somewhat decompress. My cell phone rang. It was the two new, new AUSAs. This was stupid. They were in a panic. They needed me to now brief them on the case. I couldn't understand why the previous two AUSAs couldn't brief them but to no avail. I agreed to delay my trip for a few hours on Saturday and meet them in Alexandria. I had big box on my desk containing all the evidence, except of course the drugs, and went to the office and picked up the box and transported it to the US Attorney's Office and met with the AUSAs. Then I left for the Beach. It turned out to be the most miserable vacation ever. I spent the entire time walking in circles on the sand talking on the cell phone with the frantic AUSAs who for some reason could not wait one week for me to get back to the office, and then calling squad mates trying to beg someone to bring more evidence over to the US Attorney's office. One squad mate was generous enough to go over to the DEA Lab and retrieve the drug evidence and take that over to the AUSAs. After all this panic and my ruined vacation, the two AUSAs passed the case on to a fourth AUSA, Jim Trump. Jim was a very experienced AUSA and knocked out a guilty plea from Smiley and his defense attorney rather quickly, but with less exposure than I thought was appropriate. At least it was done.

Time to move on. Sami and Mohammed and Abdelreheem got slammed by the sentencing judge and were sentenced to around 89 months each. Mohammed's plea included future testimony, but he resisted for over a year while incarcerated, and finally he just outright refused. After a year or so, we prosecuted him one more time for obstruction of justice and added another year to his sentence.

• • • • • • • •

In between cases, I had been asked to join a team of agents traveling to Indonesia to support a long-term investigation into the murder of four US citizens near the town of Timika, on the Indonesian side of the Island of Papua. Indonesia is comprised of hundreds of Islands. Java is the main island, and where the capitol, Jakarta is located. Timika is the location of a massive copper mine halfway up a mountain at about 7000 feet, owned and operated by a US company, Freeport Mcmoran. The company had established a town near the mine, which housed the mine's employees and families, and had schools and churches and stores. A full town. The native Papuans were of aboriginal stock, and generally Christian. Most lived in small tribal settings in the forest, while many were employed in the mine. For several years, the Indonesian government had embarked upon the Islamification of the Island, to which the natives objected. They formed small, primitive guerilla groups in the jungle, and would attack Indonesian army outposts. In this case they attacked what they thought was an army convoy of white SUVs driving along a curve on a steep mountain road, but which sadly turned out to be carrying teachers from the town's school heading to a picnic. Four teachers were killed and several wounded. The Indonesian army post nearby responded and began firing wildly. The rebels faded back into the jungle down an incredibly steep mountain side. I would at one point in the journey stand on the edge of that mountainside, at the site of the attack, and look down the incredible steep slope into the endless jungle from which the rebels had emerged and then disappeared into.

I partnered up with a Headquarters supervisor who had been one of the original case agents and who was relinquishing the case to another agent. Various teams of agents form WFO had been cycling in and out of Timika for over year to assist in the investigation and conduct interviews. My job would be to serve as a team leader and liaison with the Indonesian National Police and the Military Police, both of whom reportedly hated each other. The Headquarters agent and I began the ridiculously long series of flights and stopovers on the way to the final destination of Timika. Twelve hours to Tokyo, then a nine-hour stop in Singapore, then a two day stop in Jakarta to meet with the US Ambassador. The meeting with the Ambassador fortunately was a formality, because as we sat in his office, having not really slept in 24 hours, we were all falling asleep in our chairs right in front of him. Fortunately, embassy personnel are very used to travelers on official business suffering from severe jet lag. Embarrassing but understandable. Then on another seven-hour flight on a very scary airline, Garuda, to Timika.

The airport consisted of one runway, and an open wooden terminal that resembled a picnic area in a national park. The luggage was brought off of the plane on a handcart-wheelbarrow type contraption and dumped into a wooden trough. An SUV from the hotel took us to our lodging. It was a nice resort hotel—in the middle of the jungle. One of the agents had already contracted malaria, so we made sure we took our meds.

Over the next ten days we met with the Indonesian authorities in a conference room in the hotel. When the bureau personnel, about eight of us, met in the room alone, we made sure to make offhand comments about how great the Indonesians were, because we assumed the room was bugged. Funny though, because we were there to assist them in building a case against the rebels who had murdered US citizens in their country. The new President of Indonesia at the time was trying to modernize his legal system and saw this as an opportunity to learn how to prosecute cases lawfully. We had an AUSA on our team as well who would assist the Indonesian prosecutors. As much as we wanted collectively to bring the killers to justice in the US, the Indonesians were adamant in proving they could prosecute the case fairly in their own country.

We spent a few days up the mountain at the Freeport offices, interviewing witnesses and management, and employees of the school. Then we got word mass protests against the Indonesian government were planned to take place in a few days, and they were expected to turn violent. We were ordered to evacuate. So, a trip that was expected to last a month lasted just less than two weeks. We headed home. I would find out much later that the case agent and a new team, and Indonesian law enforcement personnel had eventually lured the rebels who had been part of the attack out from the jungle, ostensibly to negotiate some sort of plea deal, and negotiated their surrender and arrest. They would be tried and convicted in Indonesian court.

The Washington Post

Terrorists Hijack 4 Airliners, Destroy World Trade Center, Hit Pentagon; Hundreds Dead

Bodies Pulled From Pentagon; Troops Patrol District Streets

Bush Promises Retribution; Military Put on Highest Alert

U.S. Intelligence Points To Bin Laden Network

On Flight 77: 'Our Plane Is Being Hijacked'

'I Saw Bodies Falling Out— Oh, God, Jumping, Falling'

Jordanian Royal Police Academy, Amman, Jordan

Petra, Jordan, with FBI/NYPD instructional team

US Embassy Beirut Security Team at US Embassy, Beirut

The Corniche section of Beirut, and the Beirut Starbucks

Timika, Papua, Indonesia, site of attack of American teachers

US Mining town, Timka, Indonesia

Car Parcs in Benin, West Africa

Car Parcs in Cotonou, Benin, West Africa
Used Autos purchased in US with LH funds, shipped to West Africa, and sold to Nigerian customers

Jim Graham (deceased) and his birthday gift

CUSTOMER#: T66190719
CUST. NAME: HANJOUR,HANI,S H

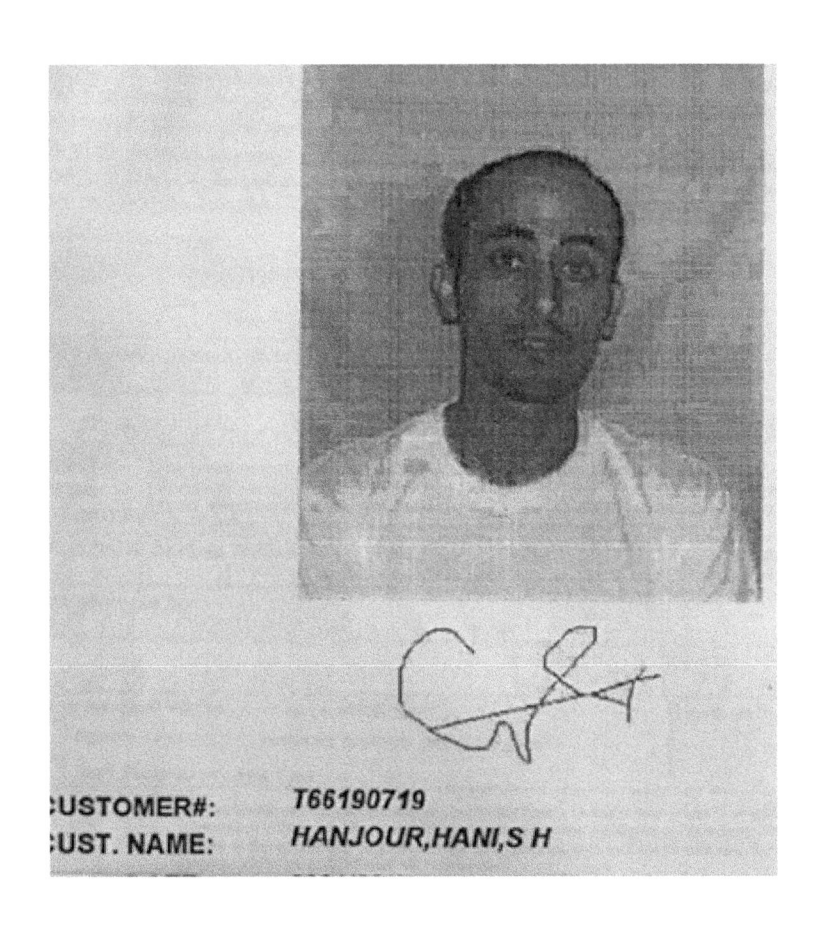

USTOMER#: A69600408
UST. NAME: ALHAZMI, SALEM M S,

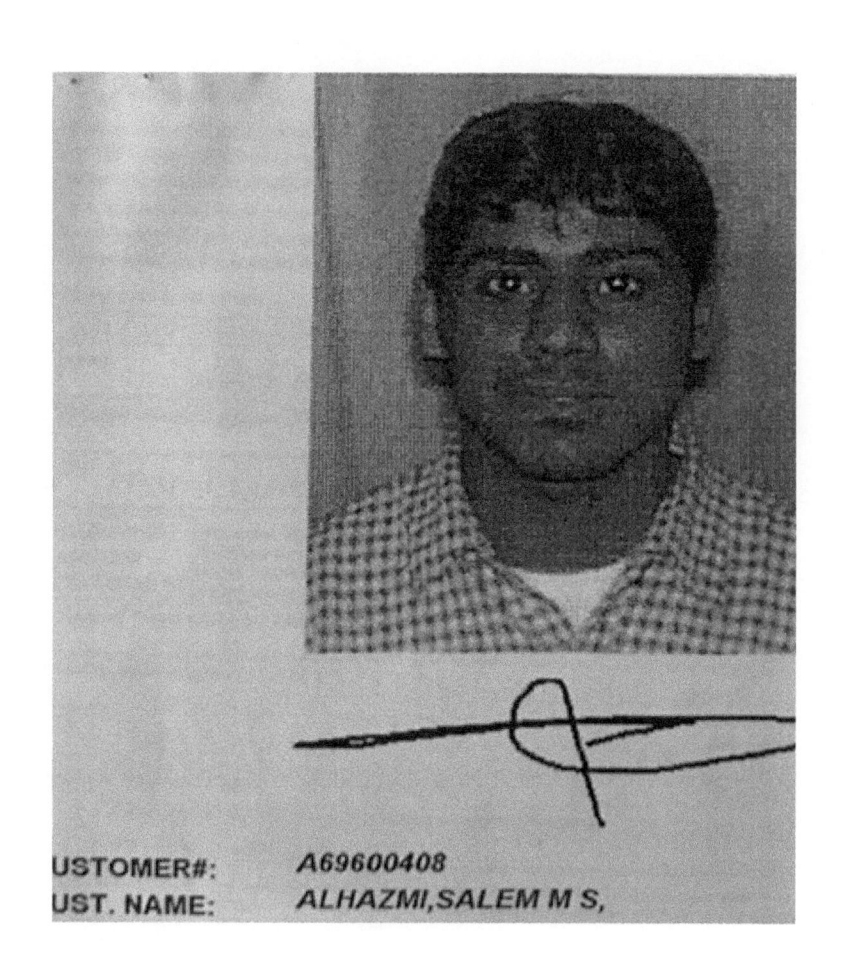

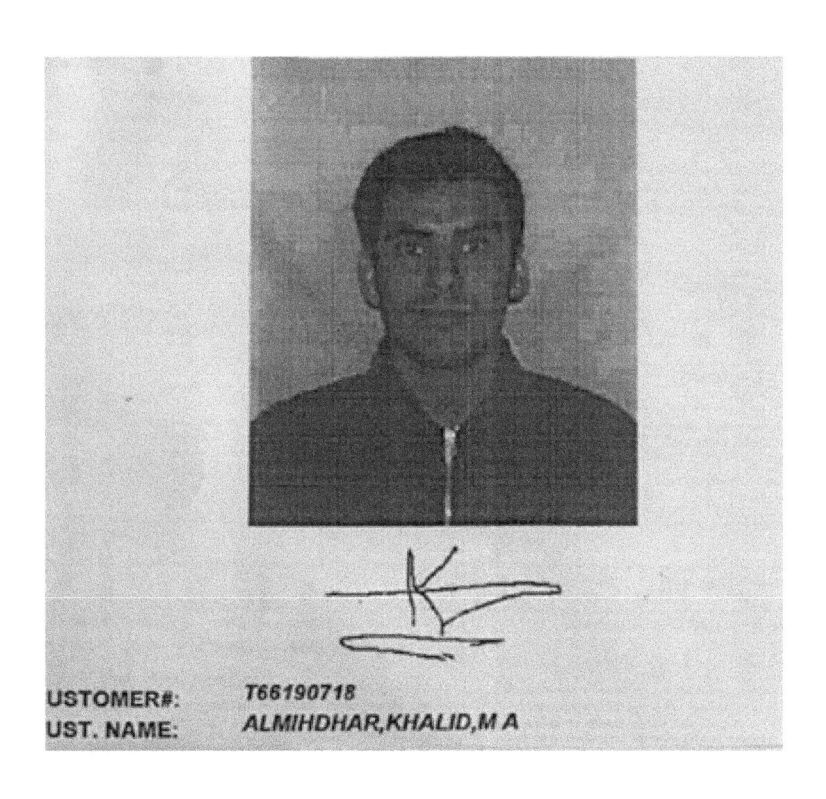

USTOMER#: T66190718
UST. NAME: ALMIHDHAR,KHALID,M A

USTOMER#: A69600405
UST. NAME: MOQED,MAJED,M.GH

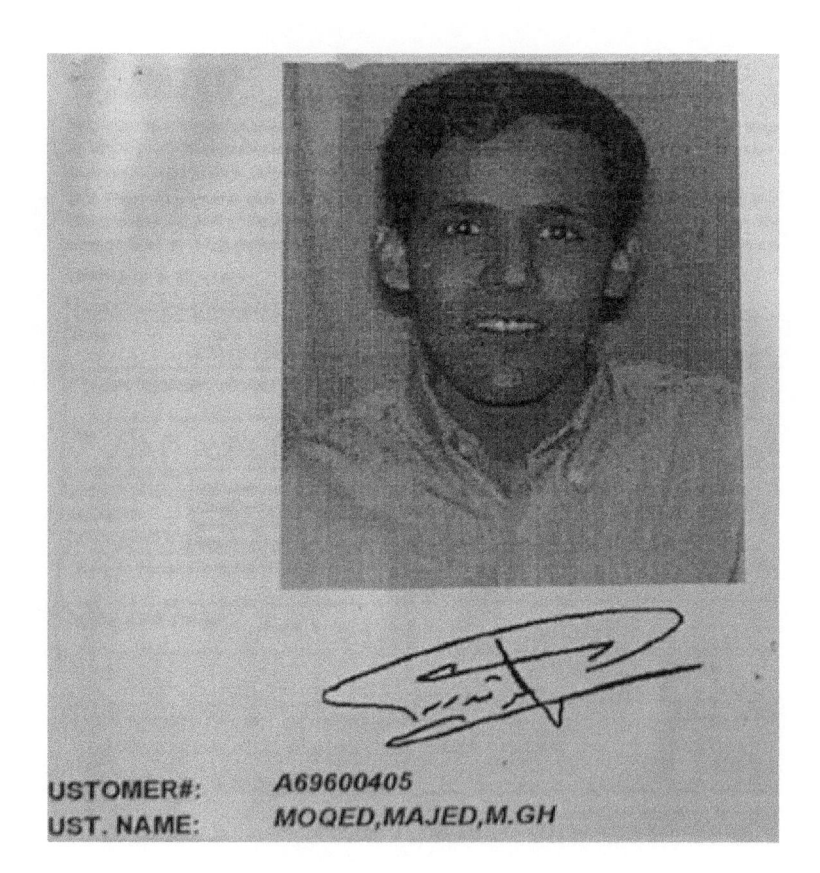

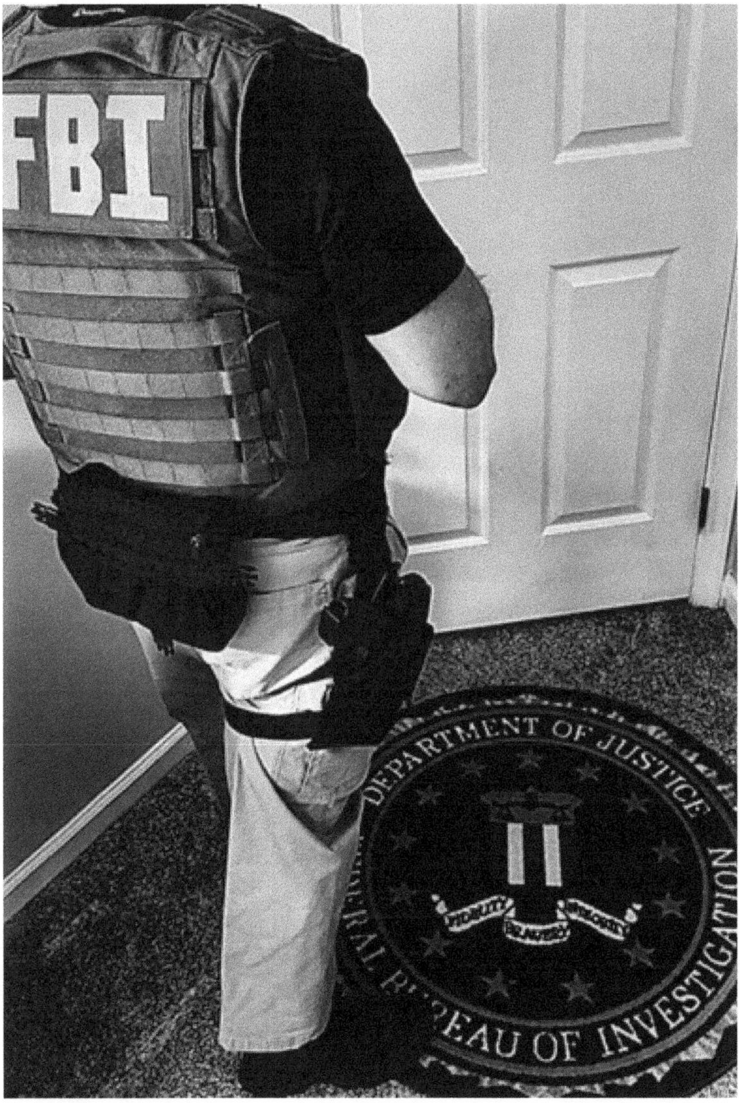
FBI
DEPARTMENT OF JUSTICE

VIII.

The Terrorists Next Door

"An FBI Agent spends years investigating Middle Eastern Men in Northern Virginia who want to sell guns, buy phony visas, and offer to procure a missile launcher. Are they terrorists—or just criminals talking big?"

My fifteen minutes of fame. I will never know how many read the article in the Washingtonian Magazine in 2009, but it was somewhat vindicating that a journalist, Harry Jaffe, was interested in the story. I will tell it in my own words here, but the article was well-written and captured the facts and the spirit of the investigation and the dynamics of the relationship between an agent and his source. That source is our old friend Yusuf. I'm using the name Yusuf because Harry named him with that alias in his article and in deference to that I will continue with that name for him. I'm just spelling it a bit differently.

I will admit Yusuf surprised me when he called me several months after having been released from prison. We met at a local mall at a Starbucks. As it turned out we both had grown up in Fairfax County, although I'm twenty years or so older. Yusuf was born in a Middle Eastern country, but he came to the US with his family as a youth. We had much in common, although my grandparents immigrated from Lebanon in the early 20th century.

Bearing in mind Yusuf had served his sentence and was not "working off charges", his expressed wish to redeem himself seemed somewhat plausible. Over the years, he would prove he meant what he said. Very rare. He volunteered to begin associating with members of the Middle Eastern Community in Northern Virginia. Yusuf could associate with members of the various mosques in the area and collect intelligence identifying possible radical Islamist threats, as well as hopefully seeking out the "good guys".

We were still early in the new decade and the bureau was going through its growing pains in its new mandate to prevent terrorist acts rather than mopping up afterwards and apprehending the perpetrators. We were driven to change our philosophy from collecting evidence to that of collecting intelligence, supposedly because prior to 9/11 the bureau allegedly was neglectful of its intelligence function. I disagreed and still do. We were actually quite good at intelligence collection--our historical emphasis on recruiting and operating sources demonstrated that. Our work largely dismantling the LCN was also the result of years of intelligence collection building out our knowledge of the LCN's membership and structure and illicit activities. What we were not good at, was the digestion of intelligence--the analysis of intelligence. Our cadre of intelligence analysts was mostly, but not completely, recruited from other support employees who might have a college degree and had shown some aptitude in their other assigned duties, which was where I started in the FBI; but there was not a defined training program, and the art of intelligence analysis was not inculcated. FBI headquarters Counterintelligence Division, for example did have some well-educated individuals who possessed a doctorate in say, Russian studies. Their abilities came from their education and not from any real FBI training.

This began to change somewhat after 9/11. The bureau developed a career path for analysts and began a training program at Quantico for analysts. The problem arose as to what the analysts' duties would be once they got out to the field. Eventually the analysts and agents would even train together in the classroom, with the idea they would work better together in the field. Unfortunately, this did not happen. Analysts were generally separated from the agents in the field offices and were encouraged to produce product more for management's benefit than for the purpose of supporting investigations. I referred to this as "writing term papers".

Under Robert Mueller, the drive to collect intelligence became an end in itself, rather than a means to an end. The new mandate now neglected the pursuit of criminal prosecution, the historic strength of the FBI and the Justice Department in general. The US Attorney's offices are reliant upon federal investigative agencies such as the FBI and the DEA to bring completed investigations for prosecution. Intelligence is generally information that is deemed pertinent to one's mission, but it can potentially go on forever never having an end goal. For intelligence collection within law enforcement to have a worth, it should be targeted towards identifying individuals or criminal conspiracies or organizations involved in the violation of US law, and developing probable cause for obtaining evidence, that is, to support search warrants, wiretap affidavits, or even to underpin an undercover operation. Fortunately, there were some Bureau analysts who got it, but it was an individual choice to develop a partnership with the case agents.

Yusuf would begin the develop a broad base of associations in the community. It helped having grown up in the area. Identifying the good guys was just as important as the bad guys. Many of the bad guys turned out to be long time from friends from his youth who had allegedly slid into Islamic radical thought and activities. Perhaps 9/11 had emboldened some, perhaps it was just the ongoing trend among a small part of the Muslim community. Some of the activity trended more towards a sense of Arab nationalism, especially among the Palestinian ex-patriot community and among some Lebanese. Designated terrorist groups linked to those two nations (I use the term nation because although Lebanon is a sovereign country, the Palestinian territories are not, yet are self-ruled and function as a separate political entity and maintain a distinct identity from Israel). Palestinian HAMAS and Lebanese Hizballah are both Islamic based militant organizations but with a public face and political operations and are distinct in their nationalism from Al-Qaeda, which is comprised of all nationalities and functions internationally in small cells.

The difference between even Sunni Muslim Hamas and Shiite Hizballah is their focus. Hamas is internally focused on regaining territory from Israel and its terrorist activities are restricted to attacking Israel and Israelis, generally not having engaged in terrorist acts in other countries, mostly conducting fund-raising outside of Israel, specifically in the US. Both Hizballah and Hamas receive funding from other Islamic countries, most notably Sunni Muslim Saudi Arabia and its key geopolitical rival, Shiite Iran. Hizballah maintains close military and financial ties with other Shia militant organizations or militias in Iraq and Yemen, all supported militarily and financially by Iran. Both Saudi Arabia and Iran finance Hamas as means toward a perceived struggle against Israel, while only Iran backs Hizballah.

Hizballah has engaged in terrorist bombings in a number of countries, most notably against Israeli targets in South America and US targets in Saudi Arabia. Hizballah operatives have been caught in multiple countries, including the US, Africa, and the far East stockpiling bomb-making materials. Both HAMAS and Hizballah have received far less attention from the intelligence community over the past two decades than Al-Qaeda, and most recently ISIS, yet they are the longest running organizations and persist today. Hizballah in particular functions as a shadow government in Lebanon, and maintains separate military, Intelligence and political organizations often in direct conflict with the Lebanese government. Hizballah keeps a massive arsenal of rockets and missiles supplied by the Iranian Islamic Revolutionary Guard Corps, or IRGC. The IRGC was extremely active in Iraq in concert with the Iraqi Shiite Militias such as Kataib Hizballah and Ansar al-Haq, and under the leadership of now diceased Major General Qassem Soleimani, was responsible for the deaths of hundreds of US soldiers. News stories covering the assassination of Soleimani by a US drone strike in Iraq largely ignored this fact. But I digress.

Yusuf began to identify several individuals who were, in conversation, becoming more radical in their religious beliefs. This concerned and then upset him. One individual, Ahmed, had become much more religious, which in and of itself is a person's personal right to belief. The problem was this individual's conspiratorial discussions related to his observation of the total lack of security on transportation systems other than the airlines, and how easy it would be to carry any type of package onto one of those systems. It was not the observation itself, but his expressed interest in carrying a possible explosive device on a train. This was still in the chasing shadows stage. Trying to assess his actual intent was difficult. Was this guy just blowing smoke and trying to impress Yusuf or was he planning something? We opened our first case based on Yusuf's reporting. Ahmed joined an Islamic organization in Maryland known to be affiliated with Hamas. This was another concerning piece in a puzzle. Ahmed eventually moved to Maryland, and we passed the hat to our Baltimore office. But several of Ahmed's friends had seemed to pick up the baton and were actively trying to recruit Yusuf to assist them in a number of concerning endeavors.

In Harry Jaffe's article in the Washingtonian, he quoted Gary Lafree, director of the National Consortium for the study of Terrorism and Responses to Terrorism at the University of Maryland:

"The FBI has changed its policy-it's trying to intervene much earlier. That creates a paradox. The public wants law enforcement to intervene much earlier, but the farther you get up the threat chain, the less crime there may be to report and the less convincing it might be to a jury".

The dilemma exists as to where to intervene. Do we wait until a subject is about to press the button on a bomb? If so, would we be able to get there in time? If we infiltrate a plot, how do we avoid offering too much help to the subject to the effect we "entrap" him? If an undercover agent or a CHS allows the subject to build an explosive device on his own, how would we be able to intercede? Very often the subject requires help in building that device. He would need to recruit someone who has that skill. If we needed to intercede, we would have to offer that assistance before the subject connected with someone else. An inert device could then be provided so that the subject could complete the prosecutable act without causing any damage. Then the undercover must appear to be legitimate but can't go too far in making suggestions or initiating any proactive acts without the subject's requesting it. I don't think the public appreciates how difficult it is to walk that tightrope.

Most terrorism cases resulting in a prosecution are based on other criminal charges. In my experience, the individuals involved in terrorist activities also support themselves through criminal activity and to finance an organization or developing plot. Hence my eventual use of what I referred to as the "Al Capone method" to build prosecutable cases.

Most counterterrorism cases do not involve bomb plots or other attacks. They are financing cases. HAMAS and Hizballah see the US as a cash cow. Soliciting donations for a legitimate cause is the right of any American. Soliciting donations to be provided to a designated terrorist organization is illegal. Both of those organizations have formed "charities" in the US for that illicit purpose. Complex money laundering networks commonly feed the "donation" stream. Outright fraud and other criminal activity feed the money laundering networks. Developing a criminal fraud case is clear cut and explainable to a jury. Demonstrating to that jury the proceeds were being provided to a foreign based terrorist organization is the tough part. Using that as a prosecution strategy even meets resistance from prosecutors. I've had to battle with AUSAs who are afraid the jury will be convinced that the defendant was just "bragging" to impress a co-conspirator, which I think is cowardly, and is really not logical. It's the prosecutor's job to convince the jury, especially when provided with recorded conversations where a subject admits to providing the funds to one of those organizations.

The truth is that the targets of these counterterrorism cases operated on a day-to-day basis the same way any organized crime enterprise or street gang operated. Criminal enterprises are focused on making money and engage in acts of violence to enforce discipline and protect themselves from informants. Terrorist cells such as Al-Qaeda have the opposite perspective--their end game is to commit acts of violence and use the criminal activity to finance the violence. Nationalist groups such as Hizballah and Hamas direct their illicit efforts and violence as much toward gaining or consolidating political and economic power.

In early 2006, two brothers and a cousin, friends from Yusuf's youth were re-connecting. Yusuf began hanging out with Akram Salih and his brother Amjad Hamed. Akram was a high school friend. Amjad had recently immigrated from the West Bank Palestinian Territory. The Palestinian TerritoriesGaza in the South of Israel and the West Bank on the border with Jordan, are administered by separate organizations; the Islamist Hamas in Gaza, and more secular Fatah under the Palestinian Liberation Organization, or PLO in the West Bank.

Akram owned a construction company, Palis Construction. He was born in Puerto Rico and then moved to Palestine when he was four years old, and then to the US after his parents divorced. Amjad lived in Akram's basement in his lavish home in Annandale, Virginia. Amjad was born in the West Bank and came to the US as legal permanent resident, or "green card" holder. Yusuf was introduced to Amjad and Amjad began to confide in Yusuf. Amjad was a bit of a partier and a pot smoker. Yusuf did not partake but Amjad was not particularly a considerate host and would smoke in front of Yusuf with the windows shut. On one occasion Yusuf was returning from Amjad's house and he called me from his car. He was stopped at a stop sign, "waiting for the light to change". Amjad's smoke had overwhelmed Yusuf. It made for a humorous but concerning conversation. Fortunately, I was able to talk him home safely.

To Yusuf's disappointment, Amjad began to regale Yusuf with his exploits in Israel. He had a brother in Israel who was in prison for bombing a movie theater. Amjad admitted he was working for the Palestinian Authority, in effect meaning the Fatah faction of the PLO, as an intelligence agent. He was seeking Yusuf's help in smuggling six associates into the US. Amjad explained these associates were close to being arrested by the Israeli authorities. For some reason Amjad perceived Yusuf as having family connections in the Middle East who could possibly obtain visas for these individuals. Yusuf realized this perception presented an opportunity, so he did not disabuse him of this idea.

Amjad was aware these individuals could not legally obtain a legitimate visa to the US for various reasons, so he assumed Yusuf would have to secure the visas through some type of fraud or manipulation of the system using his "connections" in an embassy. The specifics we will keep generic. That played out in a significant way later on.

Amjad and Yusuf began plotting how this could be handled. They met in different places—Amjad's basement apartment, and at the Pine Crest shopping center in Annandale where a Starbucks was located, known to be a hangout for local Middle Eastern men, many of them reputed to be both Islamist, and involved in criminal activity. Most often they would meet in one of their cars in the shopping center parking lot and drink coffee and chain smoke. This was a perfect location for us to conduct surveillance of the meetings. By this time, I had contacted the Diplomatic Security Service, or DSS Task Force Agent at WFO, Tim Alexandre, since visa fraud was a DSS violation if you recall "operation Eagle Strike". He would join us for these surveillances. Needless to say, Yusuf was "wearing a wire" during these conversations; both a body recorder and a transmitter so we could listen in. The parking lot location worked well for both. Their meetings in Amjad's basement proved more difficult, especially when trying to monitor the transmitter. Tim and I would meet Yusuf behind the shopping center next to several big dumpsters and I would "wire him up". We would set up in our cars around the parking lot with an eye on Yusuf's car. When the conversation ended, we would again meet, and I would remove the recording devices and debrief Yusuf. The conversations between Yusuf and Amjad were most often predominantly spoken in Arabic and would eventually be translated and transcribed by our linguists, so in order to keep track of progress of Amjad's plot, until then, I would need Yusuf's feedback. I would then have to document his debriefings on a bureau document FD-302. I hoped the eventual transcriptions matched the debriefings. As it turned out, they did. Yusuf was actually very good at recounting his conversations with Amjad, and later other subjects, even when the conversations lasted several hours. He was really a pretty good storyteller. Sometimes though maybe a little too dramatic in the retelling, but I learned to take all of that with a grain of salt.

On one occasion Amjad met with Yusuf in his basement apartment and to Yusuf's dismay, hooked Yusuf onto what Amjad claimed to be a lie detector device. The device appeared to be a makeshift, homemade machine that Yusuf did not take seriously, but he took it in stride and apparently "passed".

Along with the Amjad operation, Intelligence was being developed regarding a major exporter of vehicles to the Middle East, specifically to Saudi Arabia and to Lebanon. Both countries had significant commercial ports. Later the port of Cotonou in Benin, West Africa would also become a hugely important destination for these vehicles. I had by this point partnered with a Department of Commerce Bureau of Industry and Security Agent, Office of Export Enforcement, "OEE", Rich Jereski. We would be joined at the hip for almost ten years thereafter and became good friends. Rich joined us on the Amjad investigation and would always assist us on these surveillances. Yusuf took a liking to Rich, which helped morale in general.

For Yusuf to obtain the visas, Amjad would have to produce passports from his Palestinian associates. Amjad would pay Yusuf for the service and the visas. It took a long time for Amjad to come up with the passports, but eventually he called Yusuf and informed him the passports had arrived. Amjad arranged a meeting with Yusuf at the shopping center, but when Yusuf arrived, Amjad called Yusuf and had him come over to the apartment in Akram's basement. Fortunately, we had already wired Yusuf up behind the shopping center, so we were able to switch gears quickly. This was the most important event so far. It was going to be a bit of a struggle for me unfortunately because I was suffering from a concussion. I provided karate classes in the office to bureau employees, predominantly agents, after work several evenings a week. I was used to injuries, but this had come at the worst time and at the hands of a careless and clumsy student. The class had concluded just before we left the office for the operation, and I was pretty groggy. But with the help of a squad mate or two, I was able to push through.

We moved over to set up outside Akram's house. Yusuf went down to Amjad's basement apartment. Amjad explained the passports had been delivered by a relative who left at the front door. There were six "clean" Palestinian Authority issued passports with no stamps. In recorded conversation between Yusuf and Amjad, and quoted in the Washingtonian article, Amjad claims "a passport just as this one never left the country and was never stamped. We got everything organized and a decision was made. When we got the OK, they sent it to us. I came and found it at the front door."

In the same recorded conversation between Yusuf and Amjad, Yusuf asks Amjad if he was truly serious about the visas, and "powerful enough" to pull it off. Amjad replies "As far as being powerful I can bring you the whole universe if you want. Anything you want in the area. If you want him to go to Lebanon to bomb everyone, he will go to Lebanon." The six Palestinians coincidentally had the same last name as Amjad—Hamed. Successfully smuggling them into the US was crucial to Amjad's future plans. He assured Yusuf if the operation were to be completed, the fees would make Yusuf "a millionaire." Amjad's hyperbole became a source of some amusement over time.

Yusuf took them with him when he departed Amjad's. Yusuf then met me at the usual location behind the shopping center near the dumpsters and gave the passports to me, and he was clearly relieved and somewhat surprised he actually pulled this off. I handed them to Tim. I asked Tim to contact the DSS Regional Security Officer in the embassy in Tel Aviv, Israel, to try to verify the legitimacy of the passports and the passport holders through the Israeli authorities. As it usually happened, in the end I had to do it myself. I contacted the FBI Legal Attaché, or Legat, in Tel Aviv to further identify the passports holders. It appeared that two had already been arrested by Israeli authorities.

At this point Amjad had clearly initiated a visa fraud conspiracy. Legally it was still an "attempted" fraud. An attempted criminal act is still chargeable, but a subject must engage in some substantive act initiating or furthering that criminal act. Most often law enforcement would want to stop the conspiracy before it could be completed and cause damage—either physical or financial, or to our national security. If it were to be completed it must still occur under controlled circumstances, but still not cause damage—hence the inert bombs sometimes provided to terrorist subjects, or the fake checks we used in the bank fraud case in New Jersey. In this case we would not be able to provide visas to possible terrorist or foreign intelligence agents and allow them to enter the US. Of greatest concern, we would not be able to keep track of these individuals if they did enter the US. So how do we complete the deal without actually providing the visas? Or do we need to? And if we didn't complete the deal, how would that affect Yusuf's credibility?

Yusuf continued to play up Amjad's impression that Yusuf's family had "wasta", an Arabic term denoting influence, in the Middle Eastern diplomatic community in the US and in the US embassies in Jordan and Lebanon, both of which would be the logical embassies from which a Palestinian could conceivably seek help. Yusuf's having recently been released from prison added to Amjad's confidence in Yusuf's willingness to involve himself in a criminal conspiracy. In reality, Yusuf's recent release was his driving motivation to do the right thing and redeem himself. So far it was working out for all of us.

A few weeks later, Amjad fulfilled his part of the deal and gave us the substantive act to satisfy the statute. Yusuf met Amjad at his apartment and Amjad paid him $2500. This was a partial payment in advance for the visas. Now the question was what do we do now? We couldn't actually put visas on the passports and give them back to Amjad. If the deal were not completed, what would happen to Yusuf's credibility? We could arrest Amjad now but that would be the end of the case and would not further identify Amjad's network. Even the nature of the network was still in doubt—Amjad claimed to be an intelligence officer for the PLO. Was this a counterintelligence case or a terrorism case, since the PLO was now part of the Palestinian authority, but for decades had committed terrorist acts against Israel. Amjad had claimed in a recorded conversation with Yusuf, that Amjad had previously been a member of Force 17, the elite commando unit of Fatah, and the bodyguard unit for PLO leader Yasser Arafat. We were able to confirm that Amjad was indeed a former member of that group. Amjad claimed Force 17 was the first Palestinian unit to be used to attack Israel. Members of Force 17 were believed to have gone on to found Hamas.

Amjad was clearly enamored of the various Middle Eastern Islamist terrorist organizations. He boasted "Fatah, Hamas and Hizballah are one. We all work together. We all do operations together. Don't let people fool you". Amjad expressed his admiration for Hizballah leader Hassan Nasrullah and gave Yusuf tapes of Nasrullah's sermons. I truly believed Amjad's terrorist bona fides were pretty solid at this point.

The decision to withhold the visas became a problem. The delay in providing them caused concern among Amjad and his visa customers. Amjad was anxious to get the visas to Palestine. Amjad was as much worried about the money to be made as much as his responsibility to help his compatriots. "They called me yesterday, and the day before yesterday. I did not answer. They pressure me. We can't wait. We need to work. We need to make money."

In July, Amjad met Yusuf again at the apartment. "These passports are the biggest responsibility of my whole life" Amjad told Yusuf. "They are calling me every two weeks. I want one request from you. Call your people and tell them if they can't get the visas in two days, to return the passports."

We were forced to return the passports to Amjad. Coming up with an explanation, well really an excuse, for why the visas were not forthcoming took some brainstorming. Finally, we settled on a story. At that time, in 2006, the Israeli military and Hizballah were engaged in a month-long war in Lebanon. That provided the excuse we needed. Yusuf met with Amjad, and returned the passports, explaining his contact in Beirut was restricted in his ability to obtain any visas due to the battles going on in Lebanon. Amjad reluctantly accepted the passports back and Yusuf's explanation. But we still had our violation to be included in any future prosecution. But we weren't done yet.

• • • • • • • •

Several months went by. I concentrated on other matters for a while. The Public corruption squad had approached me to begin another undercover. This case concerned the DC City Councilman Jim Graham (now deceased) and his Chief of Staff, Ted Loza. The initiation of the case came when the DC taxi commissioner, Leon Swain, had been approached by lobbyists for the taxicab industry in DC. They began to offer bribes to the commissioner, a former DC Metro Police or MPD, officer. Leon was a straight up guy and he reported it to his former agency, who then passed on to the FBI. Leon agreed to work undercover, and then in time introduce me to the lead lobbyist, Abdul Kamus, as a wealthy businessman who wanted to obtain special legislation that would benefit my ability to purchase a taxicab company. Currently the industry was closed to new cab companies due to a glut of companies operating in DC at the time. Also at the time, the city councilman responsible for the taxicab industry was Graham.

I was introduced to the lobbyist, Abdul, and he agreed to introduce me to Loza, who would then be able to in turn introduce me to Graham to pitch the legislation. The legislation would provide an exemption to me. I would of course have to pay for it. This became a year-long "collateral duty" parallel to my ongoing investigations. After several months, I was able to wear a wire and meet with Loza. I had a briefcase fitted with a hidden camera. Also, in the briefcase was $4000 in cash to provide to Loza to gain access to Graham. Loza mumbled his way into justifying the funds as a "gift" to help defray the cost of a trip to Ethiopia on behalf of the taxi industry, whose members were predominantly of Ethiopian nationality, as was Abdul. Not sure how a trip to the home or ancestral country of a group of businessmen would benefit the industry.

After several weeks of wining and dining Loza, in several very posh DC restaurants, I was asked to meet Graham at his office in the DC City Hall. Loza and Abdul accompanied me to the meeting. I was equipped with a body recorder. I had to pass through a metal detector to enter the building. The metal detector would discover the recorder if it were on my person. I came up with a small ploy to get the recorder through the gauntlet. Once successfully through, I excused myself to the restroom and sneaked the recorder back into place. My adrenaline subsided. I then met with Graham in his office. Graham was an interesting and very flamboyant character, with matching eyeglasses and bow ties. I presented a business model for my company. The company would be a "green" company using only electric vehicles, perhaps providing me with an exemption. He agreed to consider the legislation.

Over several months I would meet Loza by himself or with Graham. This usually entailed my paying for lunches or dinners again at very expensive restaurants in DC. At one lunch, Loza sat next to me in the booth, while Graham sat across from us by himself. Graham graciously offered to have me sit next to him. Thanks Jim. Made for a much better recording.

The two case agents, both young and relatively inexperienced agents were seated nearby to observe the meeting. Sadly, the MPD detectives who were both assigned to a WFO task force, and who had brought the case to us, were being treated very disrespectfully by these two young agents. They had no clue as to how to treat members of other partner agencies and had effectively locked them out of any operational activity. The MPD detectives were parked somewhere down the street. The two agents seemed not to want to share the glory, such as it was.

At the conclusion of one notable dinner meeting with Graham, at one of his favorite restaurants, the waiter brought the bill. Graham took the bill from the tray and handed it to me with a flourish. He stood, and pirouetted, as he handed it to me. "I believe I'm the guest...and I love being the guest".

The two agents also had no clue as to how to treat a senior, experienced undercover agent who had agreed to balance his heavy case load with assisting them in their case several days a week. Many debriefings back at the office deteriorated into arguments between the case agents in front of me over the case strategy. This made it difficult for me to have any idea as to what my role would be or how I should approach future meetings. The squad supervisor, SSA Steve D'Antuono, who had been one of my trainees at the FBI Academy, did not have any control over what was happening in the operation. I would stop by the squad on a regular basis to see how the rest of the case was going. The case agents were rarely in the squad area. Lots of vacation time it seemed. After the dinner meeting with Graham and a subsequent meeting with Abdul, where Abdul actually described the cash "gifts" and "campaign donations" as bribes—"in this country you call these donations—in my country we call them bribes", D'Antuono exclaimed I had "hit it out of the park". That would be the last kind word I would receive over the remaining year of undercover.

The next question was now to move forward and prove to the court that all of the wining and dining, and a later offer to take Loza and Graham on a weekend trip to Florida, (which they at first turned down and then repeatedly tried to reinitiate), counted as bribes, solicited bribes, and public corruption. The case agents requested I arrange a meeting with Graham without Abdul being present. I opined that it would not be a good idea to cut Abdul out so early in the game, and that it would alienate Abdul and ruin our access to Graham via Abdul. They insisted, believing Abdul would make confusing or exculpatory statements. I met with Graham in his office. As predicted, he asked where Abdul was. I was stuck between a rock and a hard place—Graham was clearly uncomfortable not having Abdul there after having only met with me once before. I had to make apologies to Graham and then call Abdul and apologize to him as well. Thanks guys. Yes, I had to tell them "I told you so". No apologies on their part. The relationship deteriorated from there.

Another inroad into Graham arose when Abdul approached me to pay for a painted portrait of Graham that his taxi lobbyist group wanted to give to Graham as a "birthday gift". The price was $5000. I of course agreed. I met with Abdul and provided him with $5000 in case funds. It would mean nothing however if we couldn't make the connection between me, the businessman trying to buy his way into a city contract, and the "gift" from the lobbyists who were wining and dining Graham and Loza, and had, as I had discovered, been paying for expensive "fact finding" junkets to their home country of Ethiopia. Not sure what facts would be found in Ethiopia that would inform Graham and Loza on taxicab industry issues in DC. Not sure why that was never prosecuted either. I was able to insist that I must be present when the portrait was given to Graham in his office so that he knew I was the one who paid for the "gift". I still have a copy of the photo I had taken of he and I shaking hands in front of the portrait. Not sure why that was never prosecuted either. Graham, now deceased, was a Democrat. The DC USAO is known to be decidedly Democrat in in its politics.

Eventually Abdul was compelled to cooperate, and he met with Loza and paid him a small amount of money, $1500 which Loza assumed was from me. At the end, Graham introduced the legislation. Mission accomplished at least on my part. For an unexplained reason, (to me) the money paid to Loza by Abdul, supposedly from me, was the only charge made in the case based on the undercover operation. Loza went to prison. Graham was never charged, even though he solicited bribes, took many expensive meals, and introduced the legislation. None of what I described to you here, specifically the undercover operation, ever came out in public, and was never mentioned in any media related to the case. A year or so later, the Washington Post published an article claiming the "FBI 'Cash Cab' Investigators Tested D.C Council Member" with no mention of any of the payments or the lavish wining and dining. It did discuss the conviction of Loza, based only on the money paid by Abdul to Loza, with no mention of the $4000 I paid to Loza. It did in a roundabout way acknowledge the $5000 painting having been paid for by the FBI. In the article, Graham expressed his anger at Loza, and acknowledged that the FBI had tapped his phone and noted that an "undercover agent" posing as an investor offered him a lavish trip to Miami to discuss potential projects in the District, and the legislation he had introduced on my behalf, none of which was prosecuted.

∙∙∙∙∙∙∙

Well back to Amjad. By this time Amjad had forgiven Yusuf for the visa issue. We at least had something with which to prosecute Amjad, but he had proven himself to be someone to continue to investigate. Amjad had produced the passports, which indicated he could produce official PLA documents and had the contacts in the US. His personal history also attested to his connections to terrorist organizations and their operational activities. During the conversations between Amjad and Yusuf, Amjad explained he had been assisted in obtaining the passports by various diplomats from several Arab embassies. A "diplomat" was also serving as a courier for Amjad's network. Amjad also admitted to having been in jail in Israel three times. When asked by Yusuf, Amjad admitted his first arrest was "related to Hizballah". He added that his Palestinian superior would be coming to the US "early next year" and would then meet with Yusuf.

Amjad assured Yusuf that Hizballah is "stronger than ever now", and that Fatah does work with Hizballah, apparently to reassure Yusuf they were all in it together. Amjad explained he was actively involved in smuggling arms by ship to Hizballah in "the middle of Lebanon". Not sure how much more we needed in order to consider Amjad as a terrorist and a spy.

Amjad spoke at length about the current political situation in Lebanon and in highly positive terms about Hizballah's activities in that country, explaining

"Hizballah not only has ties to the Palestinian people but also sympathizes, supports and aids them."

Amjad spent a good deal of time boasting of his military experience and how "powerful" he was, and that he could "turn Lebanon upside down". He recited the many terrorist acts conducted by the PLO and Hamas, such as the attack on the Munich Olympics. Amjad further boasted of his knowledge of spy trade craft. Amjad went on to describe the various secure technologies used by his groups and how hard it was for him to have some equipment assigned to him, and how he would have to return items as soon as he was done using them, so another officer who needed it could sign it out. Very reminiscent of our own struggles at the bureau trying to sign out equipment. I guess we are all the same in our bureaucratic struggles.

I now had to balance the undercover operation with a reinvigorated Amjad case. In 2007, Amjad contacted Yusuf with a new scheme. Amjad had a contact with a Middle Eastern diplomat to the US in DC who was seeking to sell contraband, untaxed cigarettes. Amjad hoped Yusuf could come up with $4500. Well, why not keep Yusuf in the game? I put in the paperwork to request the $4500. It sat in Brian's in-box for weeks. He went on vacation.

The Assistant Special Agent in Charge, or ASAC, Diego Rodriguez, came to me for a briefing on the progress of the case. We sat down in Brian's empty office. Diego was a supportive and engaged manager and was looking for ways to provide me with the resources I needed. Rare. I briefed him on the most recent development. Diego was an organized crime agent for most of his career, as was I, so we both understood the value of targeting the racketeering activity used by terrorist groups, and ways to build a successful criminal case. He asked where was the request for the funds? It presented an awkward situation, but I realized this was my only opportunity to get something done. I looked in Brian's in-box, sitting next to me on his desk. There sat the request for the funds. Untouched weeks after having been submitted. The ASAC looked disappointed to say the least. He took the request and got it processed. I got the cash—but not in time to complete the deal. Amjad had by this time found another buyer. I was sick to my stomach at another lost opportunity. The ASAC transferred me to another CT squad the next week. It was a mixed blessing as I would soon find out, but he was trying to do the right thing.

As I adjusted to the new squad, located right next to my previous squad, I spent the weekend with my family. My middle son had a sports awards ceremony in Fredericksburg. In the middle of the ceremony, I received a call from Yusuf. He rarely called on weekends. I went outside on the sidewalk and took the call. Yusuf informed me Amjad had contacted Yusuf and apologized for having to sell the cigarettes but had a new, possibly better deal to pitch. Trust Amjad to always have another scheme brewing. A true entrepreneur. Amjad offered to make up for the cigarette deal gone bad, and supply guns to Yusuf. I thought, I would take guns over cigs any day. I hoped he was good for it, because buying guns was a no-brainer, and didn't present the complications of the visa deal.

Amjad was working on multiple gun deals. The first deal involved a ninemillimeter pistol. Yusuf would take any guns Amjad had to offer and was not worried about the cost. Luckily, we still had the cash from the cigarette deal. I got permission to use the "buy money" for this new deal. I had by this time briefed my new supervisor, Reid Roe, and the ASAC had backed me up on this operation. Any support from Reid would not last long.

Amjad offered the pistol for $750. On May 23, Yusuf met Amjad at the apartment in Akram's basement, and handed over the $750. Two days later, Yusuf sat in the Pinecrest shopping center lot as he had done so many times before. Amjad pulled into the lot in a small truck. Yusuf climbed into the passenger side. Amjad handed over a Smith and Wesson nine-millimeter wrapped in a cloth. Yusuf looked at the gun. Its serial number had been obliterated. Amjad was wearing latex gloves to keep his fingerprints off the gun.

Yusuf reminded Amjad that Yusuf was a convicted felon and he "can't buy a gun legally". Yusuf was good at following directions. Amjad's knowingly selling a firearm to a convicted felon was a felony. Another charge. Amjad assured Yusuf he was aware of Yusuf's legal status and explained he had obtained the gun with the serial number "erased" for him. We now had two related charges.

Yusuf informed Amjad that the gun was going to a crew of Hizballah in the area, explaining, he had to "prove himself". He questioned whether the weapons came from "Amjad's people", to which Amjad replied in the affirmative. Yusuf challenged Amjad's earlier statement that Amjad had told Yusuf that Hizballah was coordinating with Hamas. He emphasized that if Yusuf "served the Hizballah people" then he would be serving the "Hamas people" and Amjad's people.

Yusuf asked if the gun came from Amjad's own group, or did it come from "gangsters"? Amjad explained it came from "all groups", but the problem is that it doesn't have a serial number".

Amjad provided Yusuf a hand-written shopping list of guns he could supply to Yusuf and a price list. The list included an AR-15 rifle for $2400 to $2800, a fully automatic military M-16 for $3500 and a shotgun for between $1400 and $1600. Amjad claimed he could get "as many as ten M-16s, fully automatic, from my supplier."

Yusuf confirmed the money for any future gun purchases would come from Hizballah. Amjad replied "it doesn't matter".

Yusuf asked whether Amjad had connections to transport the weapons "from one state to another or one area to another". Amjad assured him "I have connections to transport from America directly to the middle of Lebanon". Amjad did have a knack for hyperbole. But could he?

Amjad, in an apparent effort to reassure Yusuf he was not alone in the effort, revealed that his brother Akram was aware of and had to approve everything Amjad did. Akram later would try to claim he was an innocent guy swept up in his brother's mistakes. Thanks, little brother.

A month later, they met again, this time in the parking lot of the K-Mart off Little River Turnpike in Annandale. We had met at the usual spot behind the dumpsters, wired Yusuf up, and arrived in time for Amjad to show up in a white van. The surveillance team was able to maintain a good distance because of the vast parking lot and clear line of sight. That would not last.

Yusuf walked over to the car and handed Amjad an envelope of cash; case funds I had given him after putting the wire on. The envelope contained $2600. Just then, a huge tractor-trailer pulled up and parked in the middle of the parking lot, and completely blocking my view of the meeting. Par for the course. We pretty much expect these stupid glitches to happen. I quickly relocated so I could regain the "eye". Several other members of the surveillance team did so as well.

Yusuf, admonished Amjad for being late, that it made it difficult for "our folks and Hizballah" and that Amjad was providing the service for both of their groups. Amjad didn't miss a beat, asking whether the "merchandise" would go out of the country. Yusuf explained that half the merchandise would stay here and half of it will go out of the country. It would depend on the quantity that Amjad would give him. Yusuf asked whether Akram was aware of the gun deals as he was the visa deal. Amjad replied that this was a different deal— it was a "military" type transaction as opposed to the visa deal, which Amjad described as being a "civil task". Yusuf questioned whether Amjad had been honest and frank about where the weapons would go, because Yusuf was following Amjad's advice by "walking down the right path" and providing the weapons to the "right people". They engage in a small debate concerning Amjad's purported contacts and Amjad's opinion of Hizballah and its leader, Hassan Nasrullah. Yusuf questioned Amjad whether he believes Hizballah "does it for the belief and cause" but that they also do it for the money? Amjad replies in the affirmative, to which Yusuf then confirms that they were "the same thing". Amjad agrees that yes, that they were "all at the same line". Yusuf again confirms that he will deliver the guns to the people of the "Hezb" (party) here. He questioned whether Amjad could provide a quantity of "guns or machine guns or whatever" if he wanted to get them out of the country. Amjad assures Yusuf he could do so and "this is going to be a good deal".

Amjad departed the parking lot and returned about 15 minutes later. Usually giving money to a subject and allowing them to depart is a risk. In this case Amjad had already proven himself to be reliable and we could always arrest him later if he scammed Yusuf. Besides the money was not a particularly large amount as far as contraband buys go. As Amjad left the parking lot, part of the surveillance team left with him and followed Amjad to his and Akram's house. They observed the van park in front of the house, and subsequently depart the house carrying a bundle. They then followed him right back to the Kmart. Amjad gestured Yusuf over to the van. In the back of the van was another blanket-wrapped bundle. This time it concealed an SKS sniper rifle outfitted with a scope, a bi-pod stand, and a laser finder. Amjad handed the bundle to Yusuf; it also contained an eight-millimeter pistol. Amjad dangled the next shipment to Yusuf—to include something special.

The recorded conversation went this way:

Amjad: "Are you still interested?"

Yusuf: "I want it".

Amjad: "A missile".

Yusuf: "Don't play with me—is it true?"

Amjad: "It's true".

Yusuf: "What is it? Rocket? Missile?"

Amjad: "Missile".

Yusuf: "Does it come –pay attention—does it come with equipment to shoot it out or only the missile?"

Amjad: "No, no, no, when I say missile, it is with everything—with the controls if you want to hit the Pentagon."

Yusuf: "With the controls? What? You want to hit the Pentagon?"

Amjad: "You can put the bottle on it—the blue bottle and hit the Pentagon".

Yusuf, knowing by now how slow the government can be in approving an operation, and especially providing the funding, explained it would take at least two weeks for the next deal. Yusuf did not want to look bad in front of his "Jemaa" (army) which is big and powerful". Amjad revealed that Akram and Ibrahim had seen the guns in the garage, and Amjad did not want them to know about the impending gun deal.

As always, Yusuf met me and several members of the team back behind the shopping center and we took possession of the guns, and the recording devices. I turned the guns over to Bob Poole, the ATF agent assigned to one of our task forces to have his agency analyze the guns, check for fingerprints, and to affirm the serial number was illegally obliterated.

Later that month, Amjad and Yusuf talked again about the proposed M16s and the missile. Yusuf reiterated he would need two weeks to get the money. Amjad had made an off-hand mention of his cousin, Ibrahim Hamed as though Ibrahim may have some involvement in the deals. This was now appearing to be a conspiracy. We decided to have Yusuf contact Ibrahim and set up a meeting. Might as well see what he has to say about it all.

Yusuf gave Ibrahim a call. Recorded of course. Ibrahim confirmed he had provided the guns to Amjad but was angry with Amjad and Akram that they had only given him $200.

They met at the Pinecrest Starbucks. Ibrahim played the gangster to Yusuf. Ibrahim claimed to have provided all of the guns to Amjad. "Everything he gave you came from me. I'm the one that gave him everything, the 9 and the 11. Yes, it came from me. He begged me to give him some. Do you think Amjad knows anything? Amjad is the dumbest one in Virginia." Ah, a rivalry. It causes bravado and boasting, and in this case, a new defendant whose admissions implicated himself for us. Another charge.

Ibrahim claimed Amjad had no connections. We knew better, based on bis ability to secure the passports from the Palestinian Authority. But nevertheless, Ibrahim continued to boast he had brought all of the guns from Florida—illegally transporting guns interstate is a felony. Amjad had allegedly screwed up a deal for AK-47s.

Ibrahim exclaimed if he had known the weapons were going to Hizballah, he would have "gotten him the newest shit that could turn a handgun into a machinegun." This conversation was actually spoken in English. The surveillance team all overheard it at the same time. Over the radio there was laughter among the team as they broke in and acknowledged we now had Ibrahim dead to rights. The best evidence is always the subject's own words. On tape. With witnesses listening in.

Ibrahim dug himself deeper. He stated he was aware Yusuf was negotiating for a missile. Ibrahim was hoping to cut out his cousin and deal directly with Yusuf. It was apparent that Amjad and Ibrahim fully believed Yusuf's affiliation with a terrorist organization, in this case, Lebanese Hizballah. This clearly was motivation for them to continue conspiring with Yusuf, rather than backing away.

In January 2006, Amjad and Yusuf met again. Yusuf eventually reiterated he was procuring the firearms and shipping them overseas on behalf of Hizballah. Yusuf admonished Amjad "you know the objects I bought from you, the weapons and the rest, are going to Hizballah and our people we are all one these days.

Is that right or not? Ibrahim replied "yes, right". Yusuf then explained his people had complained about the 8-millimeter pistol. When we had processed the gun as evidence, we had found a bullet lodged in the barrel. It was also an unusual Italian caliber, which made it less usable. Yusuf further explained his people were also not happy with the delay in obtaining the missile and the additional military rifles.

Amjad had not yet produced the missile. He did not rule out the deal, he was just having trouble obtaining it right now. The conversation was, let's say, rather lively. Lots of waving hands and rapid fire, loud exclamations. The car was actually bouncing. Cigarette butts were flying out the windows. The normal Arab way of engaging in conversation. At one point, Tim broke in on the radio, clearly concerned that the conversation was taking a dangerous turn. He asked if we should intervene. I responded calmly, no Tim, that's just how Arab guys talk to each other, nothing to worry about. Tim and the rest of the team got a laugh out of that. I will admit to having a tee shirt given to me by my wife that states "I'm not yelling, I'm Lebanese".

Amjad advised he had been stalling in completing any further gun sale because "his people" were being watched by the government. The second issue, he explained, was that these items are very expensive". One of Amjad's people, a "big guy" had to cut a ticket and leave.

We were at a crossroads now. We had plenty of charges to apply to Amjad and Ibrahim. We had visa fraud charges, conspiracy, and illegal gun trafficking.

Was the missile for real? If so, how much more investigative effort should be put towards completing that transaction?

Amjad's brother, Akram gave us renewed reason to continue the investigation. He asked to meet with Yusuf in May 2007. Akram's construction business was not his only business pursuit. He, along with apparently half of the Arabic community in Northern Virginia was purchasing used cars at various auto auctions and exporting the used cars to the Middle East and to Africa, very often as a side hustle to their primary businesses. We were still keeping an eye on several identified suspect car dealers, and they would turn out to be the nexus of the next vast terrorist money laundering network linking one specific dealer with Akram, and with their sometime business partner, Mohammed Abdelaziz. Eventually it would link dozens of Middle Eastern men across the US, extending to their partners in Lebanon, Jordan, Saudi Arabia, Benin, and many countries in Europe. At this point, the subjects we had identified were all Palestinian—some from the West Bank, and some from Jordan, which has a large Palestinian expatriot community. The Lebanese would show up soon enough.

The war in Iraq was raging. Vehicle born improvised explosive devices, or VBIEDs were a massive problem. A VBIED factory in Fallujah, Iraq was raided by the US military where all of the vehicles being outfitted with explosives had turned out to be Chevrolet Suburban SUVs. The vehicles were traced to a used car company in California, Tripoli Auto. Our Los Angeles Division had an open case concerning Tripoli Auto. The Suburban was a common vehicle used by the military and other US government civilians and security contractors. It would make sense that the Suburban would be used to infiltrate a US facility. Why ship cars to Saudi Arabia and West Africa? We would answer that question much later. Yet it would also become more complex and difficult to counter.

Akram wanted Yusuf's help in collecting a debt related to his used car business. Yusuf would have to fly to Chicago and collect from a Jordanian car dealer, who owed $38,000 to Abdelaziz. Abdelaziz in turn owed $20,000 to Akram. Akram could skip a step by collecting directly from the Jordanian in Chicago. Akram was aware the Jordanian was in Chicago attending a car auction. Akram provided Yusuf with the man's itinerary, cell phone number, and his description. Akram was clearly angry and frustrated, and very graphic as to what violent methods Yusuf should employ to convince the now victim to pay up, ordering him to "step on his neck!". It took us a little while to formulate a plan, and coordinate with our Chicago office. In the meantime, Akram was becoming anxious, and pressured Yusuf to go get the job done, because if he couldn't, Akram would have to send "another team" up to Chicago "to do the job".

I contacted the Chicago FBI field office and spoke with an agent who had previously been assigned to WFO, and with whom I had previously been acquainted. The agents in Chicago were successful in contacting the Jordanian and interviewing him. The man confirmed he conducted auto business with Abdelaziz, and they were engaged in a lawsuit over the shipment of two vehicles, for a total of $38,000, which matched Akram's claims. The Chicago agents informed him of the plan to have the money taken from him by force and explained he would need to go along with the FBI's plan to convince Akram that had happened if he was to communicate with Akram. The FBI would provide funds to Akram via a person who was cooperating with the government. That person, he was told, would make Akram believe it had come from the Jordanian and he would have to explain he was beaten up by "a big Arab guy" to collect the money if Akram followed up with him and asked. Once the Jordanian returned to Jordan it would be his responsibility to resolve the lawsuit on his own. It appeared the Chicago agents had convinced him that bis cooperation was in bis best interest.

There was no need for Yusuf to actually go to Chicago. Yusuf laid low for a week so as to appear to have traveled there. We provided Yusuf with $10,000 in FBI case funds. That was as much as any of us wanted to give to Akram in taxpayer funds, but we needed to give him enough to convince him Yusuf had done the job as best as he could. Yusuf met with Akram at the Kmart parking lot on Little River Turnpike and gave him the $10,000 in cash. Yusuf explained he had traveled to Chicago, knocked the Jordanian man up against the wall and beat him up as Akram had asked. Yusuf described the beating rather graphically, to Akram's glee. Yusuf explained the man was only able to come up with $12,000 by taking Yusuf to a friend's house to borrow the money. Yusuf kept $2000 to defray his travel costs and as his fee. Akram was clearly not happy with the amount but had to accept what he could get. The whole

$38,000 was not Akram's to claim anyway. He kept the $10,000 as his cut from the deal with Abdelaziz.

Now Akram wanted Yusuf to turn on Abdelaziz and collect the remaining funds from him. It was becoming a circular firing squad. Abdelaziz, also known as "Abu-Jameel" around town, had given Akram several checks from his used auto export company, A and M Auto, that had all turned out to be bad checks. The account had been closed, coincidentally, shortly after the checks had been made out to Akram. Akram admonished Yusuf that anything done to Abu Jameel would have to be discreet because he was "in town". Yusuf tried to convince Akram to try to exhaust all legal methods first before resorting to force. Well done.

Akram and Yusuf again met at Akram's house, where Akram complained Abdelaziz had been "jerking him around" and still owed Akram $17,000. His father had lent Abdelaziz $40,000 and was also involved in the conflict. Akram reiterated his demand that Yusuf accept a "contract" to collect the cash from Abdelaziz "using whatever force is necessary". Akram gave Yusuf $400 as a down payment (and a substantive act towards an attempted extortion) and promised him 15% of the amount collected. Strike two.

At a third meeting with Akram, Yusuf begged off of the contract, explaining that "Abu-Jameel" was well known in town, was too powerful, and Yusuf was personally acquainted with him and would be too exposed. Yusuf added that he did not want to just be a "gangster" and wished more to be supporting the cause. No need for us to complete the contract because the attempted act had already been proven under the statute with the provision of the down payment.

The investigation got a boost from Yusuf's accomplishment. Yusuf became known as the go-to guy to get things done under the table. Yusuf spoke with Abdelaziz by phone and set up meeting at the usual spot. The conversation began with Yusuf asking Abdelaziz about what was happening between him and Akram Saleh. Abdelaziz was surprised that Yusuf would bring up the subject. Yusuf revealed he was the one who "took care of Chicago". Abdelaziz replied he thought that "Ibrahim Hamed had taken care of this". Yusuf described what he had done in Chicago and the money he had collected. Abdelaziz asked Yusuf to describe the guy. Fortunately, the Chicago agents had provided us with a description of the Jordanian car dealer at our request, and we had briefed Yusuf on those details. He went on to describe the Jordanian as being short and balding, which Abdelaziz confirmed was correct. Abdelaziz explained the car dealer had returned to Jordan and had been under arrest for two days. Yusuf admitted he had been sent to Abdelaziz by Akram to collect what was owed using whatever force was necessary, but he assured Abdelaziz that he was only there to warn him and not to harm him. Abdelaziz was understandably angry, and began "cussing everyone out", threatening to put out his own "contract" on Akram.

Month or so later, Yusuf attended Amjad's wedding. The wedding took place at a Chinese restaurant located in, of all places, the Cullmore area of Falls Church. Also attending the wedding were Akram, Ibrahim, and "AbuJameel". At one point during the reception,

Abdelaziz took Yusuf aside and now asked him to make a collection of funds from an unidentified individual. Later that day, Yusuf related the conversation with Abdelaziz to Akram. Akram realized things were getting out of hand and decided they all needed to sit down together and discuss the matter.

In a subsequent conversation with Ibrahim, Ibrahim confirmed he had also been involved in the whole Abu-Jameel issue. Ibrahim had on behalf of Akram, visited Abdelaziz in order "to give him a message". If Abdelaziz did not come up with the money, he would "make him disappear". Ibrahim bragged he had warned Abdelaziz that he "had a sniper outside the house". Ibrahim did tend to overplay his hand it appeared.

Abdelaziz now approached Yusuf for another deal. Culturally, in the Arab community, once you perform a task for someone, you are never off the hook from thereon. Abdelaziz introduced Yusuf to an Egyptian national named Sameh Ibrahim. Ibrahim was the subject of a civil immigration proceeding. Marriage fraud. Sameh needed help with Immigration and Customs Enforcement. It amazed us that once Yusuf succeeded in completing illicit gun deals, and a believed extortionate credit transaction, he was perceived to be capable of performing any task requested. How could Abdelaziz and Sameh Ibrahim think the previous transactions would translate to now bribing an ICE agent? But they did. Maybe even though the visa deal did not work out, the perception Yusuf still had wasta held firm. Strange logic for sure, but it worked to our benefit.

Abdelaziz was already of interest in relation to the whole auto export question, which was growing exponentially as a separate avenue of investigation, so we wanted to pursue this angle for more than just another quick criminal charge against another target. Abdelaziz met with Yusuf at one of two usual spots, the Pinecrest parking lot. As usual, Yusuf was wearing a wire and transmitter. Sameh was introduced, and he explained he had botched the paperwork filing for a marriage benefit with ICE. He was about to be deported. Sameh wanted Yusuf to make sure the American woman he was allegedly marrying would not blab to ICE that the marriage was a fraud. He also hoped Yusuf could somehow bribe the ICE agent into dropping the case. Magic. Another conspiracy charge, along with attempted bribery.

Relying on Yusuf's reputation for wizardry, Sameh also needed him to obtain fraudulent driver's licenses for his two sons. Yusuf agreed, for a fee of $4500 total. Sameh provided copies of the ICE paperwork charging him civilly with marriage fraud. The name of the ICE agent was included in the paperwork. I was concerned if we continued with the scheme, it could conceivably damage the agent's reputation. I contacted the ICE agent and explained the situation. Our respective management and the agent and I all met to work out the details. I hoped we could complete the deal and benefit ICE as well. I explained we were able to boost the ICE case from a civil case to a criminal case based on the recorded conversations between Yusuf and Sameh. Sameh had provided Yusuf $500 as a down payment, which fulfilled the attempted bribery and fraud statutes with an overt act. Reid and I did have to hold the line in that the ICE supervisor seemed to be pushing for ICE to run the rest of the investigation. I had to gently explain the case had been going on for several years and was much larger than the marriage fraud. ICE was welcome to be a partner, but we had much bigger fish to fry going forward and there were many more substantiated and potential violations that the bureau was responsible for and was going to continue to pursue. The meeting ended cordially. Diplomacy sometimes works.

Abdelaziz was not finished. They met again. This time Abdelaziz revealed the identity of the man from whom he wanted Yusuf to collect $20,000. The man was a Libyan whom Abdelaziz wanted Yusuf to "shake him down and threaten him but not hurt him yet". If that didn't work, Abdelaziz would tell Yusuf what to do next. He added that Akram's father, who resides in Tampa, Florida, was also involved in the car shipment with Abdelaziz and the Libyan. Yusuf had to admonish Abdelaziz as he did with Amjad, that he did not want to be a gangster, but rather wanted to help with "the cause". Abdelaziz advised him that if he wanted to be part of the cause, he would have to do him a favor. Another favor? When would it be enough? Yusuf would now have to obtain a US passport for him because Abdelaziz was tired of being stopped at the airport every time he traveled, and that "the FBI is blocking his passport". Abdelaziz did not seem to appreciate the fact he was not a US citizen and was not eligible for a US passport. Abdelaziz wanted the passport "right now" and would pay cash for it.

The Sameh Ibrahim family wasn't finished either. Abdelaziz called Yusuf to set up a meeting between

Yusuf and Sameh and his two sons Bassam and Ayman. The sons needed help too. They were also involved in marriage frauds. The apple doesn't fall far from the tree. The Ibrahims piled into Yusuf's car. The conversation was short and productive. For us. Both sons admitted to having made false statements to ICE and complicity in marriage frauds.

It was several months before Yusuf and Abdelaziz would meet again. Yusuf had been pushing him to bring him a couple of passport style photos of himself, but Abdelaziz had been procrastinating. Yusuf also instructed Abdelaziz to fill out the required application forms and get them to Yusuf as soon as possible. Apparently Abdelaziz expected Yusuf to do everything for him. That wouldn't work. The passport would cost a total of $10,000, but Yusuf would be willing to collect the funds from the Libyan and use that money to pay for the passport, to which Abu-Jameel readily agreed. Yusuf was a proactive guy. We followed him to the nearby CVS where he practically dragged Abdelaziz into the store and helped him take two passport photos.

DSS was now happy again. They had a piece of the pie. Visa fraud is a State Department violation as opposed to marriage or any other immigration fraud, which comes under the purview of ICE. DSS prepared a phony passport for Abdelaziz for delivery to him as the last criminal act that would result in a "buy bust" arrest.

We had arrived at a crossroads—again. We had solid charges against Amjad for illegal gun trafficking, including the sale of a firearm to a convicted felon, the trafficking of firearms interstate, the sale of a firearm with an obliterated serial number, and I think most significantly the visa fraud, on behalf of a terrorist group. We still had the distinct possibility we could get that missile from Amjad, who was still holding out the possibility he would have the missile soon. He and Ibrahim were both pitching additional weapons sales. They claimed they had connections at an unidentified military installation in North Carolina for automatic weapons.

Reid was building his resume for a promotion at that time. He began to pressure me to shut the case down. At the top of his lungs. Seven anticipated arrests would certainly look good on his promotion packet. That's all he apparently cared about. We argued. I felt that we—Yusuf and I—had invested several years in the case, and we had succeeded in building a multitude of prosecutable cases. We certainly had the possibility to take more guns and a missile off the street, as well as determine the source of any stolen or contraband military weapons, we could wait a little more. I was overruled—loudly. Reid needed his stats. We began to plan the take-down.

We met with the prosecutors at the US Attorney's Office at the Eastern District of Virginia in Alexandria. By this time my fraternity brother, Neil Hammerstrom was in charge of the National Security Section. He had assigned Jeanine Linehan as the AUSA. I had by this time drafted several arrest warrant affidavits for the seven subjects upon whom we had built cases. A separate affidavit was drafted for Amjad charging him with material support of terrorism. This was the sticking point with the Department of Justice writ large. Considering the extensive conversations between Yusuf and Amjad where Amjad readily agreed to provide weapons to Hizballah, his attempts to obtain illegal visas for members of Fatah and Tanzim, and his detailed statements detailing his prior terrorist activities in Israel, it seemed a "slam dunk" that his various deals with Yusuf would constitute material support. That was not to be. EDVA was on board with the charge. Main Justice in DC, specifically the Counterterrorism Section, or CTS, made every excuse not to approve the charge. The now common excuse used by CTS was always that the defense would be that the defendants were just making up their expressed connections to a terrorist group "to impress and intimidate their co-conspirators". The truth is that they would have to do extra work in order to have that charge approved. This excuse became a standard for DOJ/CTS for the remaining years I worked counterterrorism.

The debate as to whether these cases were "just criminals talking big", or terrorists funding their organizations, would dog every FBI CT case for years to come. Another reason why most case agents learned to pursue the underlying criminal activity rather than material support. We all knew the truth— we knew our subjects were supporting terrorist networks because we had all worked hard to develop the intelligence to identify the networks and had followed the money to the finish line. What mattered was that we would do what we could to get them "off the street", and at least temporarily neutralize their particular conspiracy.

On the night of September 29, 2008, arrest teams assembled near the various locations where we would find all of our targets. Most of the subjects were to be located at home, however Akram and Abdelaziz would be meeting in person with Yusuf at the Kmart. We had fed them the plan that they would meet with Yusuf in his car in the far parking lot where Yusuf would provide Akram with $5000 he would have ostensibly collected for him, and Yusuf would kill two birds with one stone by providing Abdelaziz with the passport.

At 8:00 pm, Yusuf pulled into a prearranged parking spot at the far end of our now favorite location at the Kmart, up against a curb that would contain any vehicle that pulled in next to his car. We had a plane up filming the festivities in infrared, due to the darkness. It made for some fascinating video for later presentations. Surveillance and take-down teams were positioned in a semi-circular pattern surrounding the site, camouflaged among the cars already parked in the lot. Everyone was focused on Yusuf's massive old Lincoln Continental. The various exits from the vast parking lot were covered by chase team cars. We had, as in the past, surveyed the lot in advance, picked out the spot, and practiced the take-down with our vehicles. This time it would work out flawlessly.

Much later I Would take Harry Jaffe on a tour of the parking lot and a rundown of the arrest operation.

About 15 minutes passed, when a large SUV arrived and parked among the cars in the lot, several rows away from Yusuf's car. And two cars away from one of our surveillance teams. The two agents scrunched down inside their car. Akram and Abdelaziz emerged from the SUV and ambled over to Yusuf's car. They climbed inside. Yusuf was of course wearing a recorder and a transmitter. His instructions were to provide Akram with $5000 in case funds, allegedly collected from the Libyan as part of Akram's share of the debt, and then provide the fake passport to Abdelaziz. Upon completion of the transaction, he was to say, in English this time, "are you happy now?" This would be the signal for the arrest teams to move in and contain the scene and make the arrests. Yusuf would also be "arrested" in order to maintain his cover for at least awhile, or until he possibly had to testify in the future. When he and I were planning this out, I realized we needed some redundancy in the takedown signal, knowing for one that transmitters are notoriously finicky, and we might not hear the signal. Also knowing he and his friends were all somewhat chain smokers, I instructed him to also throw his cigarette out the window. It was nighttime. Would I see the butt going out the window? How about also stomping on his brake, and flashing the brake-lights?

Turns out three's a charm. We could hear the conversation going on over the transmitter. The traffic over the radio among the teams blanked out the code words. During the conversation, cigarettes were flying out the window on all sides. They showed up on the infrared video as black, pulsing blobs on the pavement. We could not tell which was which. But signal number three worked like a charm. Yusuf was a big guy. The lights flashed as he stomped on the brakes, and with a touch of humor, the car bounced up and down, kind of reminiscent of a low rider. We were ready to move in. I had a team of good agents I trusted from my new squad and my old squad. As to be expected, there was glitch. A motorcycle was parked right in our path. It would obstruct our moving in close to Yusuf's car.

The idiot driver arrived to climb on his bike just as the Continental was bouncing. He sat on the bike and pulled out his cell phone. If we moved in, we would most assuredly run over this guy. We held our breath. He finally finished his call and drove away. We moved in quickly. Akram and Abdelaziz were already climbing out of the Continental. Three cars moved in—my car was in the center of the triangle. I was seated in the passenger side to be positioned to call out to the subjects and instruct them towards our handcuffs. I called out. I didn't bother with the PA system. Adrenaline can make up for that. I'm loud anyway, and the acoustics in the vast parking lot were pretty good. Tactically, we pushed our vehicles in a car length away from Yusuf's car. Close enough to block them in and call the subjects back toward us, walking backward.

First, we needed to get Yusuf out of there. Bobby Wells was in the car on my left. He called Yusuf out of his car and back towards Bobby. Bobby struggled to get the cuffs on. As I said, Yusuf is a big guy. Yusuf looked over his shoulder, laughing quietly, and said "Bobby! Use two handcuffs dude."

Yusuf was secure. I called out to Abdelaziz to stand up and Akram to kneel down so I could have a clear view of both of them. Either my instructions were just not clear, or we had a language problem. Or both.

Akram stood up and Abdelaziz kneeled down. Yikes. I reiterated my instructions, and it worked the second time around. I could now see both of them.

I called Akram back, knelt him down again and placed the handcuffs on. I removed the $5000 in cash from his back pocket as I searched him for weapons or contraband. I pulled him around to the back of our car. Abdelaziz was last but not least. The car to my right held two squad mates who were also SWAT team members. Ian and Baker, both good young agents were "tact-ed out" to the max. All of us wore bulky body armor, and most carried our sidearms low on our thighs in tactical holsters, along with whatever we could hang off of our vests, such as handcuffs, batons, etc. Ian's vest looked like a Christmas tree with more stuff than I could identify hanging off his vest. Better to have it and not need it than need it and not have it. Both agents I trusted to handle subject number three's arrest, and then clear the car to make sure no one was hiding in the car, or any evidence left behind. The aerial video of the arrest operation certainly highlighted our tactical skills.

The remaining subjects, Amjad Hamed, Ibrahim Hamed, Ayman and Bassam Ibrahim were located at home. Father Sameh Ibrahim was located and arrested at work.

Between September 2008 and February 2009, all seven subjects pleaded guilty. Akram was sentenced to 12 months incarceration. Amjad was sentenced to 18 months. Ibrahim was sentenced to ten months. Sameh was sentenced to 10 months. Ayman and Bassam were sentenced to four months each. All except for Akram, a US citizen, were scheduled to be deported. All very light sentences, considering the overall number of charges, the clear connection to terrorist organizations for Amjad and solicited acts of violence on the part of Akram. The US Attorney's office unfortunately has a habit of low-balling charges, often ignoring multiple charges, and only picking out the easiest charge to prove in order to obtain guilty pleas. The worst example of this was Abdelaziz. We had solicitation of extortion against multiple intended victims, including the overt act of paying an advance fee, along with passport fraud, solicitation or attempted bribery of a federal agent, and conspiracy to commit immigration fraud with the Ibrahims. The only charge brought forth against him was the attempted bribery. The sentencing judge, US District Court Gerald Bruce Lee, astonishingly seemed to sympathize with Abdelaziz in the attempted bribery, speculating there was a "cultural element" involved, and that in Abdelaziz's home country, "bribing a public official was an accepted practice". He did not seem to take into consideration that it was not an accepted practice in America and is illegal. He sentenced Abdelaziz to a three-year period of probation. He was never deported. What about US law? What about all the other charges?

The final point made by Harry Jaffe in the Washingtonian article:

"Terrorism cases aren't easy to prove. Investigators have to gather hard evidence such as weapons or bombs. Prosecutors have the burden indicting subjects for violating specific crimes and proving beyond a reasonable doubt that a suspect was plotting to perform a terrorist act."

Abdelaziz would continue to be a central figure for years, along with dozens of others in the growing phenomenon of the use of used auto exports and Lebanese banks and currency exchange houses to fund Hamas, Hizballah, and AlQaeda for years to come. That would occupy my time for years to come.

IX.

All Others

Al-Qaeda had become the overwhelming concern of the intelligence community and federal law enforcement since the day of 9/11. AL-Qaeda is organized along the lines of small cells scattered around the world. As of 9/11, it was headquartered, for lack of a better term, in Afghanistan. A trend emerged over time whereby other Islamist terrorist groups such as Boko Haram in Nigeria, and Abu Sayyaf in the Philippines, would eventually pledge allegiance to Al-Qaeda's leader, Osama Bin-Laden. Yet Al-Qaeda, a Sunni Muslim, Wahabi extremist fundamentalist group was a relative, although vicious, newcomer in the realm of Islamist terror. The longest existing organization has always been the Lebanese Shiite organization Hizballah. The various Palestinian terrorist organizations such as Hamas and Palestinian Islamic Jihad, or PIJ, would come in a close second. The Iranian revolution in 1979 changed the complexion of terrorism forever, in that prior to that event, the majority of international terrorist groups were based upon leftist or communist ideology, such as the Bader Meinhoff gang, or Red Army Faction, in Germany, the Red Brigades in Italy, and the original Palestinian Liberation Organization, or PLO.

Hizballah and Hamas, in contrast to Al-Qaeda, are Islamist, but with a nationalist basis. Hamas is internally focused, anti-Israel, and focused on gaining a Palestinian homeland. Hizballah in Lebanon functions as an Islamist militia, a political party, a sophisticated intelligence organization, a well-armed army, and an international organized crime enterprise. Both organizations support themselves through ex-patriot fund-raising and donations, funding from Iran, and a vast network of criminal activities. Actual membership in either organization requires extensive vetting based on family reputation, religious fidelity, and other factors. Those willing to provide donations or engage in racketeering activity to raise funds may feel an allegiance to these organizations for different reasons, are considered supporters, but are not considered members. These individuals comprised the bulk of subjects in the US providing material support to Hizballah and Hamas, and other similar groups. The fact that we had difficulty in identifying individual subjects as "members" of a terrorist group, although clearly functioning as operatives on behalf of those groups, presented a sticking point in a multitude of investigations. Many of these cases, rather than being designated as "international Terrorism-Hizballah", or

"Hamas", were lumped into the category of "IT-All Others".

Case agents, that is the agents in the field with investigative duties rather than supervisory, administrative, or full-time instructor positions, are a rare breed. Many "old school" "street" agents choose to remain in the field as case agents and spend their career developing a particular area of expertise. A handful of counterterrorism agents fit this profile. In the past, agents assigned to investigate La Cosa Nostra, also more commonly known as the Mafia, or the "mob", are of the same mentality. It takes years to learn the identities all of the members of a vast organization which makes every effort to keep its membership a secret. Management tends to frequently change investigative priorities. Being forced to "switch gears" frequently, after spending much time and effort in developing an expertise can be very demoralizing. Often the changes are in response to changes in funding. Many agents give up or give in and never flourish. Some remain stubborn and continue the struggle against the whims of changing priorities that seem to have no real logical basis, and they keep at their mission despite facing much "push-back". I guess I'm one of the stubborn ones. I saw Hizballah, in particular for the massive beast it is. It has active supporters and members world-wide, in particular in certain cities in the US, such as Dearborn, Michigan, the Chicago metro area, New York/New Jersey, and in the Northern Virginia area outside of DC, my territory.

Hizballah was formed roughly in 1982, although its actual founding was not a formal process, but an evolution, so there is no exact known date of its founding. Until 9/11, its members and supporters were responsible for the deaths of more Americans than any other "militant" organization. The Iranian Islamic Revolutionary Guard Corps, or IRGC, infiltrated Lebanon and helped organize and supply the nascent cells of now Shiite, Islamist Jihadists, centered in the Shia strongholds of the Bekaa Valley in the North, the South of Lebanon below the Litani River, and the South Beirut neighborhood known as the Dahieh. The newly formed clandestine group, at first identified as the Islamic Jihad, later identified as Hizballah, or "Party of God" was responsible for the truck suicide truck bombing of the US embassy in West Beirut, killing 63 Americans, and the truck bombing of the US Marine Corps barracks in Beirut on October 23, 1983, resulted in the deaths of 241 Marines.

Since that time, Hizballah has maintained its weaponry, even after the end of the Lebanese civil war involving a multitude of constantly changing factions and alliances that ended around 1990. Hizballah and the Lebanese Armed Forces remain the only officially armed organizations in Lebanon while all the other factions, specifically the Christian militias such as the Lebanese Forces and the Phalangists, or Ketaib, were forced to relinquish theirs.

Lebanese Hizballah assisted the IRGC in organizing the Shiite militias such as Ketaib Hizballah and Ansar Al-Haq in Iraq, who were engaged in fierce fighting with US troops beginning in 2003. The IRGC, led by Quds Force Major General Qassem Soleimani, and Lebanese Hizballah in particular were directly responsible for the deaths of over 600 US service members.

Hizballah engaged in decades of kidnappings and assassinations in Lebanon of foreign nationals, including Americans, and of Lebanese political rivals. Over the years, in concert with the IRGC, it also directed the bombing of a Jewish synagogue in Argentina, a bus transporting Jewish tourists in Bulgaria, and the Khobar Towers bombing in Saudi Arabia, killing US service members.

Throughout the current Syrian civil war, battle hardened Hizballah troops have fought alongside Syrian Army and Iranian forces against Syrian rebels, as well against the Sunni Muslim Islamic State. Hizballah maintains as many as 50,000 missiles and rockets, although estimates may be as high as 100,000. It has tanks. During the 2006 war with Israel, Hizballah fired a Chinese silkworm shore to ship missile, striking an Israeli naval vessel. Hizballah maintains its own private fiber optic communications system underneath Beirut, which became the source of a short conflict between Hizballah and the Lebanese government, when the Lebanese government attempted to have Hizballah shut the system down. Hizballah won.

What gave the US government a legal inroad into Hizballah operations however was its banking system. Hizballah controls a number of banks, or local branches of those banks when the branches are located inside Hizballah territory, specifically in the South Beirut Dahieh neighborhoods. Currency exchange houses are also the prime method of transferring illicit funds into the banks or to operatives around the world, as far away as Africa and China. One of the greatest successes, although having a limited lasting effect, was the combined efforts of the FBI, DEA, The US Treasury's Office of Foreign Asset Control, or OFAC, the US Department of Commerce OEE, and even the US Secret Service, in sanctioning the Lebanese Canadian Bank, the Elissa Exchange, the Halawi Exchange, the Rmeiti Exchange, and several others for money laundering. The exact illicit origin of the funds was always open to debate and believe me it was vigorously debated among the various agencies, including the CIA and the Department of Defense. Over time, we were able to identify numerous criminal schemes engaged in by Hizballah members or supporters, often in tandem with Hamas operatives or supporters. These schemes included but were not limited to trade-based money laundering through the purchase at auction of used autos and their export to Lebanon and to West Africa. That became our number one priority for a variety of reasons. We also discovered the counterfeiting of US currency and Euros, drug trafficking (which caused the most adamant disagreements between law enforcement and the intelligence community), bulk cash, diamond and gold smuggling, arms smuggling, and various financial frauds and scams. But it all started with the cars.

As a result of the Mohammed and Sami Said case, we were starting to target the exporters of vehicles to the Middle East and as it turned out, to West Africa, specifically to the port of Cotonou, Benin. Several sources were becoming aware of several Lebanese individuals in the Northern Virginia area who were also involved in that business. A third source was already selling cars locally and was bumping up against several car dealers of interest.

Interestingly enough, several of the Lebanese individuals were Christian. That confused us at first, because all of us across the bureau who were working this issue were of the belief that Lebanese Christians were opponents at best, and enemies at worst of the Shia militias groups such as Hizballah and Amal; but we later concluded that although most of these subjects were primarily just out to make money, the particular Orthodox Christian faction (out of about 16 commonly recognized sects) they belonged to in Lebanon, the Syrian Social Nationalist Party, or the SSNP, had been historically allied with Hizballah. It took a while to learn this, but it did fill in some of our questions. The constantly changing nature of political alliances and conflicts in Lebanon just left us confused most of the time.

Over time, I was able to connect with agents all across the bureau who were investigating Middle Eastern criminal conspiracies underlying possible terrorist cells. The dilemma, as always, was whether these investigations were one or the other. Or both.

During my time in North Jersey working the Middle Eastern criminal networks, the curtain was just beginning to open on this issue. I began networking with other agents in other divisions who turned out to be looking at the same types of subjects. We put together a conference in Rochester, New York. The attendees were working criminal and CT cases. Interestingly enough, the criminal agents, both "white collar" investigators, and like myself, organized crime investigators all had substantive cases with definable violations. We each gave presentations describing how we developed the criminal cases and prosecutions. The CT agents pretty much had little to say at the time. They were chasing shadows, simply trying to develop any intelligence that could demonstrate their subjects were supporting a terrorist organization. Now I was in the same boat to some extent, trying to develop that same intelligence, yet also find ways to disrupt them by pursuing their criminal activity, which almost all of these targets were using to fund their organizations. As result of the horror of 9/11, the current FBI Director, Robert Mueller had mandated we now had to prevent terrorist acts. He never really provided any guidance or definable policy as to how to accomplish this. This lack of guidance would cause much conflict between agents and management over the next ten or fifteen years.

At first, it appeared the Palestinians, specifically in Northern Virginia and Maryland such as Abdelaziz dominated the car export business. The car dealer associated with the Saids was sending cars from the port of Baltimore to Saudi Arabia. Right next to Iraq. Were his vehicles being moved across the border from Saudi Arabia into Iraq to be turned into VBIEDs? Cars were also being shipped from the port of Norfolk as well as Baltimore. Other FBI divisions were looking at subjects in their territories using local ports in Florida, New Jersey, and elsewhere. We were starting to connect with each other. The FBI Headquarters unit known as the Terrorist Financing Operations Section, or TFOS, formed in response to 9/11, was was brought into the mix to ostensibly coordinate these cases bureau-wide. It met with mixed results over the years.

The key event for me, and what may have initiated the interdivision cooperation, was when I was contacted by a former student of mine from New Agents training at Quantico, Wayne Gerhardt in the Birmingham Division. Wayne was looking into the auto auction in Birmingham and several of the Palestinian auto dealers. I agreed to help out and flew down to Birmingham. I attended the auction and observed several groups of Arab men clustered together and appearing to coordinate their bidding on cars. They turned out to be uninterested in meeting me and were clearly very insular and wary of a newcomer, regardless of his (my) apparent similar ethnic background.

Wayne and I returned to the office and began to compare notes. He provided additional background on his subjects and their connections to Hamas and possibly Saudis. We exchanged notes on our now clearly similar investigations. His and my subjects were similarly Palestinian and had Saudi connections. There were many other similarities. We continued to collaborate for several years thereafter, and gradually expanded our network of bureau agents and investigators from other agencies. We were all collectively trying to coordinate over 100 similar or interrelated auto-export, trade-based money laundering, terrorism investigations.

A key bureau agent with whom I partnered and became good friends, was a Baltimore agent, Dave Rodski. Dave was the liaison to the port of Baltimore. Dave was one of those rare agents who had great sense of humor, had no ego, and was sincerely interested in helping other agents. He also succeeded in building good relations with other agencies, specifically with ICE and Customs and Border Protection, or CBP, which had the federal law enforcement jurisdiction over imports. My colleague and friend at Commerce, Rich Jereski, had the mandate over exports. Yes, the law enforcement community can be quite complex.

Dave was able to arrange a tour of the port, and one of the massive cargo ships used to transport the vehicles to their destinations in Lebanon and West Africa. Rich accompanied me along with Amy L., whose CHS, was assisting us in identifying vehicles as they left the country. I will admit the ship was fascinating. The decks could move upward and downward in order to accommodate different sized vehicles, large construction equipment, and even a 20foot yacht. There were generally two methods for shipment of cars. The cheaper, older "beater" cars being shipped to West Africa were loaded directly onto the ship by drivers who would pack the cars so tightly they would have to slide across the seat and exit out the passenger side. The more expensive cars destined for Beirut such as BMWs, Mercedes Benzes, and Jeep Grand Cherokees, would be loaded into large shipping containers. Generally, the shipping containers should only accommodate two cars. The exporters were clever. They would suspend two additional autos from the ceiling using large straps or even used seatbelts. In violations of export laws, other items and contraband would often be secreted inside the trunks. Over time we would discover that firearms, cash, and even illegal drugs were being smuggled, hidden inside the gas tanks, the tires, the seats, or the inside door panels.

During the process of figuring things out, we observed the sale of a few SUVs to the car dealer. We would attempt to track their movement overseas. The vehicles were to be shipped from the port of Norfolk to Saudi Arabia. We put together a team of FBI, Commerce and ICE agents, and our AUSA, Jeanine Linehan, and piled into a Bureau prop plane leaving out of a small airport in Virginia. It was a noisy ride, but it didn't take too long to get to Norfolk. Rich drove his government car down separately. He didn't like to fly. I will admit it was an interesting few days. We had a good group of people including a few key technical folks from the bureau. We had a way of possibly tracking the cars. We never saw the cars again. Eventually we determined the cars never left Saudi Arabia for Iraq and eventually we discovered the truth; the vehicles were not for VBIEDs but were the basis of a world-wide, billion-dollar trade-based, Hizballah and Hamas money laundering scheme. The cars were the money.

We began a multi-track effort to identify the players, the methodology, the beneficiaries, and an effective strategy for combating this international terror financing cabal. It took several years to get a handle on the exact nature of the scheme. The majority of the agents across the country were at first concentrating on their local cases. We began organizing conferences where the case agents could present their cases and compare notes with other agents working almost identical investigations.

Our significant car dealer and Mohammed Abdelaziz were first on my radar but fortunately information from reliable CHSs, began to help us identify a most wanted list of local Middle Eastern subjects who were all engaged in the same business model. This was where the Lebanese came to the fore and eventually eclipsed the Palestinians. It was becoming clear that the Lebanese had begun to muscle out the Palestinians and were buying up all of the used cars at auctions around the country and had begun shipping vehicles to the port of Beirut and to the port of Cotonou in the country of Benin, West Africa. Notably, most of the subjects in the Washington metro area were employed in other businesses—including a hair salon for one, and had become involved in the auto export business as a "side hustle". That side hustle would prove to be far more lucrative than their day jobs.

In the meantime, I was contacted by a DEA Agent, Jack Kelley, at the DEA's sensitive Special Operations Division. DEA had been looking into almost the same network but of course with an eye towards international drug trafficking and money laundering. Many of their targets were bumping into our targets. DEA automatically assumed every target was involved in drug-related activity—as the saying goes, if you are a hammer, everything looks like a nail. Now we had more conferences to attend.

The FBI's TFOS, as mentioned earlier, had started to coordinate the bureau's cases across the country, and would continue to arrange conferences several times per year. The bureau's International Terrorism Operations Section, or ITOS, would find itself competing with

TFOS to supervise the best cases. The end result was that the coordination became disjointed and uncoordinated. The left hand did not know what the right hand was doing. Some FBI cases were designated as Hamas cases, some were designated as Hizballah cases, some strangely were considered Al-Qaeda cases, and many were captioned as, yes, "All Others", not being sure which terrorist organization was involved. This caused a lack of coherent and coordinated analytical support. Some of that lack of intelligence analysis came from a lack of analysts. Some of that came from a lack of analysts who were trained properly to conduct analysis.

The pattern of each case remarkably seemed to be the same. It took the case agents' networking with each other to eventually start mapping out the vast sea of co-conspirators in the US and a myriad of other countries. Many of these case agents were as dogged as I guess I was, and we formed a close bond that lasted many years. The many conferences became, as we joked, as much like support group sessions as working groups. So many of these agents were the best of their kind and sadly many eventually gave up, partially because of the lack of support from DOJ, and the feeling we were hunting ghosts half of the time.

X.
Following the Money—Following the Cars

We eventually found that each and every target of a TBML investigation, regardless of their nationality, were:

Using the same shipping companies,

Using the same currency exchange companies in Lebanon,

Financing each other's auto purchases and shipping fees,

Purchasing cars for each other as straw buyers to conceal the number of purchases of each dealer over time, and in violation of their licenses.

Laundering proceeds for each other,

Using hundreds of rotating bank accounts.

DEA, on the other hand, was delving into the currency exchange houses, believing the money was proceeds from drug trafficking networks, specifically on behalf of what they described as a Hizballah drug trafficking conspiracy beginning in the South American "Tri-border area" where Brazil, Paraguay, and Argentina meet. The area, specifically the commercial area known as Ciudad El Este, is widely considered by international law enforcement to be the center of criminal activity of all varieties, and by the bureau specifically as a center of Hizballah and IRGC recruitment and financing activity. DEA had observed what were more than likely drug proceeds funds generated by a Lebanese drug trafficker in that area, Ayman Joumaa, move through the banking system and other means into the Lebanese currency exchange houses of Elissa Exchange, and several others. The funds eventually found their way into the Lebanese Canadian Bank in Beirut.

On a parallel track, the Bureau case agents were observing the same phenomenon in the US, but in reverse. Subjects of bureau investigations were receiving funds into their US accounts from the same banks and exchange houses. Ellissa Exchange, Ayash Exchange, Halawi Exchange, Rmeity Exchange, and Yasmin Trading were several of the exchange houses identified by bureau agents. The key bank was the Lebanese Canadian Bank, or LCB.

Our CHSs had connected with Lebanese individuals in Northern Virginia with whom they had already been acquainted over the years. Both had been approached to become involved in the auto export business, specifically to help finance auto purchases at the multiple Mannheim auctions in Virginia, Maryland and Pennsylvania.

A significant boost to our intelligence base came when, based on multiple source reporting, an individual was identified as having a significant financial relationship with a half dozen or so local auto dealers identified as being involved in the network. I won't identify the nature of that relationship any further to protect the source. Even more fortuitously, I discovered that the individual had recently been arrested by the FBI locally for some sort of financial fraud. That was easily confirmed with a quick name check in our system. Yes, he was arrested by another WFO agent, Mark Stanley. I knew Mark pretty well by that time. We were both of the same generation, had the same work ethic I believed, and Mark had a welldeserved reputation as a competent and hard-working case agent. I spoke with Mark at first in a short phone call to confirm the arrest, inform him of his defendant's role in my investigation, and express my interest in possibly interviewing the defendant if he was willing to cooperate. About a week later, Mark called me and told me the subject was willing to cooperate and had offered up some preliminary information. Mark admitted he had "no idea what the guy was talking about". When an opportunity like this presents itself. Jump. Quickly.

This began several days of debriefing. This guy was a potential gold mine. But of course, I did not want to damage or forestall Mark's prosecution. Mark was extremely gracious and was willing to let his defendant, whom we shall use the alias Jules, get a deal, as long as he pled guilty. Jules had an aggressive and I must say, obnoxious defense attorney, but it worked out in the end in court, so he now owed me. And I owed Mark for being an agent who cared about the greater good.

Part of the deal with Jules was that Jules's best friend from Lebanon would also be part of the package. The friend, whom we will call Maurice, was a wellconnected and very wealthy businessman and was a dual US and Lebanese citizen. We got him to the US as quickly as possible. Another gold mine of information. Maurice knew many of the players in Lebanon and his access within Lebanese society was astounding. He also had extensive information regarding Hizballah members. That's just Lebanon for you.

Together Jules and Maurice identified targets in the US and Lebanon, and eventually West Africa, and would go on to develop detailed information regarding the various exchange house owners, money launderers, and Hizballah financiers.

Jules was identifying, and thus corroborating a good portion of what other CHSs were reporting. They all knew the same personalities in the Lebanese and Palestinian communities in Northern Virginia.

We began to identify the currency exchange house and banks in Lebanon involved in the now widely recognized, among law enforcement and the intelligence community, vast money laundering network for Hizballah and Hamas, and presumably Al-Qaeda. This information served to confirm much of what DEA was seeing in Lebanon and West Africa. We would eventually go to Benin and fill in many of the blanks, with extensive photos to match. Both Jules and Maurice would prove to be highly reliable, and surprisingly dedicated to assisting the US government. Even someone who commits a crime can still be a patriot I found. Also being demonstrably anti-Hizballah helped motivate both of them. Jules was a survivor of the 15-year Lebanese Civil war, so that clearly colored his perspective. Both turned out to be intelligent and gracious and easy to work with.

Maurice was a bit arrogant and opinionated, but he was articulate and extremely detailed in his debriefings, bringing with him copious notes he had to smuggle inside of his luggage from Lebanon. We developed a very cordial and professional relationship, and I actually enjoyed meeting with both of them, often together. Rich and other agents were present at a lot of these debriefings, as well as many of my squad mates. Maurice spent quite a lot of his own money in order to socialize with significant Lebanese officials and businessmen. This unfortunately would present the one complication administratively, and of course, with Reid, who felt the need to reflexively roadblock almost every request for funds or operational approvals, no matter how detailed and appropriate or necessary the request. This ongoing conflict would wear me out over the five years I spent on that squad, and it resulted in many knock-down drag out arguments between us with Reid literally shouting and spewing insults in the squad area in front of my colleagues.

On one occasion, I needed to reimburse Maurice for expenses. Far less than what he actually deserved. Reid stalled for weeks to submit the request to the ASAC. Maurice was preparing to return to Lebanon. I had to remind Reid multiple times about the request. It was a significant amount of money, but not unusual for this type of operation and was much less than had been paid to other high level operational CHSs. The request was finally approved just as Maurice was on the plane preparing to take off from Dulles airport in Chantilly, Virginia. There was no way I could get the funds to him at that point. Another argument with one of Reid's multiple personalities. It was too late. I then had to return the funds. The relationship with Maurice was damaged for a long time thereafter. Not that he needed the money, but it was a matter of courtesy and respect. I was just trying to do my job. Let no good dead go unpunished. Of course, the paperwork for returning the funds was worse than that for requesting the funds.

I was much later able to re-request the funds when Maurice returned the US for a personal business meeting. I swallowed hard and asked Reid to reinstate the request. It had been finally approved at the last minute before, so I felt it was appropriate to ask for it again. In the middle of the squad area, Reid turned red faced and began berating the request, and me. It took a closed door "conversation" in his office. I did not give in to the verbal abuse and held my ground, until I talked him off of the ledge.

I got the funds approved, met with Maurice, and repaired the relationship. Bearing in mind the administrative headaches of handling sources, the cadre of CHSs was growing as was the strength of the effort to "identify, disrupt, and dismantle" an astoundingly complex criminal enterprise. Unlike we often see in police shows, we don't treat sources as "snitches", or whatever. These are human beings and I believed in treating them as such. If you treat someone with a modicum of respect and common courtesy, most often (but not in every case of course) they will respond in kind. I found this worked very well with my sources. They became surprisingly loyal and put themselves in actual danger on many occasions.

We were getting a clear picture now of how things worked, and it was almost overwhelming. From the FBI's perspective, we were now observing funds being wired into the accounts of our domestic subjects from the identified exchange houses and LCB, now identified as being controlled by Hizballah. Maurice was recognized bureau-wide, although his true identity has never been revealed except to a very select number of FBI agents and a few others such as Rich Jereski and a US Secret Service agent, Mike H. (who I will cover shortly). His work led us to identify the internal workings of LCB, and its complete control by members of Hizballah. His work led to the first US Treasury, OFAC and FinCEN designations against several of the exchange houses, the dismantling of the bank, and the seizure of millions of dollars.

Jules was able to provide detailed insight into local subjects' financial activity, and the convoluted maze of auto action purchases, shipping methodology and routes, and movement of funds back to the US. He obtained a business card from one of those local used auto exporters, George Noufal, from an exchange house in Beirut, the Rmeiti exchange house, that was a prime distributer of funds. Noufal, the owner of a hair salon in Alexandria, admitted to Jules that he entered the business with "seed money" from Hizballah, and the funds had been sent to his bank account from Rmeiti exchange. We opened a case on Noufal.

Paralleling Jules and Maurice, Yusuf had also been approached by Noufal to join him in the auto export business. The twist was that Noufal had asked Yusuf if he was interested in smuggling cash to Lebanon. This got our attention.

Rami was at it too. He had been approached by Mufid "Mark" Mrad, with the same scheme. We opened a case on Mrad too.

Both Yusuf and Rami had begun to portray themselves as money launderers for both Hizballah and Hamas. This seemed to draw in various schemers. Of note, both Noufal and Mrad were Lebanese Christians. This at first baffled us somewhat. As I mentioned earlier, we were surprised and a bit confused because we would not expect Christians would support a Shiite militia and terrorist organization, especially after what had occurred during the civil war in Lebanon. We eventually accepted the fact that many of the Christians were just businessmen trying to make a buck, and not caring about where it came from, while several of them turned out to be members of the Syrian Social Nationalist Party, or the SSNP, which has been historically aligned with Hizballah.

The combined intelligence from all of our myriad CHS's was filling in the map. We now knew that once the funds arrived in the domestic accounts, commonly in $100,000 increments, the money would be used to purchase the vehicles at auction. The dealers would then contact their shipping brokers—one of whom was our identified car dealer, on whom we had recently opened a separate case after the conclusion of the Said case (this car dealer was never prosecuted which is why I have not identified his name). The broker would make the arrangements for the vehicles to be transported to the port of Baltimore and placed on a ship. The ship would then be destined for either the ports of either Cotonou or Beirut and offloaded there. The Cotonou destination was the most popular and lucrative in that the cars being shipped were cheaper and brought a greater profit. At the port of Cotonou, the vehicles were off loaded from the ships and driven nearby to vast mostly dirt parking lots known as "car parcs". Buyers from neighboring countries, predominantly from Nigeria, would arrive daily to purchase the cars and drive them back home.

The dilemma faced by the operators of the car parcs would be that of moving the profits out of Africa and back to the US. And the need to peel off Hizballah's share of the profits. The banking system in West Africa was finicky at best, and it was very expensive to wire transfer funds out of Benin to other destinations. The universally used method was to smuggle cash, in millions of dollars, or gold or diamonds having been converted from cash to next door Togo, and then onto an airliner from Middle East Airline, partly controlled by Hizballah. The pilot would in this case be a member or supporter of Hizballah, and he would take possession of the cash contained in a suitcase. The flight would return to Lebanon, and then cash would be picked up by a Hizballah member. The cash would then be deposited into one of the exchange houses, thus far identified as the Ellissa Exchange, Ayash Exchange, Rmeiti exchange, Halawi exchange, and Yasmin Trading. We determined Noufal had a direct financial relationship with Yasmin trading. Two other banks located in Africa, Prime Bank Gambia, and Middle East and Africa Bank, could often be the first stop before being transferred to Lebanon. Both banks were controlled by a publicly well-known Lebanese Shia Businessman and Hizballah money launderer, Mohammed Bazzi. Bazzi became the subject of many news articles describing his international illicit business dealings and connections to Hizballah and government officials in the Middle East and Africa.

Each car parc was connected to an informal money transfer business and network known as a "hawala". Hawalas operated outside of and independently of the formal international banking system. Hawala operators, known as "hawaladars" are connected with other hawaladars most often in other countries where the banking systems are unreliable or primitive. One hawaladar would receive cash from a customer who wished to transfer funds to perhaps a relative in his home country. He would then deposit cash with his local hawala and the hawaladar would then contact his counterpart the destination country. The counterpart would then take the same amount in cash from his account and hand it to the recipient. No money is transferred from one location to the other. The end hawaladar would then balance his books when someone on his end needed to transfer cash at the other end sometime in the future.

In Cotonou, the car parc hawalas were almost all controlled by Hizballah. The charge for cash transfers out of Africa on behalf of Hizballah supporters was generally 2.5%. DEA had an undercover operation ongoing that was also corroborating most of the intelligence that the various FBI case agents were collecting. Both agencies had solid sources reporting on the details of the car parcs' involvement in the laundering of Hizballah funds. DEA was tracing the funds from South America. We were tracking the money coming into the US from overseas, predominantly from financial institutions in Beirut and others in Europe. Both agencies had sent sources to Cotonou. Jules was one of the first CHSs of either agency to travel to Cotonou and fully identify the car parcs, and pinpoint the ones connected to Hizballah.

Jules had known George Noufal for many years. As did Yusuf, so they were able to corroborate each other, unknowingly of each other's cooperation. Noufal was trolling around for investors in his auto export business. He had approached both Yusuf and Jules to invite them to join his venture. One of our many CHSs had the wherewithal to travel to Cotonou ostensibly to conduct his own inspection of the car parcs so as to determine whether he wanted to get involved with Noufal. We were able to obtain extensive photos of the port and the car parcs. Each car parc had a large sign identifying itself. The names of the car parcs included the Ellissa Group, owned Ali Kharroubi, Parc Rmeiti, owned by Kassem Rmeiti, Yasmine Car Parc, and Trading Africa Group, owned by the most significant Hizballah financier in the world, Mohammed Bazzi. Bazzi would eventually become the number one target of the combined agencies. The car parcs bore the same names as did the exchange houses in Lebanon that we were in the process of identifying and targeting now for Treasury sanctions. Jules had hit it out of the park.

By this point, I had to combine all of the cases, such as Noufal, Mrad, Abdelaziz, and a few other related cases, into one case.

We had another meeting at DEA in Northern Virginia. There were bureau agents from our office and my squad, and from Baltimore and Philadelphia, and from FBIHQ-TFOS. The FBI's Philadelphia office had initiated a major Hizballah investigation and was well ahead in tracing funds around the world. The Philly case was initially well supported by its management, and the entire squad was assisting the case, unlike at WFO, where I was all by myself. The Philly squad supervisor, Charles Dayoub had experience in working Hizballah in his previous office, and we had been corresponding for several years as he transited through WFO and then arriving at Philadelphia. He had a deep bench on the squad, including a young agent, Brad Lewandowski, with whom I would continue to coordinate on related matters long after his squad had concluded its parallel case, and a Task Force officer from the New Jersey State Police, Fred Fife, who actually became the lead investigator for the bulk of the operational activity and who was adept at recruiting and handling many of the CHSs supporting the case. Fred had initially picked up a lead that no one else had been interested in, and in doing so, launched a massive Hizballah arms trafficking investigation that led to multiple operations in several European countries. Fred certainly racked up some frequent flyer miles.

∙ ∙ ∙ ∙ ∙ ∙ ∙

While Philly was pursuing its case, our CHSs were connecting with similar domestic Hizballah supporters. Yusuf had agreed to work with Noufal. Noufal offered to smuggle cash in a vehicle to Lebanon for Yusuf, believing the cash was destined for Hizballah. Of course, we would not actually provide any cash to a terrorist organization and the Justice Department would never approve such a thing. But the story used by Yusuf drew Noufal in, seeing an opportunity to expand his own Hizballah money laundering business.

Noufal began to direct Yusuf in planning how to smuggle the cash to Lebanon. These meetings would occur frequently at the Landmark shopping mall, where Noufal operated a hair salon. They would meet and plan multiple times over a year or so, until they finally agreed on a plan. Noufal explained two methods to get the cash to Hizballah. Everything, as always, was recorded by Yusuf. Noufal explained the slow but safe way was to use the cash to purchase cars and ship them to Cotonou, where the car would be sold, and the proceeds would be smuggled to Beirut and provided to Yusuf's counterparts. Yusuf informed Noufal he was going to send $70,000. Noufal was somewhat skeptical at what he considered to be a small amount of cash. He exclaimed that if the money was for Hizballah, "it should be a million dollars". Yusuf explained it was test amount because he was just getting into the business.

Noufal explained the second, faster but higher risk method, which would entail purchasing one vehicle at either the Mannheim auction or the Adessa auto auction in Northern Virginia near the Dulles airport. These were the same auctions, we found, used by Abdelaziz, and other money launderers. The cash could then be secreted inside the car, placed on a ship, and would arrive in about two weeks, in contrast to the West Africa method which would take a few months.

Our decision was an easy one. We were willing to use government funds to purchase the cars. We were not willing to smuggle any real, government cash out of the country, in effect giving it away to someone in Lebanon. We didn't need to. I had our lab at Quantico dummy up bundles of paper to resemble stacks of cash. I wrapped the bundles in duct tape (the greatest invention after the wheel and fire). We would have Noufal hide the "cash" for Yusuf in a cheap used car that we would provide the funds for, and have the car shipped to a contact of Yusuf's in Beirut. I had previously met the contact on a trip to Amman, Jordan a few months earlier.

Noufal, along with his hair salon at the Landmark shopping center in Alexandria, Virginia, operated a trading company, Noufal Trading, an auto company, Mrouj Auto, and a hidden owner of shipping company, Global Business Link Shipping. The trend was to own the dealer's license for the purchase of vehicles, and to own or partner with a shipping agent so as to control the actual placement of vehicles on the cargo ships and the end recipient for the vehicles. Noufal, admitted to Yusuf, that "seed money" of $100,000 for his car export business was provided by Hizballah controlled business entities Yasmin Trading and Rmeity Group. Noufal was specific in stating to Yusuf he was "working for Hizballah-that's how I make my money". Yusuf informed Noufal that he had obtained a large sum of money from a mutual associate. He explained they happened to be "doctored (counterfeit) bills". Noufal agreed that the associate was linked to Hizballah and that there were rumors that "they" are watching him. Yusuf later informed Noufal that he had laundered the counterfeit bills.

He explained that two hundred thousand was laundered—and "they" had brought him "seventy thousand." Noufal asked Yusuf what his share would be out of that. Yusuf informed Noufal that his share would be twenty percent. Yusuf explained Noufal could put the cash in the cars here and send it to "the Hizballah group over there". Yusuf further explained the money would be "revenue" from Hizballah. Noufal speculated they could send several hundred thousand dollars in a car. The plan would be to launder them—turn them into cars, then turn them back into cash and return it to them. Noufal proposed that Yusuf could give the cash to him, and in turn he would launder his own funds.

Over several months, Noufal and Yusuf met several times again. Noufal was worried that someone would be after Yusuf. Yusuf explained that he had instructions from the "Hizballah people" that no money can leave his hand without their knowledge. Yusuf emphasized that he could be eliminated as well as people he cared about.

At a final meeting, Noufal instructed Yusuf; the contacts overseas should watch where the money is going and who is transferring it the first time; if they transferred it to Yusuf it would be fine. The second time he would want them to transfer the money to Noufal's account.

Noufal further explained it would be better if they gave Yusuf the money in cash. Noufal emphasized they are moving their money from here to Lebanon and they make their money on the cars that are shipped there, because they have the money here and not in Lebanon, and that they are transferring the money to you. Noufal felt that this approach worked for them, especially since they take 2.5% for a transfer, with one billion dollars of transfers a day. Noufal finally admitted definitively that he was working for Hizballah, and the money smuggling was his business. He explained that only if they would transfer the funds to him, he could buy cars, and he was completely reliant on Hizballah cash in order to purchase the cars.

Noufal had previously provided a business card for Rmeity Group to Jules and acknowledged to Jules the Hizballah connection as well. Noufal's own statements over a period of months confirmed over and over again—Noufal was materially supporting a terrorist organization.

Noufal also explained he was involved in stealing cars and having them shipped to West Africa. Free money. In mid-2011, Yusuf provided $4000 in case-funded cash to Noufal for the purchase of a car at the Mannheim Auction. A few days later, Yusuf picked up an SUV from Noufal and promised to return with the cash in a few days. Several days later, Yusuf contacted Noufal and arranged the next meeting. I met with Yusuf behind a bookstore in Springfield, Virginia. I had the fake cash. Yusuf had the SUV. Yusuf had brought an empty box of crackers in which to hide the "cash". As always, I put the body recorder on Yusuf. Rich and a few members of my squad, including Eric G., followed Yusuf to the vicinity of Noufal's million-dollar house in Springfield. Rich would always be there for me for years going forward. I hoped we would be able to prove some Commerce, export related violations that would make his involvement worthwhile for him. Eric would serve as co-case-agent sporadically over the next few years when he wasn't deployed with the Marines for a year or more at a time.

Yusuf parked in the driveway and went inside. A few minutes later, the garage door opened and Noufal and Yusuf were observed standing in the garage. Yusuf walked down the driveway, climbed into the SUV, and drove it into the garage. The garage door closed. We waited down the street. It was dark by now. About 45 minutes later, the garage door opened, Yusuf and the SUV exited the garage. Yusuf drove it out of the area and returned to our initial meeting spot behind the bookstore. I had instructed Yusuf to not leave the vehicle with Noufal. Firstly, he needed a car to go home in. Secondly, we did not want to take the chance Noufal would remove the cash and keep it for himself and lie to Yusuf when shipping the car. Plus, it was not real cash. Needless to say, we had no reason to trust Noufal.

I met Yusuf at the SUV. He briefed me as to the conversation with Noufal, and the logistics of secreting the cash inside the vehicle. Yusuf explained that Noufal had removed the inside side panel of the passenger-side door and had taped (yes duct tape) the bundles onto the door and replaced the panel. Noufal had left the electric screwdriver he had used with Yusuf, so we used that to open the panel, inspect the bundles, and take photos. We all went home and met again in the same place the following morning.

The next morning, the same team met behind the bookstore. Yusuf arrived in the SUV and got wired up. We again followed him over to Noufal's house.

In the meantime, I had contacted Dave in Baltimore to inform him of the operation and that we would be coming into Baltimore territory—the port. I called Dave and let him know we were on our way. Dave had arranged for his squad to take over the surveillance inside of the port where Noufal would take the SUV to have it loaded onto the cargo ship. Noufal had access to the port being a dealer and exporter. We did not.

Noufal, in his Mercedes, and Yusuf following in the SUV, drove like bats out of hell toward Baltimore. We had to work hard to keep up, and we almost lost them in the toll booth. We finally arrived at the port. I had to switch radio channels to Baltimore's channel and let Dave and his team know to take over while we waited outside of the main gate for the delivery to be made. Unfortunately, Dave's team had lost sight of the SUV.

Dave Rodski, to be clear, is one of my favorite people in the FBI. We were able to pick up on Noufal's Mercedes as it exited the port, so no harm no foul. Dave apologized profusely. I had no need to forgive. These things happen all the time. Years ago, I had been doing an undercover, ten kilo heroin deal with several Turkish members of the Russian mafia. I had to drive around Paterson New Jersey with a CHS and three bad guys in the car negotiating the deal. They were making threats, warning if the deal didn't go right, they would "start shooting at everyone". As I drove down the street with the idiots in the car babbling about the deal, I passed my surveillance team driving in the opposite direction. I won't forget the look of panic on the face of the lead surveillance agent who also had realized they had lost me. The team eventually regained the coverage. No harm no foul. This situation at the port was minor compared to that.

We followed the Mercedes, now with Yusuf in the passenger seat. He was not happy with Noufal's driving. Neither were we, but we were all happy the operation had succeeded. Noufal dropped Yusuf off at a shopping center parking lot, where a friend of Yusuf's met him and took him home. Mission accomplished. Now we needed to confirm the retrieval of the SUV in about two weeks at the port of Beirut. We weren't done yet with Noufal. In the meantime, we had many other schemes to make sense of.

XI.

A Week Blowing Up Cars

This brings us to multiple associates of various subjects who were now coming out of the woodwork to assist us. That was a story in itself. Around 2004, when we were first trying to track the vehicles going overseas, I had bumped into a new Joint Terrorism Task Force (JTTF) Special Agent from the US Army's 902 Counterintelligence Branch. He had been talking with another bureau agent with whom I needed to talk to as well. Army Special Agent Joe Simon. His first question upon learning my name was "are you Lebanese?" Of course, we Lebanese recognize each other right away. We already had about a half-dozen agents at WFO who were of Lebanese decent. Several were naturalized citizens. My father, whose last office in the FBI was WFO, was the first Arabic speaking agent in the FBI as he told it. My Arabic sucked. Joe joined the "Lebanese mafia" at WFO, and we became joined at the hip for years thereafter, and he became my travel partner to the Middle East. Joe liked to travel. But I admit, so did I.

Joe began to work with me and several sources. He was assigned to a separate JTTF squad, but he practically became an adjunct member of my squad. His initial interest, from a military point of view, was in the possible use of the vehicles being shipped overseas as VBIEDs. Joe and Rich, both Special Agents from other agencies, were my most reliable partners, in the absence of any long-term assistance from my squad members. Amy L., also assigned to another squad, remained a dedicated part of the team.

Early on, when we were trying to assess the reason for the cars going overseas, Amy and I and two other agents spent a week blowing up cars. I learned to plug blasting caps into C-4 plastic explosive. Got to admit it was fun week. In late 2004 Joe and I headed to Jordan. This would be my second trip to Amman. The first overseas trip I had taken on official business came only a few months earlier, when I was privileged to teach at the Royal Jordanian National Police Academy. The Jordanians are some of America's best and most reliable allies in the Middle East, and they treated us like royalty. The FBI Legal Attaches in the embassy had also taken good care of us. The hotels in Amman are surprisingly some of the most beautiful I've ever stayed in.

Of course, the administrative hoops we had to jump through for this trip were epic and sadly expected. Joe and I were on the tarmac, ready to take off, waiting for authority to travel. We were sweating this one out.

At the last second, of course, the approval came in. We took off. Our stopover was Frankfurt, Germany for two days. Then on to Amman. The Legal Attaché, or Legat in Bureau parlance, was Andre Khoury. Yes, Lebanese. When Joe and I admitted to also being of Lebanese descent, he laughed, and responded "what is this?"

His Assistant Legal Attaché, or Alat, was Don Borrelli. I had met Don on my first trip to Amman. Don was sharp, low key, and was very helpful. It was Don with whom we worked on the operation. Because of my good experience on my first visit, Amman was the easy and logical choice for this operation. When I showed up for the second time, Don was our again our host. He looked at me and commented something to the effect "back so soon?" Andre was more of a figurehead. Don provided us with an embassy vehicle. The operation went well. Can't say more than that.

Amy's CHS was continuing to do business with the car dealer/broker. This was actually how we determined the vehicles were not being moved into Iraq, and we were able to move on to other issues with the auto exports, specifically the money laundering aspect.

Dave in Baltimore had recruited an important CHS who finally clarified the overall Hizballah auto export issue. This CHS claimed to be a former Hizballah member who had a falling out with Hizballah and was providing information to the FBI in retaliation. This CHS explained we were all missing the point of the cars, and that the cars were the money. He further elaborated on what we later learned from Noufal, that the money used to purchase the cars in the US by the target auto dealers, was wire-transferred by Hizballah from Lebanon to the dealers for the purpose of laundering the funds. The cars would be exported to West Africa and sold, and the cash would find its way back to Hizballah coffers in Lebanon. The auto dealers in the US would receive a profit from the sale of the cars and would eventually build their own profit margins along with the laundering. We needed to look at the banks and exchange houses who were sending the funds to the dealers in the US.

DEA was looking at the same financial institutions. We were colliding. For better or for worse.

• • • • • • •

Along the way, we had also started developing information from multiple CHSs that Hizballah had begun a massive counterfeiting operation in tandem with the Iranian IRGC in the Bekaa Valley of Northern Lebanon. Enter the US Secret Service. The USSS had been a solid, reliable partner in our JTTF, which comprised several squads at WFO. The JTTF had members of dozens of federal State and local agencies. Each agency contributed one or more investigators on a semi-permanent basis, often for several years at a time. Some agencies, such as Immigration and Customs Enforcement, or ICE, were reluctant partners and their members' presence at the office was sporadic at best. USSS agents were dedicated and available, and actually took on cases.

Because of the new counterfeit issue, I had reached out to the USSS Agent on one of the nearby JTTF squads. Unfortunately, although we developed a good relationship, he transferred over to Alcohol Tobacco and Firearms a few months later. I didn't take it personally. His replacement, Mounir Khoury, jumped in and I worked him into the mix. As it turned out we had already met during the aftermath of 9/11. Mounir, born in Israel, was a native Arabic speaker, and had been assisting in translation during interviews. Mounir was unpretentious and humorous, and my CHSs liked him. I introduced him to several of my CHSs. Of course, after a few months, Mounir was transferred to the JTTF in Richmond. Hard to hang on to a good partner.

As it turned out, three's a charm.

We were collecting so much intelligence on the Hizballah-IRGC counterfeiting, USSS headquarters counterfeiting unit became involved. Thankfully. We had a meeting at my office. I was introduced to Special Agent Mike

H. (Mike has asked me to not use his full name due to his current employment). Mike has been assigned to the protective details for three US presidents. One claim to fame was that he was the "bike buddy" for President George W. Bush. Mike was gracious, professional and very much the happy warrior. And really tall. We remain close friends today, and coincidentally, live within a few miles of each other. The USSS lab was made available, and I got a tour of the lab. I received a great, fascinating tutorial on counterfeiting. It helped a lot in understanding the whole counterfeiting enterprise element of the now Hizballah-centric government-wide operation.

Mike and I and his supervisor, Mike D'Ambrosio, determined the Department of Defense was interested in the whole Hizballah issue. We tried hard to coordinate with DoD, specifically with US Central Command, or CENTCOM, and US Special Operations Command, or SOCOM, down at MacDill Air Force Base in Tampa. It was a painful experience. DoD had reached out to us and USSS and invited us down to discuss working together against the Hizballah threat. The counterfeit issue had gotten CENTCOM's attention, as well as the auto export trade-based money laundering, or TBML, issue.

We found we were dealing with "J2" intelligence analysts who talked in circles, and never offered anything of value. Neither element of the Combat Commands really had any operational capacity, and the meetings never resulted in anything other than our sitting around conference tables while individual analysts spouted generalities about their knowledge of Hizballah. They had put together some very complex and interesting charts, but that really didn't help us further our investigations. Bearing in mind they had invited us down, the most exasperating thing we experienced was their asking us "what they could do" for us. My question was always, "I don't know—what can you do for us?". After numerous meetings up in DC and down at Tampa, we eventually gave up. I hate to admit that after I retired from the Bureau, I worked for CENTCOM and then SOCOM for five years as a liaison back to the FBI. Funny. Mike and I decided we were on our own.

The one bright spot of the many trips to Tampa was an activeduty Army Special Forces Major assigned to SOCOM, Mike Lipsner. Mike tried hard to square away the DoD folks, to no avail. Even better, I was thrilled to eventually recruit Mike into the bureau as a Special Agent. His first assignment was on a squad right next to mine at WFO.

So, we were now spread pretty thin. We had another conference in Tampa. Then another at Nellis Air Force Base in Nevada. That was the only trip on which I was able to invite Rich, despite his long involvement and dedication to the whole effort. Commerce didn't pay for many conferences.

By 2011, we had cases bureau wide. Mike H, Rich, and other agents from a dozen other divisions, folks from TFOS, and Jack Kelley from DEA-SOD became regulars at these conferences.

Because of the banking issues, we had recruited OFAC. John Moses (yes, another Lebanese guy-see a pattern here?). Most of the conferees became friends over time. We were all suffering the same slings and arrows. Jack on the other hand, although clearly having a strong intellect, and having an encyclopedic knowledge of Hizballah and of the entire DEA effort against Hizballah, was relentlessly combative and lost his temper frequently when challenged on any minor issue. Over time, He alienated everyone involved. When we eventually began to have some successes, Jack would take the credit for everyone else's contributions.

Whenever a press release was issued, Jack made sure DEA would take all of the credit, even though we, the FBI, usually contributed at least 50% of the evidence or intel. Most of the bureau's contribution came from my half dozen or so CHSs, and from Fred's numerous sources. Thanks Jack.

The predominant, most contentious issue among the agencies was whether Hizballah as an organization was directly involved in drug trafficking. DEA of course was adamant that it was. But they characterized Hizballah as a "narcotrafficking organization", similar to the Mexican drug cartels. CIA and DOD elements disagreed vehemently, claiming that the leader of Hizballah, Hassan Nasrullah had declared that drugs were "haram" or forbidden. The Office of Naval Intelligence, or ONI, sided with DEA, based upon their own intelligence regarding the shipping companies controlled by Hizballah. I fell in between. I reminded the naysayers Nasrullah had in the past issued a "fatwa" that it was acceptable to sell drugs to the "infidel", but I saw Hizballah as a multi-faceted organized crime enterprise, with drug trafficking being only one many of its illicit activities. The debate was never really resolved to everyone's satisfaction.

I had credible source information from Maurice, who had direct contacts with several high ranking Hizballah members. He also was reporting on several Shia leaders in the Bekaa Valley who were by their own admission, in the illegal heroin business, and while their tribe may have not been themselves Hizballah, they answered to Hizballah leadership for permission to traffic in drugs. Hizballah would in turn provide their money laundering services for a significant fee.

In DEA's eyes, they needed justification to remain relevant in the post 9/11 Patriot Act era, citing the proliferation of "narco-terrorism". If you are a hammer, everything looks like a nail, right? I tended to support DEA, in that I believed Hizballah is a multi-headed dragon, and it functions as many things; as a political party, an army, a highly sophisticated intelligence operation, and a world-wide criminal mafia involved in a myriad of illicit activity, including drug trafficking, money laundering, arms smuggling, and sophisticated frauds. I had at least a half-dozen CHSs by this time reporting on Hizballah activities in Lebanon, Africa, South America, and the US, and they would support, with specific details, the drug trafficking allegations, but would not paint Hizballah with the same broad brush that DEA painted.

• • • • • • • •

By this time, the counterfeiting issue was becoming a significant investigative avenue. My sources had all, completely separate from each other, begun to focus on the counterfeiting issue . All three were able to obtain samples of the counterfeit dollars and some Euros as well. The first samples each brought back were perhaps mid-level in quality, but over time the samples became increasingly of better quality. I would accept the bills from each, return to the office, administratively place them into evidence and then turn them over to

Mike, who in turn would submit them to the USSS lab. Eventually the counterfeit would be designated as the "Middle Eastern bill". Bear in mind it is difficult for Secret Service to do much of anything about counterfeiting in foreign countries, at least in terms of criminal enforcement. The bureau was most interested in identifying the OCONUS networks, so they could be targeted in other ways. We were able to obtain some OCONUS intelligence identifying the smuggling of, and delivery of, very large shipments of counterfeit from Lebanon to Iraq. Counterfeit US currency can be used to fund terrorist groups and hostile militias, and to purchase drugs, weapons and other materiel.

Hizballah and its benefactor and partner, the IRGC Quds Force were operating in the Shiite stronghold of the Bekaa Valley of Northern Lebanon, and in the Shiite neighborhood of South Beirut, known as the Dahieh. The counterfeiting operations were generally operating in the same locations as were the drug production facilities. Maurice and Yusuf, involved in completely separate efforts, were able to pinpoint these operations. Hizballah was now also developing massive and sophisticated military capabilities in the Bekaa, including significant military installations and missile sites supported by the IRGC.

An operation involving Yusuf became somewhat famous among the bureau agents working the Hizballah effort, and especially among the headquarters folks who had to review it. The report of the of the operation read almost like a Clancy novel. The intelligence it provided was invaluable. I have to keep this information very generic of course, but the work Yusuf eventually did overseas was so significant, I truly wish I could tell the tale in its fullness, but it may work better being told in a future novel. Enough said on that.

• • • • • • • •

Back to the money. The financial institutions, and then later, the various interconnected shipping companies located in the middle of the cycle of money laundering presented the common denominator among the various agencies' interests. Now it was up to John Moses and OFAC.

Investigating any criminal activity outside of the US is a tricky business. For the FBI, and really for any US government law enforcement agency, DEA included, it was necessary to connect that activity to a domestic target. Many US agencies assist foreign governments on their own soil with a two-fold purpose; it served to aid an ally in and of itself, but to also stem the activity from entering the US. The sheer number of Federal law enforcement agencies can be a two-edged sword. Our various overlapping jurisdictions can create conflict or engender cooperation. When we all do cooperate, as in the venue of a JTTF, each agency can bring its own expertise to the table. In the middle of the 20th century, DEA was struggling with the explosion of drugs being smuggled into the US by newly sophisticated criminal organizations, but they had limited resources. The FBI was finally going after the Mafia, which had historically been a major international drug smuggling and distribution network. The DEA understood drugs.

We understood racketeering enterprises. The FBI and DEA and several other agencies successfully teamed up on some ground-breaking cases, such as the "Pizza Connection" mafia heroin trafficking case. Great things can be done if agencies put aside their territoriality and work together.

In this case, I made sure I shared everything I had with everyone involved.

The consensus among the partner agencies, which now included FBI, DEA, ONI, Commerce OEE, and ONI, was to "follow the money", as had been the mantra since 9/11. The banks and exchange houses were the targets. OFAC was the lynchpin, because to effectively go after foreign business or financial entities, Treasury sanctions would be our main weapon. We would need to effectively shut down the conduit for the money laundering and financing of the terrorist organizations' operations. This effort would not result in criminal prosecution. That would be the responsibility of the many agents in the US. Some overseas operations, coordinated with cooperating host governments have the potential to result in criminal prosecutions in that country and in some cases, extradition of those defendants back to the US for trial.

XII.

From Baltimore to Beirut

From my personal perspective, moving forward it would be a mixed approach. I had prosecutable cases against Noufal, and Mrad, and later, against another admitted Hizballah arms smuggler, "Sam" Ghanem, all in Northern Virginia. I had not given up on Abdelaziz and his crew, but I needed to concentrate on the sure things. Rami had been approached by Mrad, again inquiring as to whether Rami needed to smuggle any cash to Lebanon, and offering to make the arrangements for of course, a fee. Rami reported back to me, and I decided to try the same tactic we had used with Noufal, who was at the same time, trying to work out another money laundering deal with Yusuf.

Rich and I met Rami behind a shopping center off of Route Seven in the Tysons, Virginia area, and wired Rami up. It was just Rich and me, as usual. Eric was supposed to join us, but we had no idea where he was.

Turned out he did arrive just as we were heading out to Mrad's house behind Rami. Mrad lived in a large, apparently million-dollar house in Vienna. Rich and I parked a few streets away, but with a view between two houses. As it turned out one of those houses was owned by a Washington Redskins player (yes it was still called the Redskins back then). As we were sitting in our car for several hours while Rami conspired with Mrad, a Fairfax County Police Officer pulled up next to us. She was very professional. I identified myself, and explained we were in the area on an operation. We are not obliged, nor should we give any specifics, and she did not expect any. She did explain the neighborhood had a lot of Redskins players living there and the house we were sitting in front of was one of those.

Rami finished his meeting and departed. We carefully followed him out of the neighborhood and back to the shopping center. Mrad had schooled Rami as to how to smuggle cash inside of a vehicle and offered to handle any amount Rami would like to ship to Lebanon. Rami had presented himself as being in the business of laundering money for both Hamas and Hizballah. Mrad explained he was in the same business, laundering money for anyone who required it, regardless of affiliation. Rami was by now an experienced undercover, having made several cases for me over a seven or eight-year period, including two cases where he and I worked undercover together to assist other agents. That included a case for two WFO drug agents, both solid agents and former squad mates, Glenn Mai and Gus M.

We scheduled another meeting with Mrad to discuss the fees and the amount of cash to be smuggled. We provided Rami with case funds. Mrad, whose sole business was the used auto export business, would purchase a cheap car at auction, and then they would meet again to secrete the cash, in this case "$100,000", inside the car. I had the lab dummy up more bogus cash. A week or so later, Rami met Mrad at his house again, and pulled into the garage. The entire process of hiding the cash in the car's dashboard was recorded on video. Mrad was fully informed as to the cash going to Hizballah.

The next day, we followed Mrad to, of all places, the office of our aforementioned car dealer. He was also, as we discovered, a shipping broker. He would be the one who handled the shipping of the car from the Port of Baltimore to the Port of Beirut. Rich was with me again. His expertise in export law helped us determine when the actual export violation occurred. Rich is also an attorney in his own right. We observed from afar the car being placed onto a small car carrier and depart down the road. That was all we needed to complete the violation for Mrad. In this case we did not need to follow the vehicle all the way to the port. The recorded conversations between Rami and Mrad would do the rest. The car would be shipped to an associate of Rami in Lebanon who got a free car out of it.

Later on, Mrad would admit to both Yusuf and Jules that he was in negotiations with an unnamed individual who claimed to have a million dollars to launder on behalf of Hamas. It certainly demonstrated his involvement in terrorism financing, by his own admission.

It would be a while before we would need to indict and arrest Mrad and Noufal. We had one more transaction to complete with Noufal, and I still had to support the OFAC designations.

Rami and I had a follow up meeting at the Starbucks in Springfield. As we were talking, in walked Akram. Fortunately, I saw Akram walk in. He saw me too. If looks could kill. Rami was able to scoot out a side door and not be seen. I left shortly thereafter, and Akram stared angrily out the window at me as I drove away.

• • • • • • •

Attempting to develop intelligence concerning illicit activity in a foreign country is a complicated effort for federal law enforcement. It requires the handling of CHSs who are capable of overseas travel. It requires extensive authorizations from FBI headquarters, DOJ, and approval from US intelligence. It's no secret the CIA is charged with OCONUS collection of intelligence and the recruitment of sources in foreign countries. For us, operating a source who actually resides in a foreign country is even trickier and more sensitive and requires even more approvals and concurrences. The FBI and DEA have both been very adept in recruiting sources who have access to countries connected to US investigations. The CIA cares less about DEA operations because those are criminal, drug related, and although not completely out of CIA priorities, because the CIA does engage in counter-narcotics collection, it is most interested in counterterrorism and national security related collection. Because the FBI is engaged in both criminal investigations and national security investigations, any operations conducted overseas impinge more so on CIA territory, and therefore require much closer coordination. In truth, the FBI is more diligent in jumping through the required hoops. I found that of their own admission, DEA tends to ignore a lot of those approvals. Lucky them.

Over time, since 9/11, I had been fortunately able to recruit a cadre of sources who were able to report on Hizballah, Hamas, and Iranian criminal and terrorist activities. I have to keep the details somewhat general in order to protect these "sources and methods". Some sources, although US citizens, lived in Lebanon, and had vast access, as I described earlier, volunteered to assist us. Some also had associates in the Middle East who were willing to assist us because of their opposition to those groups. They all had differing motivations and accesses.

XIII.

I'm Here to Change Your Lightbulb...

In June 2005, Joe and I headed overseas to meet two new potential sources, identified to us by Yusuf. We were to meet them in the embassy in Amman.

The trip actually had a two-fold mission.

The second half of the trip was completely different. A CHS I had assumed from Brian had returned to the US from the Middle East. He was a truly loathsome individual, and who I believed to be a casual Hizballah sympathizer. He was alleging he had met two Iraqis who had worked at one of Saddam Hussein's arms depots, and who claimed the depot was a storge facility for tons of chemical weapons.

The CHS, who we shall call Jamal, provided copies of documents from the depot to me. The documents had been given to him by one of the Iraqis and contained details concerning the purchases of loads of cyanide from a European country for the Iraqi government.

Some of the documents appeared to be scientific papers detailing experiments with the deployment of the cyanide using small animals such as rabbits. Jamal met us at the embassy while we worked on getting the Iraqis into Jordan. They were taking a taxicab from Bagdad all the way to Amman. It took more than a day for them to arrive, having met some resistance at the border. After a tense night, and many frantic phone calls, the following day they showed up at the embassy. The two Iraqi men were ushered into the compound with the help of our good friend Alat Don Borrelli and introduced to us by Jamal.

We were assisted by an embassy attaché who was an American of, yes, Lebanese descent who was an Arabic speaker. I did not trust Jamal to translate honestly. The embassy attaché represented another government agency that required its analysts to produce Intelligence Information Reports, or IIRs on a regular basis. This guy proved to be more obsessed with authoring an IIR than actively responding to the information these Iraqis were providing. The two Iraqis detailed how the depot where they had been employed still stockpiled hundreds of tons of Cyanide and could be used to attack US soldiers. They claimed to have had stolen five, fifty-five-gallon barrels of cyanide from the depot and had hidden it in a garage in the Shiite part of Bagdad known as Sadr City. We implored the attaché to contact a partner military unit in Bagdad to at least retrieve the barrels as proof, and to prevent the contents from being used in VBIEDs. He continued to stall, and stammer, and repeat his need to "get out an IIR". Joe and I were sincerely close to punching the guy out. We were so frustrated we had to back away and move on to the next issue. Sad. Nothing was ever done about the WMD, but the IIR went out a few days later to the general intelligence community. Great.

The two Iraqis also claimed the depots had stored rocket warheads that were configured for Sarin gas but had been driven around in large trucks when the inspectors arrived in the months prior to the US invasion in 2003. Just before the invasion, the warheads were smuggled into Syria and out into the Saudi Arabian desert. We were never able to get any US government assets to address the Cyanide. As far as I know those tons of cyanide are still sitting in a warehouse in that unattended depot, and the barrels of cyanide are still in the garage. I found out shortly thereafter that the CHS had met with a CIA case officer during his initial trip to Iraq. The case officer deployed from Iraq and never followed up. My subsequent report upon returning home fell on deaf ears.

The next day we had a better day. The two new contacts arrived, and our go-to guy Don Borrelli assisted us again in getting them into the embassy. This meeting resulted in more good intelligence, and a better feel for their capabilities. At the end of one long day, Joe and I were sitting in my hotel room, which to Joe's dismay was larger than his room, allowing me some brotherly ribbing. There was a knock at our door. It was Yusuf. He was grinning sheepishly, but evidently feeling nervous about being there. He knew he was really not supposed to be seen with us at the hotel. But he had a message to pass on from the other visitors. It was a note. I took the piece of paper and hid it in my suitcase. Yusuf took off and I did not see him again until we got home.

About a half-hour later, we got another knock at the door. It was a hotel employee with a large ladder. Or that's who he said he was. He explained "I'm here to change your lightbulb." Joe and I looked at each other and rolled our eyes. He placed the ladder underneath the large five or six bulb, ceiling chandelier. None of bulbs appeared to require replacement but he climbed up that ladder and changed one of the half-dozen or so bulbs. Guess it was an emergency. Can't have a single bulb out in a five-star hotel room. We were impressed that the hotel management was so diligent in maintaining our lighting. The bottom line we surmised, was that even our allies such as the Jordanians still want to keep an eye on us while we were in their country, or so it seemed.

The next trip, to Beirut, had a significant meaning for both of us, in that both of us were of Lebanese descent, and neither of us had been to Lebanon. My grandparents immigrated from Lebanon over 100 years ago in the big immigration wave from Mediterranean countries around 1910. My grandfather served in the US Army during World War One, and thus earned his citizenship. A "Doughboy". Joe still had cousins living there. We arrived at the Beirut airport and were picked up by an embassy employee in an armored SUV. The security situation in Lebanon was still dire. We were more than likely identified by Hizballah members working at the airport.

The embassy resembled a forward operating base, surrounded by barbed wire and surrounded by heavy security. We had to stay in a hotel-type complex within the embassy compound. The room was stocked with bottled water, and we were instructed not to drink the local water or even let it into our eyes in the shower. We hadn't eaten all day. There was nowhere to go to get something, because we were not allowed to leave the embassy compound and the embassy canteen was closed. Joe was able to call a cousin who brought us shawarmas from a local restaurant. Best shawarmas I've ever had.

We were able to quickly tour the city the next day, again in an armored SUV with armed guards. They kindly drove us around the city and allowed us to literally jump out and quickly take a few photos before frantically beckoning us back into the SUV. The city by this time had been essentially restored to its previous glory after the conclusion of the Lebanese civil war. It even had a Starbucks. One notable location we visited was the sight of the assassination of the former Prime minister, Rafiq Hariri. His convoy had been destroyed by a massive car bomb as it drove by a well-known hotel. The huge crater was still there. The front of hotel had been obliterated. Hariri had been greatly responsible for the rebuilding the city. Hariri had also been openly anti-Hizballah.

That evening we were able to get out of the embassy, accompanied again by armed guards, by visiting relatives of Joe's in the nearby Christian neighborhood of Aukkar. The families lived in an apartment building where each family lived on a separate floor. We had a truly epic Lebanese dinner. In typically Lebanese fashion, they would not let us stop eating. Not that I wanted to.

The next day, the two new potential sources arrived at the embassy, and were escorted into a small building in the middle of the embassy grounds. This was functionally an interview room. Earlier that morning Joe and I had met with the CIA Chief to brief him. He assigned one of his people to join us in the interview. We found out much later with an eye towards stealing our sources. Over the years I have had three rather unpleasant meetings with three different Chiefs, usually to argue over source recruitments and other issues not to be discussed here. The interviews went well enough, and we went home with some helpful intel. Much later we found out the spooks had approached our CHSs to try to recruit them out from under us with offers of large amounts of cash.

A few months later, war erupted between Hizballah and the Israeli army. The city of Beirut had finally been rebuilt and restored after the civil war in the 1980s and the downtown area, and the ritzy section called the Corniche, were beautiful. That sadly was somewhat reversed over the next 40 or so days of Israeli bombing. Joe had, coincidentally, been so enthralled with our trip he took his family on vacation to Beirut. One morning, they were awakened by the sound of military aircraft and explosions. They were able to make it to the US embassy and were placed on a helicopter to Cyprus, and then flown home from there. Having contacts in the embassy cultivated on our previous trips helped a lot in just getting entry into the embassy.

The third meeting took place with the group and a new third member, in Limassol, Cyprus. That was a long trip. Cyprus is somewhat in-between being a

Middle Eastern culture and a European culture. It is split between the Greek ethnic majority population in the South, and the Turkish minority in the North. The FBI Legat in Athens covers Cyprus. For this trip, I dragged Amy with me. It was an experience for both of us. The hotels in Cyprus are actually very good, much better than in Europe. Cyprus is a popular vacation spot for British and Germans. Yusuf travelled separately and found a hotel about a quarter mile away. We found a hotel lobby in a hotel midway between our respective hotels and met Yusuf and the whole group. Two were already US citizens and could come to the US any time. They had begun collecting and reporting on criminal and terrorist activities in Lebanon and Jordan, and possibly in West Africa. It made for a long and very detailed report when we returned home.

Cyprus is only about a 40-minute ferry ride from Beirut. It is known as a place where spies and terrorists meet, and spy on each other when they are meeting with other spies and terrorists. We were looking over our shoulder the entire time. Once or twice, I got the distinct impression that we were being followed. At one point, I walked down a hallway lined with glass display cases, and I observed what I thought was the reflection of someone who appeared to be following me. Just because you're paranoid, it doesn't mean they aren't out to get you.

I would return to Cyprus one more time in 2008 with three other WFO personnel to debrief two sources, in the exact same hotel lobby.

• • • • • • •

The OFAC sanctions effort was gaining speed by 2011. I had traveled to Paris at the end of 2010 to meet Maurice. I took Eric with me. We were able to set up a meeting in the US embassy. The DSS Regional Security Officer, or RSO was responsive and helpful, and smoothed the way for Maurice to enter the embassy and meet us in a secure room. The debriefing took over five hours. He provided us with details of how the Lebanese Canadian Bank was completely controlled by Hizballah. We were later able to identify the employees known to be Hizballah members. He also provided details concerning the Ayash and Halawi exchanges that would contribute to additional sanctions. All of this information would be made available to John Moses and to DEA.

Fortunately, when developing a sanctions package, OFAC, and its sister Treasury agency, the Financial Crimes Enforcement Network, or FinCEN, could use classified information that would not be required to be made public. Maurice's contribution, just in this matter, would substantially put us over the top in making the OFAC sanctions stick. A combination of intelligence from Maurice and Jules, who would travel frequently to Lebanon, would provide supporting evidence to bring sanctions against first, the LCB, and then against a multitude of other exchange houses and suspects. John and his supervisor spent several days in my squad area, reviewing all of the CHS reporting that would be used in the sanction packages. I had met several times with Jack and his colleagues at DEA SOD and shared the same information so that we were all "on the same sheet of music", and they were up to speed on everything being included in the sanctions. Fed Fife in Philly had also provided a significant amount of source information that corroborated our information and what DEA had accumulated. Jack was excited to now have the holy grail information DEA did not have, especially against LCB. They needed what we had. He took the information, coordinated with OFAC, and took all the credit.

DEA did put together the evidence related to the South American leg of the money laundering trip in an impressive effort. Ayman Joumaa had been proven via an extensive undercover operation to be a major cocaine smuggling kingpin. He was Lebanese, living in South America, and was moving his cocaine to Europe through West Africa. His proceeds were traced to LCB. Joumaa was DEA's top target. He was indicted in the Eastern District of Virginia, and was included in the sanctions, but has never been arrested. Some international criminals are just sometimes out of reach. Way back to my case with Fahim Sabr, as an example, I was just lucky. Joumaa was never definitively proven to be a direct member or supporter of Hizballah, but it was pretty clear to most of us he certainly had a business relationship with them by way of the Hizballah controlled international money laundering cartel. This whole situation was also now beginning to show up in numerous media reports, and naming names, notably ALi Kharroubi, Ayman Joumaa, and Mohammed Bazzi.

The tracking of the funds led to the car parcs in Cotonou, and eventually traced to the FBI targeted used auto dealers in the US, such as Abdelaziz, Noufal,

Mrad, several other subjects located in Northern Virginia, and later Ghanem, as well as most of the FBI subjects across the country. The key to it all was the LCB and the exchange houses; Ellissa exchange, Ayash exchange, Halawi exchange, and the Rmeity Exchange, all of whom controlled the car parcs and the transferring of funds from West Africa to Lebanon. They then in turn controlled the movement of the funds directly into the US-based correspondent accounts held by our Hizballah-supporter used auto dealers and exporters. The correspondent banks, such as the Bank of New York, would then transfer the funds into the actual accounts at local banks. We were able to trace approximately $330 million from four banks into the US accounts. The Federal Bank of Lebanon, LCB, Blom Bank Lebanon, and Middle East and Africa Bank with branches in Lebanon and The Gambia were the prime movers of the funds. Moving backward so to speak, $845 million was traced from West Africa into those banks, much of it coming from Ayman Joumaa.

First to fall, in January 2011, was the Elissa Exchange and Ellissa Holdings, controlled by Hizballah supporter Ali Mohammed Kharroubi. Next to fall was the Ayash Exchange, owned by Hasan Ayash. They were all designated by OFAC as "Significant Foreign Narcotics Traffickers" under the "Kingpin Act". Most Treasury designations are released to the public. These designations were no exception and were the subject of lengthy news articles.

A month later, LCB was designated by FinCEN as an Institution of Primary Money Laundering Concern under the "311" statute of the Patriot Act. Ayash was identified as a significant source of US currency to LCB. Ellissa conducted massive transactions via LCB without any oversight by the Lebanese Central Bank, whose head, Riyad Salameh was in league with Hizballah. Between 2007 and 2011, Ellissa, in concert with its many subsidiaries, was found to have transferred $329 million to US used auto dealers.

Kharroubi, and his brother Jamal Kharroubi the owner-operators of Ellissa Exchange, Elllissa Holdings, and a slew of other related companies, were designated as individuals under the same Kingpin statute.

LCB and the exchanges were at least for a while, neutralized. But the US government was going to get its pound of flesh. In December, the US Attorney's Office in the Southern District of New York, or SDNY, filed a civil money laundering and forfeiture suit for $300 million against LCB. This entire government-wide effort did receive extensive publicity, specifically in the New York Times.

According to an article in the Wall Street Journal in May 2023, A French Judge issued an international arrest warrant for Riyad Salameh after he didn't show up for questioning in France on corruption charges. He was supposed to appear before French prosecutors as "part of a continuing European probe". The article goes on to state that a European judicial team from France, Germany and Luxembourg has been conducting a corruption investigation into an array of financial crimes they allege were committed by Salameh and a long list of his associates from Lebanon's Central Bank, as well as Lebanese commercial banks and auditing companies. The allegations include illicit enrichment and laundering of $330 million. Salameh had been at his post for almost 30 years.

• • • • • • •

Several months after the meeting in Cyprus, the third member of the group came to the US. That turned out to be a mistake. Over time, I found that he was duplicitous and untrustworthy, and would provide just enough valid and useful intel to stay in our good graces, while dragging out his cooperation. Even more so after the demise of a counterfeiting deal in Eastern Europe I will describe next. The dilemma I faced was that the general intelligence he provided turned out to be relatively reliable, but every time he promised to do something operational, he would stall and obfuscate.

It was an operation that could have been epic, but sadly did not end well. This became a recognizable pattern with this source. He informed Mike H. and me that he had a contact in Lebanon who was on the verge of obtaining a tranche of counterfeit US dollars from two Hizballah members. The contact could broker a deal, but negotiations and eventual purchase of the counterfeit would have to take place in a third country. He did identify the two alleged Hizballah members by name and provided their cell phone numbers. That gave us some confidence to move forward.

Mike and I researched to identify in which country we could facilitate the deal. Over time we learned some allied countries would allow a non-attributable intelligence operation, but not a law enforcement operation that could result in a prosecution. Some countries would allow a law enforcement operation on their soil, but the eventual prosecution would have to remain in their country, which didn't really help us much. Finally, we were able to settle on a friendly Eastern European nation whose government was amenable to allowing us to complete an entire operation, and even extradite the subjects back to the US for prosecution. I reached out to our Legat in that country. Mike spoke with the USSS attaché. As it turned out, the FBI, CIA, USSS and DEA all had a good relationship and were willing to work together on this. It actually can happen once in a while.

The local federal law enforcement agency was very cooperative, hoping to curry favor with the US government, and demonstrate it was no longer a third world country. The USSS would provide technical assistance.

The counterfeiters would be willing to sell $30,000 face value of counterfeit dollars for 30% of the face value. The deal was ready to go. Mike and I packed our bags. We would head out in two days. Then it was suddenly radio silence from the counterfeiters. Nothing. They were supposedly in transit to a third country. We had already had to delay the whole operation for several weeks because the partner country law enforcement had to take their summer vacations. That definitely caused additional complications with our timeline. Now we had no idea what was going on. It never got any better. We unpacked our bags and waited for any new information. We will never know the true story.

XIV.

Another Bite at the Apple

Our problem CHS had been working with a few auto exporters, trying to get into the business. He had found two car customers in Beirut who had sent $20,000 for the purchase of two used BMWs. This was an opportunity for us to use someone else's money to complete a deal with a subject, similar to what we had done in New Jersey with the Fahim Sabr case. The plan was to approach Noufal and have Noufal handle the purchase of the cars and the shipment to Beirut. It would be explained the money came from Hizballah and he was trying to prove himself with them with a first time, small deal. Over time, Yusuf, himself exasperated that a guy he brought into the mix was not performing, volunteered to step in, and not for the first or last time.

Yusuf met with Noufal and explained the need to launder some more funds for Hizballah. Yusuf further explained he was interested in trying the other method, meaning using the purchase of cars with the money to be laundered, but the cars needed to be sent directly to Beirut to the recipients and not to West Africa. Since we had already completed a prosecutable deal with Noufal, and he had explicitly described his money laundering relationship with Hizballah, we would not be entrapping him.

The second deal went off smoothly. The cars were shipped to Beirut, and we had another violation with which to charge Noufal. Federal law would see these two transactions as "attempted money laundering", still a viable charge. The AUSA was now Ron W.

In between all of the sanctions, and various actions against the international leg of the Hizballah criminal enterprise lay the final nails to be put in the coffin of our local money launderers. In early 2012, I met with the AUSA at his office in Alexandria armed with volumes of evidence to present for his prosecution.

As a side note, by this time, I had been able to keep one of my CHSs here in the US and through an agonizing process, obtain his "green card" with the help of an ICE Homeland Security Investigations, or HSI Special Agent John G. Coincidentally John and I had worked with Mark McGraw up in New Jersey and had reconnected at WFO. Mark and John had both been in the hotel room next door when we did the take-down of the Palestinian bank fraud subjects. Mark was now the Deputy Special Agent in Charge of the ICE office in the DC area. I tried to include John in our Hizballah cases, but ICE was going its own way in its own parallel investigation that mirrored the operation that the rest of us were pursuing. We had several meetings with HSI several times and compared notes, but sadly never really partnered up.

The meetings with the AUSA were interesting to say the least. Ron was a very bright and cheerful guy, but just could not stay focused on any conversation at hand. I was trying so hard to fill him in on the details of the operations with Noufal and Mrad, and present to him the extensive evidence we had. It would take 45 minutes of Ron chatting about anything other than the cases before I could reel him in and get to the reason for the meeting. I usually only had an hour before I had to move my car before it got towed. I handed him the volumes of transcripts, hoping that at least he would study them after I had left. I had also spent the extra effort to write simplified summaries of the calls and noted the violations they supported. I even tagged each page and highlighted each significant conversation as it occurred. It took a herculean effort to keep him focused on the evidence. He lost the folders several times and I had to help him find them in his own office.

Along with the money laundering admissions to Yusuf, Noufal in particular made numerous specific admissions to his involvement with Hizballah. Noufal stated definitively that he was himself a Hizballah financier. Eventually, after several meetings at the US Attorney, we would have to settle on the two counts of attempted money laundering and bulk cash smuggling.

Mrad had admitted in a conversation with Rami that he and Noufal were both laundering funds for

Hizballah via cash smuggled out of the country using used car exports. Still not enough for a charge of material support.

• • • • • • •

Our problem source got one more chance and flubbed that as well. The next operation he initiated went well enough at first, but only because I was able to salvage it with the help of the London FBI Alat and a likeable and helpful British MI-5 officer. He had provided some information that would potentially benefit the UK authorities and the US jointly with either the USG or the British authorities taking the lead.

Our CHS was willing to assist in the operation in the UK. He would have to obtain a visa to the UK in order to travel there. I instructed him to apply for the visa, while I arranged with the London Legat office for myself and another agent on the squad to travel to London and set up the interview.

Our travel was approved, and I and the other agent, Dave S., traveled to London, and met with the Alat. I did my best to get some cool trips for my squad mates.

We made it to London, but of course the CHS procrastinated for so long, he could not get the visa in time to join us. The Alat arranged a meeting in the embassy with a CIA officer and the MI-5 officer. We figured we could still make this work. The CIA officer, a woman, breezed into the meeting, looking like she wanted to punch someone, and proceeded to contradict everything we proposed operationally. We were all a bit taken aback. The Alat later explained she had a reputation for being difficult. She never lightened up.

I provided the information we had to the MI-5 Officer. Under the circumstances, this would be a "handoff" to MI-5 and the CIA. The operation would remain in the UK. It was still a win for the USG and the UK as far as I was concerned. After returning home, I received a cryptic email from the Alat informing me that MI-5 and CIA had continued working and it was moving forward. Mission accomplished. The MI-5 officer sent his personal thanks for the handoff. Nothing from the CIA.

• • • • • • • •

In October of 2011, In the middle of all this, our squad was pursuing a Syrian intelligence operative who was operating in the Northern Virginia area. This was just before the Syrian dissident movement exploded, literally, into a fullblown civil war. The cooperative witness in the case was also from Syria and had family members in Syria who would be arrested or more likely killed if the witness testified. The subject had been videotaping protesters in front of the Syrian embassy and sending the videos to the Asad regime. The witness would not testify unless the USG rescued his family members from Syria. JP B. on the squad had become a fluent Arabic speaker and was tapped to travel to Amman and set up the escapes of eleven relatives. The witness's mother, two brothers, and their families. Reid was at first sending him alone to accomplish this task. That was completely irresponsible and dangerous, especially in sending a relatively new, although talented agent overseas solo, to handle eleven strangers. Reid sheepishly approached me and asked me, "a senior agent", if I could accompany JP to Amman. Of course, I would.

I would have to make all travel arrangements and fly out of Dulles International airport in about five hours. I was not going to let a squad mate be left hanging, but this sucked. We were told it would be a week's trip. I packed for a little over a week, just to be sure. We arrived in Amman, met up with the Legat and a new Alat, Kevin Fisk, found a hotel, and started planning out the operation. We secured a safehouse in town for the families. It was an apartment building with four furnished, empty apartments. Kevin really stepped up to make sure were being provided for. He provided us with an armored SUV from the embassy, but JP and I ended up not using it. It would draw too much attention around town. Coincidentally, Kevin later would end up at TFOS as my Unit Chief for a short time, and one of the TFOS members who recruited me for the post-retirement CENTCOM/SOCOM position.

JP and I would end up spending most of our time in one of the apartments, baby-sitting the families. We would leave our hotel and hail a taxi to take us to an unrelated hotel near the safe house, and then walk carefully to the safehouse so as not to identify the location to anyone watching. The unrelated hotel was under extensive repairs as a result of a bombing there a year earlier. Welcome to the Middle East. When we went back to the hotel, which was only every few days, we would walk to the other hotel and do the reverse. If we had to go to the embassy for a meeting, we would take a circuitous route as well. Several times we observed a black SUV with two Middle Eastern males parked in front of the apartment building. Jordanian intelligence keeping an eye on us? Hopefully not the Syrians.

The CIA folks of course insisted we could never get this done. As usual they were wrong. Always great to have your support folks. The families started arriving from Syria, with a stop in Beirut. We met them at the airport and transported them to the safehouse. Only one family member, a brother who was a known dissident refused at first to leave Syria.

We proceeded to obtain visas for the families to come to the US. JP and I sat at the table in our little apartment filling out the extensive paperwork to request Special Immigrant Visas from the State Department. As we completed the paperwork and submitted it back to the US, obtained all of the visas for the families, and prepared to go home, the brother at the last minute decided he needed to escape Syria. That meant another week to get him to Jordan and put together all of the paperwork. He left Syria. The next day it was reported that the Syrian army had blown up his house.

We went back to our hotel and washed our clothes in the sink and bought groceries at a local store called "Seven-Eleven" of all things.

After almost three weeks, the families headed to the US, and JP and I headed home too. We pulled it off. Not one word of thanks when we returned to the squad. Back to the "car cases" again.

On June 5, 2012, we formed up our arrest teams at 5:00 am in the parking lot of a church nearby to Mrad's stately home. I was equipped with an arrest warrant and search warrant. I had gone by the house the night before to confirm his car was in the driveway and the house was occupied. It was. I drove by again the first thing in the morning before we formed up in the staging area. I actually had the whole squad on this one, and of course Rich. I also had two computer experts, Special Agent Steve Bongart, and Specialist Conroy Jett who were going to help us with technical issues. No one wants to miss out on an arrest.

Reid never missed an opportunity to micromanage something. We had every reason to believe Mrad was at home, but oftentimes the subject just isn't home, and we have to come back later. It just happens that way. Reid was in a panic for some reason in fear Mrad wasn't home at 6:00 am. I had Mrad's cell phone in case we needed for some reason to call him. He was not a young guy, and we wouldn't have to look far for him if not there. We all knew Reid had virtually no arrest experience and it showed. I had to talk Reid off of the ledge, and we proceeded to knock on Mrad's door. He was there, in his underwear. Ian and Baker were right there at the front door with me. I grabbed Mrad, handcuffed him and passed him off to another agent, who placed him a bureau car. We proceeded to clear the house, and then began the search.

We found $37,000 in cash in his safe, which we seized and later forfeited judicially. Then we brought Mrad back into the house to let him get dressed and Rich and I sat him down at the kitchen table to be interrogated. Mrad grudgingly admitted he had assisted Rami in smuggling what he believed to be $100,000 in cash in a vehicle he then arranged to have shipped to the Port of Beirut, and he acknowledged that he had broken the law. This would be an easy prosecution. We would never secure any further admissions, but that was expected. They only admit, if at all, to what we can already prove, and then claim they cooperated and should get a reduced sentence.

In July, Mrad pled guilty to money laundering and bulk cash smuggling in violation of federal law and was sentenced to 14 months incarceration later in October. Mrad's family was present at his sentencing. The sentencing proceedings were interspersed with the sounds of family members wailing and shouting expletives—at me and Rich mostly. At the conclusion of the hearing, they followed us out of the courtroom wagging their fingers and yelling "shame" in Arabic—one of the few Arabic phrases I understood. Rich and I maintained our professional demeanor and got out of there as fast as we could. Noufal was next. On August 23, 2012, my 55th birthday, we formed up again near the massive apartment complex where Noufal now lived equipped with an arrest warrant for Noufal, and a search warrant for his office at his hair salon at the Landmark shopping center in Alexandria. As always, it was a tactical fashion show, which I always enjoyed and admittedly participated in.

Up to this point, I had to battle with Reid again over the arrest plan. In spite of the fact I had been working this case for several years and knew everything possible about our subject, had done extensive surveillance at the apartment complex, was almost at the 30-year mark in my career, had participated in around 300 arrests over that time, was SWAT certified, was a firearms instructor for over 20 years, was a tactical instructor at both then FBI Academy and at WFO, Reid insisted on counter-manning my rather simple arrest plan. I had planned to both arrest Noufal at his shop first thing in the morning and execute the search warrant in his tiny office right there at the shop, which would take 20 minutes. I would know he was there because we would have one of the women agents on the squad call ahead and make a hair appointment with him for a set time on a Friday, when I knew he would be working at the salon. Easy.

Nope, Reid, who had clearly not made an arrest in ten years, if ever, for some unexplained reason insisted we would have to make the arrest at Noufal's apartment on the 11th floor of the apartment complex. The apartments had limited access at the front gate and multiple entrances to the building— all would be locked with only card key access. Then we, or another team would have to move over to the shop before it opened to conduct the search warrant, which would require the Fairfax PD to accompany us to gain access to the mall. Another unnecessary, complicated step. I had even run my plan, compared to what Reid was insisting upon, with several SWAT agents and a former Hostage Rescue

Team member. Everyone thought Reid's plan was, well, stupid.

I lost the battle, but as usual we got it done "in spite of" it all. FPD helped us gain entry to the apartment building. The elevators were small and cramped, and could only accommodate four agents at a time, all bulked up with body armor and breaching equipment (Ian was there so that meant lots of gear on the vests). We had eight agents on the arrest team, so that meant we could only go up the elevator four at a time, which meant two trips up to the 11th floor before we could form up at Noufal's apartment door. So much for the element of surprise. Reid had also insisted, irrationally, that rather than just knock on the door, I would have to call him on his cell phone to come to the door. Again, so much for the element of surprise. This also contradicted his insistence during the Mad arrest that I have Mrad's home phone on which to call him because if we called on the cell phone, "he could answer it and not be home". As luck it would have it, Noufal answered his phone, and came to the door. We hooked him up right there and took him inside to, as usual, get dressed. As per protocol, we did a quick protective sweep of the apartment and found a loaded rifle on his bed. That's why you don't call ahead. Luck is not an acceptable tactic.

At the kitchen table, we had a chat with Noufal. Albert S., a new, Arabic speaking agent on the squad assisted in the debriefing. And of course, Rich was right next to me. Noufal fessed up to both deals with Yusuf but insisted he had never engaged in any other smuggling deals. We turned him over to a transport team and moved over to the shop. Again, the FCPD opened the mall for us, and we entered Noufal's office. There was room for only two agents. We searched his desk and a small file cabinet. Nothing really of use. 20 minutes at best. Done. Happy birthday to me.

Noufal pled guilty to two charges of attempted money laundering and bulk cash smuggling in US District Court in Alexandria and was sentenced to 12 months home confinement. Yup, that's all he got. Judge Gerald Bruce Lee again. Noufal's many family members were present in court on both occasions. It should be noted that pleas and sentencings are done on Fridays, and the courtroom is filled with other defendants waiting for their sentencing, members of the press, the public, law students, and family members.

I moved on to several other Lebanese and Palestinian auto exporters and expanded the list of subjects. We identified those terrorists and gangsters and bankers via source information Treasury reports and banking records. They were intimately involved in the Hizballah-Hamas-Al Qaeda trade-based money laundering enterprise. It would never end. But it would end for me.

• • • • • • •

On top of everything, in late 2013, I was asked to take on an undercover in Birmingham, Alabama. The role would be similar to the one I had assumed in the DC taxi-Jim Graham undercover. One of the case agents, Ashley H., had just transferred from WFO to Birmingham. The second case agent, Mike F., turned out to have been one of my New Agent trainees at Quantico. My first meeting with them took place in an underground parking garage. I had already spoken with Ashley via a video conference, so I recognized her. Then Mike stepped forward. "I know you". When I instructed at Quantico, I had regularly reminded my trainees that I was not going to teach forever, that I would be returning to the field shortly, and that I was training them to be my partner. That turned out to be more accurate than I had ever anticipated.

The undercover would last almost a year. My last undercover meet in my career would happen three weeks before I retired from the bureau. I was introduced to a middleman who suffered from extreme anger management issues. I can't go into the details of the case but suffice it to say dealing with this guy was a nightmare. Every phone conversation and every in-person conversation, usually concerning how much I was paying him to make introductions, ended with his screaming at the top of his lungs over some perceived slight or insufficient payment. Once or twice, it would involve his threatening me physically. He was a big guy, much taller than I, and clearly violent. I hold an eighth-degree black belt. It would have been interesting, but my job was not to fight with a subject, but to calm him down and get on with business. Another guy I had to talk off of the ledge.

I would be balancing the undercover, traveling down south every two or three weeks for almost a year, while handling all of the various CHSs, traveling overseas for several different operations, and preparing to retire. Sadly, for me the operation went much longer than we planned for, and I was at mandatory retirement age, so I would eventually have to hand over the undercover role to another undercover agent.

XV.

The Bankers

Back to the bigger picture again. Halawi Exchange and Rmeity Exchange were both designated by FinCEN in 2013. The Rmeity designation was done as a direct result of information from mine and Philadelphia's FBI CHSs. Kharroubi, Ayash, and Mahmoud Halawi, all eventually petitioned OFAC or FinCEN to have themselves and their companies removed from the sanctions list. Fortunately, by early 2014, I had finally gotten off of the squad and had moved to a Human Intelligence, or HUMINT squad and had brought all of my CHSs with me. The squad supervisor, Jeff Jones was a breath of fresh air, and was humane and supportive.

The skeevy attorney got himself right into the mix of things. He stepped in with our concurrence, to offer his assistance to Ayash and Halawi in setting up meetings with representatives of the US government.

This allowed us to offer to meet with them outside the US.

The meeting was set up for Rome. Both Ayash and Halawi would travel to Rome, separately, and each would have a day in the embassy to give us an explanation as to why they were not bad guys and should be taken off of the OFAC sanctions lists. They would be required to provide actionable information to the USG regarding Hizballah's financial activities. We had definitive source information that they had direct knowledge of those activities. The source information was essential to the various Treasury sanction packages.

This time I needed John to accompany me to Rome because of his extensive knowledge of the specific sanctions against Halawi, Ayash, and the others, and his general knowledge overall concerning sanctions and OFAC regulations. I was also able to convince another agent, Assad H., a new squad mate, and a native Arabic speaker, to assist us in any needed translation. Yes, he is Lebanese too. It just kept working out that way. A DEA agent from their New York Office also showed up to sit and watch mostly.

John, Assad, and I arrived in Rome in March 2014. The Alat in the embassy set up an interview room in the embassy for us. We maintained contact with the attorney. The first interview involved Hassan Ayash. He was a major player in the whole scheme and was outed extensively in the media based on his Treasury designation, so this was a significant interview. We were hoping to get some solid confirmation of the involvement of Hizballah.

TFOS by this time had consolidated the cases into a single initiative, nominally coordinated with Homeland Security and DEA. TFOS was hoping to lean in on the interview. I collaborated with an intelligence analyst at TFOS, Josh L., on a roadmap for the interviews. Josh, throughout the entire Hizballah auto export and money laundering effort, was the only bureau analyst who was sincerely invested in the effort to assist the field, and in himself being part of the team.

We decided we needed to shore up the "specified unlawful act", or SUA, that would support a targeted Racketeer Influenced Corrupt Organization, or RICO charge underlying the overall auto export scheme. At a minimum we would have money laundering charges to bring. At that point we were relying on DEA's assertion that the funds being moved from Cotonou, Benin, West Africa, were derived from drug trafficking or comingled with drug proceeds. We also needed to connect the US-based used auto dealers to those funds and prove that their activities benefitted Hizballah. By then, I felt the Noufal and Mrad cases had in a small way, proven or at least demonstrated that the domestic dealers were knowingly laundering Hizballah funds. Noufal's specific admissions to both Yusuf and Jules, were proof of that. Other identified targets I added to the effort were in effect identical to Mrad and Noufal in their activities.

We also needed to flesh out the full cycle of the trade-based money laundering, the knowing involvement of the banks and currency exchange houses in Lebanon and identify the individuals behind the scheme. DEA had admitted its intelligence gaps. They were missing the details of the functioning of the car parcs, their ownership, management, business details, etc. Several other bureau agents and I had substantially answered those questions by sending CHSs to Cotonou. These sources had met with the car parc operators and taken detailed photos of the car parcs, including the signs at the entrances of the car parcs. All of these efforts served to demonstrate the ownership connections between the car parcs and the exchange houses. In my case that was a source's trip to Cotonou. Detailed information from bureau sources also had proven or demonstrated the Hizballah control of Ayash, Ellissa, Rmeity, and Halawi exchange houses. Again, in my case it was our sources' reporting that accomplished that, along with source information from other bureau sources. Now we would hopefully get the proof from the horses' mouths.

Hassan Ayash, the owner of the now Treasury designated Ayash Exchange, interview lasted nine hours.

Over time we detailed and confirmed the movement of bulk cash from Africa to Lebanon. Bribes were commonly paid to various Beninese officials to allow the money to exit the country over the border to Togo.

We discovered a new twist in the way money was moved in furtherance of the Hizballah money laundering enterprise. It involved currency manipulation and the illicit movement of funds among banks to conceal the sources of the funds and the end recipients. Cash deposits were commonly not kept in cooperating banks in Lebanon overnight so that there would be no record of the deposit of the funds.

Cash was moved around between the exchange houses. The exchange houses' sole business model was in the acceptance of deposits and re-deposits of bulk cash, often from other banks. The funds are finally deposited into the exchange houses' individual accounts held at the banks. Even more revealing was a description of in-house transfers of funds into client accounts so that no record of the deposit into the clients' accounts would exist. This scheme would serve to conceal the massive amounts of cash and help to avoid scrutiny of the clients' businesses.

The exchange houses were handling cash from Africa for the car dealers and the transfer of those funds on to the US accounts. Thus, answering one of TFOS' key questions, and corroborated much of what we already knew and had been made public.

By this time Joumaa had been indicted for drug trafficking and had been sanctioned, along with his business, New Line Exchange. That had also been described in media accounts. Ayash had handled approximately $100 million for Joumaa. Joumaa had been approached by another individual in Lebanon to move "several hundred million" into the US. He had not consummated that deal as of yet.

We confirmed that Ali Kharroubi and Kassem Rmeiti had formed a partnership in Africa, as a way for Kharroubi to circumvent the sanctions already placed upon him and the various Ellissa holdings. Bingo. This new information would give John new probable cause for additional sanctions against Kharroubi and Rmeiti. These eventual sanctions again garnered significant publicity. Especially when the exchange owners filed suit against the US government to have themselves taken off of the sanctions listings.

Finally, we dug up a nugget that would later assist a DEA agent in Providence, Road Island, Dave Carnevale, in having OFAC designate the Abu Merhi shipping line for involvement in the Hizballah trade-based money laundering. I would later spend many hours on the phone with Dave helping him in my own small way in his effort against Abu Merhi. I guess Dave and I bonded as only old school street agents could. We saw eye to eye on the whole effort and knew the value of interagency partnership. Add another guy to coalition of the willing. Dave retired shortly after I did.

The Central Bank is the government entity that controlled LCB and other banks. A Central Bank employee had been directed to move up to $ 1 million at a time to LCB. The money was transferred around the world to Kuwait, the United Arab Emirates, and other countries via US based banks, and then back to LCB. Sounds like Hizballah-initiated money laundering to me. More sanctions to come. A great deal of this information was later included in additional sanctions packages and released in public press releases by the Treasury Department. Anything considered classified was not included in this telling.

We also determined that the Middle East and Africa Bank, controlled by Mohammed Bazzi, the subject of numerous news stories, was completely controlled by Hizballah. We were all already aware that MEAB was a key bank in the transfer of funds ending up in the accounts of the US based used car dealers. We confirmed Kharroubi's continued business activities in Africa. Kharroubi was at that time petitioning the Treasury to have him removed from the sanctions list. This was publicly available information. Kharroubi had sold his business interest to Rmeity for $1.5 million but actually kept his true share under the table.

We also identified several other Hizballah affiliated businessmen in Lebanon and Africa, and their business interests. The Beirut airport was being controlled by Hizballah.

It rained the whole time we were in Rome, but John, Assad and I got out and tried to catch the main attractions in Rome before we returned home. I think for John and me the Vatican was the most important stop. We're both Catholic.

XVI.

Unfinished Business

As had been the case throughout the Hizballah TBML effort, we were all insanely multi-tasking. The bureau agents who were still fighting the good fight were balancing their local "car cases" with trying to aid the broad international effort against the flow of Hizballah funds from Africa to Lebanon to the US and back again. We had taken out many of the financial institutions funneling the money throughout the world, and a number of the businessmen behind the criminal enterprise. Hizballah had such a historical grip on the financial sector of the Lebanese economy, it was like playing Whack-a-mole in trying to prevent a slew of new exchange houses from popping up and preventing the sanctioned businessmen from simply investing into a new house as a silent partner and continue laundering funds. Hizballah's business empire had a lot of money to move around, and it was not going to stop.

The 800-pound gorilla in the room was Shia Lebanese businessman operating in Africa, with close ties to Hizballah leadership, Mohammed Bazzi. Trying to police the banking system in Lebanon, or the few Lebanese-based banks in Europe or Africa was a herculean effort. Hizballah's infiltration of and control of these banks, both by inserting its own sympathizers or members into these institutions and its ability to threaten and intimidate others, made it all the more difficult for us to keep up. What we were able to do at least in the short term was to deny them access to the US banking system. The USbased used auto dealers who had been receiving funds via this system had to find other banks in the US in order to receive their proceeds from the sale of the cars overseas. They also knew by now federal law enforcement was digging heavily into their activities. One solution was for a dealer to partner with unrelated businesses and use their bank accounts to receive money from overseas. The one catch to that was that funds still had to make their way into their personal accounts.

I had made a concerted effort to identify and subpoena the bank accounts held by my subjects. Analyzing the accounts at least partially fell to several Financial Analysts in my office. The sheer volume of accounts held by each individual auto dealer was mind boggling. Over 100 accounts held by only about five of my subjects. The accounts were all fed by LCB, Ayash, Rmeity, Ellissa, and others.

Every federal agency, both law enforcement and intelligence, had a bead on Bazzi. He became "enemy number one", with each agency focusing on him for different reasons--suspected drug trafficking, money laundering, support of a terrorist organization, or operation of a banking institution in violation of various laws and sanctions.

In May 2018, according to a US Treasury press release, OFAC designated "Hizballah financier Mohammed Ibrahim Bazzi and Hizballah's representative to Iran, Abdallah Safi-Al-Din as specially designated Global Terrorists", along with five companies owned by Bazzi located in Europe, West Africa, and the Middle East. These companies were linked to the Central Bank of Iran which was "complicit in facilitating the IRGC-Quds Force", headed by Major General Qassem Soleimani, "in accessing hundreds of millions of dollars in US currency". The press release linked Bazzi to Ayman Joumaa, who is still at large. "Bazzi and Safi-Al-Din worked to expand banking access between Iran and Lebanon". The press release revealed that Bazzi, whose businesses spanned Belgium, West Africa, Lebanon and Iraq, "maintains ties to Hizballah financiers Adham Tabaja, and Ali Youssef Charara, whom OFAC had designated in 2015 and 2016. These final actions came after I left the bureau as a special agent. I returned to the bureau six weeks after retirement as a CENTCOM and then SOCOM liaison to continue to pursue Hizballah as a RICO case. That lasted five more years. The entire government effort seems to have faded out, especially from the bureau's perspective. This is partially due to the lack of effective prosecution or interest in the prosecution of any additional used car exporters. The tepid sentences given out by US District Court Judges everywhere was maybe the last straw.

XVII.

A Parting Shot

The last significant subject targeted was initiated by CHS information starting in the FBI's Richmond Division, coupled with early reporting by our friend Rami. Rami had identified Haithem Rafiq "Sam" Ghanem, a Lebanese Druze auto exporter in Springfield, Virginia, and the owner of Washington Movers. Strangely, we had developed some information regarding Washington Movers' possible fraudulent activities as early as around 2003.

Rami had provided information linking Ghanem to the export and money laundering scheme and to several of the subjects we had been targeting. Ghanem was also linked to the owners of a Lebanese restaurant in Alexandria, located just several blocks from the US Attorney's office. The owner of that restaurant had been identified by Rami, and then later confirmed by Yusuf, to be involved in money laundering and drug trafficking.

Ghanem was reputed to be involved in arms trafficking to Lebanon, using his freight forwarding business to smuggle gun secreted inside of vehicles being shipped from the port of Baltimore to the Port of Beirut.

The Richmond agent, Bill V. was a relatively new bureau agent but had prior federal experience, so he was wise beyond his years. He was apparently gaining a reputation as a solid "street agent" when we partnered up on what became the Ghanem operation, eventually involving three field divisions, Commerce, and HSI. Bill was handling a reliable CHS in Richmond who had become acquainted with several Lebanese military personnel who were training at Fort Lee in Virginia. Eventually conversations between them turned to the general availability of firearms for purchase, and then to the possibility of their obtaining guns with the assistance of the CHS. After a while they admitted the guns would be smuggled to Lebanon through a contact in Northern Virginia. Eventually they also revealed the guns would be provided to Hizballah in Lebanon.

The Lebanese soldiers informed the CHS they would be returning not Lebanon shortly, and before they left, they would introduce the guy who would be handling the shipments of guns to Lebanon. The meeting took place at the Lebanese restaurant in Alexandria. Bill and another squad mate, Steve C. and a surveillance team from Richmond, met me at a hotel in Oldtown Alexandria. The CHS was in a room being wired up for the meet with the Lebanese soldiers and their contact. The source headed over to the restaurant, while Bill, Steve and I drove over to a spot across the street to get eyes on the meeting.

The restaurant was clearly a poplar place and was very busy. Cars were parked all over the place and up and down the street. Many were "cruising" the parking lot. That made it difficult for the surveillance teams to find safe perches to observe the meeting. Our spot turned out to be a pretty good perch. We had eyes on the front entrance and were able to observe the CHS enter the building. As happens sometimes, both agents were actually good company.

The meeting concluded after about 90 minutes and the CHS exited the restaurant and met us back at the hotel. The contact was introduced as the owner of a freight forwarding company named Sam Ghanem. We already had him on our radar. This was a lucky turn of events.

We had a meeting down in Richmond a few weeks later to discuss a plan to go forward with possibly setting up a smuggling deal with Ghanem. The CHS kept in contact with Ghanem while we ran the hypothetical operation up the chain. Then the territorial issues began to raise their ugly heads. Richmond management decided the case would have no venue in the Richmond division, because the target, Ghanem, resided in Springfield, WFO's territory, and his business, to make things even more complicated, was located in the Baltimore area. The logical move would be to transfer the case to WFO. At this time, I had not yet moved off of Reid's squad, so of course he refused to take the case, with no legitimate explanation other than "give it to Baltimore". I guessed he just didn't want any more work on the squad, especially if came from me.

The case was transferred to Baltimore division, and the case was assigned to Michael Fregeau. The case languished for months, until during a briefing with Rami, he reminded me he had at one time was acquainted with Ghanem. Rami was, however, not on good terms with Ghanem. We had information that employees of Ghanem's had to quit their job after several weeks because, not unexpectedly, Ghanem would not pay them their salary. I guess Ghanem believed in slave labor.

Rami did express a willingness to approach Ghanem with a business proposal on our behalf. Rami would offer to begin shipping cars to Beirut through Ghanem. Ghanem would see a business opportunity to make money from the fees charged to ship those cars. We would carefully then test him out to assist Rami in a less risky venture, that of smuggling some cash in a car, and eventually moving up to a gun smuggling shipment if Ghanem offered or was willing to do so.

I contacted Michael in Baltimore and we partnered up. We were also at this point still dealing with the fallout from the Mrad case. Several family members were making threats. As I described earlier, those same family members had attended Mrad's sentencing and had pursued Rich and I out of the courtroom screaming at us "aib aleki" in Arabic, meaning shame "on you". We certainly felt no shame.

So, Rami was now the star of the show. My last show. He contacted Ghanem and set up a meeting at Ghanem's house in Springfield. We met in the parking lot of the Starbucks across the street from the Springfield

Mall, and wired him up. The meeting went well, and we planned to purchase one cheap car and conduct a test shipment to a contact in Beirut.

The shipment went as planned. Time to up the ante. Rami met with Ghanem again in the evening a few weeks later. This time he inquired if Ghanem would be willing to help Rami move some cash to Lebanon. We already had demonstrated Ghanem's predisposition to smuggle guns to Hizballah based on the meetings with the Richmond CHS, so we were not steering toward any entrapment at this point, but we had to be careful.

In October 2013, we again met Rami at the huge parking garage next to the mall. Michael, Mike R. and several other Baltimore agents met us there and they placed the wire on Rami. Because the case would eventually be prosecuted in Baltimore, they would be responsible for any evidence, including consensually recorded conversations. Rami again headed over to Ghanem's house and went inside. Ghanem agreed to help Rami secrete the money inside another car for shipment to Beirut, but with some trepidation. His hesitation tended more towards admonishing Rami to hide the money so it would not be easily found. They settled on Ghanem's suggestion as to where the bundles of "cash" would be hidden inside the vehicle. This would have to be done at Ghanem's shop in Maryland, near the port.

A few fays later, we followed Rami to the warehouse of Washington Movers located in District Heights, Maryland. Rami drove the car to be shipped into the warehouse, where they took apart the seat and secreted the bundles inside of the seat. Ghanem handled the rest. The car went to Beirut without a problem.

The next proposition would be the main event. In late November 2013 Rami again met with Ghanem at his house. This time Ghanem claimed he had been asked to obtain and ship "two pieces", meaning handguns, to Lebanon for an unnamed Lebanese government official. "He didn't follow through" because he would have had to put it in his name, and that was "too dangerous". This gave Rami the opportunity to bring up his interest in getting into the gun smuggling business. It was well known at the time that the market for guns—handguns in particular, was big business in Lebanon. Guns coming from the US were especially prized, everyone assuming they were of good quality and very available in numbers. Ghanem was at first hesitant, mostly because he was uncertain as to how he planned to secrete the weapons in a shipment going to Lebanon. Ghanem also knew that it was illegal to ship guns to Lebanon without a specific export license.

After a lengthy discussion, Ghanem came up with a plan that he felt comfortable with. He advised Rami to purchase several junk cars and loose car parts, and Ghanem would hide whatever guns Rami wanted to ship inside of the junk cars. The junk and guns would then be shoved into a metal shipping container and sealed, and then loaded onto a ship to Beirut. Ghanem would handle the shipping logistics, which was his business model anyway. Rami would need to pay Ghanem $3000, wired into his account, to pay for the service.

Ghanem decided since he was going ahead with the deal, he might as well send a few of his own, and asked Rami to pick up a few handguns for him as well to add to the shipment.

By this time ICE Homeland Security Investigations was brought into the case, and they volunteered to supply the firearms to be shipped. They would have to be inert, but real. HSI had a warehouse that stored just such items for use in undercover stings. The illicit shipment of guns to another country would be in violation multiple federal laws. HSI produced a cornucopia of weapons to be placed in the shipment: 10 handguns,10 semi-automatic AR-15 rifles, and 18 optic sights, none of which were legal for export. All of the weapons had been made inert in some fashion, and although appearing to be the real thing, could not fire.

In the first week of December 2013, I was attending a function for WFO firearms instructors. I got a call from Rami. Ghanem was preparing the shipping container. This initiated a flurry of calls to Michael, Rich and in turn, his calls to HSI. We were starting to scramble a bit. HSI had to go pick up the weapons. We had to decide how soon we could put this together. After about an hour or so, Rami called and sounded a bit dejected. Ghanem had postponed the deal because he wasn't ready for an unexplained reason. We would have to wait. That would not be the last postponement.

A week or so later, Rami called and gave the green light. All hands, on deck. We all made it to the District Heights area and met at a school parking lot. It was of course Saturday. In the middle of a blizzard. We could barely see out of our windshield as we arrived at the staging area. The snow was piling up, but we didn't mind, because we were about to do the fun stuff. Rami made a call over to Washington Movers. We waited for the go-ahead. It again did not come. It didn't come until a week later.

A few days later, Ghanem contacted Rami and informed him the junk cars and car parts were in the warehouse, and ready to be loaded into the container. On December 21, and on a much nicer, sunny day, Rami, supplied with a large duffel bag containing the handguns, rifles and optics, arrived at Washington Movers. He was wired up as usual. He and I maintained contact—a bit risky, but we had no other options if we wanted to know when the deal was completed and move in for the arrest.

Another squad mate and I were in a car down the street in view of the parking lot of the warehouse. Surveillance teams from Baltimore were scattered around the area. The Baltimore SWAT team was in reserve for the takedown. Now we had to wait. For the entire violation to be complete, Sam would have to finish hiding all of the weapons into the junk, and shove it all, using a forklift, into the container. Rami kept me informed as things progressed. The transmitter was not working well. Ghanem proceeded to wrap the items in cellophane and then started placing them into various car parts, such as the inside door panels and in and among engine parts.

Finally, it was done. Rami was starting to get anxious to leave. His car, parked in the warehouse parking lot, was blocked in by a large truck. The truck appeared to be making a delivery of some kind. He couldn't leave yet. We all held our breath. The SWAT team was chafing at the bit to hit the place. I didn't want Rami to be in the middle of this one. There were several rough looking guys working in the warehouse and the SWAT entry could be a bit tricky.

Finally, I could I could let my breath out. The blocking truck moved out from in front of Rami's car. Rami had told Sam to move the truck. Smart. Rami was out. The call went out on the radio, it was a go. The SWAT team hit the warehouse, and had to chase down a guy or two, but it went well. Those of on the perimeter had moved in to cover the various egress points. No one came barreling out of the back door, so we were done. The various teams moved into the parking lot across the street from the warehouse to observe the sweep of the interior. I knew a number of Baltimore agents from past operations and conferences and such, and from an undercover involving illegal technology transfers I had done years before for that office. And there was Dave Rodski. I won't say that was the highlight of my day, since this was a very successful operation involving many months and many moving parts, but it was a fine ending to see Dave.

Ghanem would go to trial in 2014. It would be a hung jury. There was some suspicion he had bribed a juror, but we will never know. It wasn't until May of 2015, after I had retired and returned to the bureau as a Department of Defense Liaison that Sam Ghanem was tried again in a five-day trial in Baltimore and this time convicted. In August of that year Ghanem was sentenced to 18 months incarceration, again another low sentence imposed by a US District Court Judge, for violation of the Arms Export Control Act and the International Traffic in Arms Regulations, committed in both the Eastern District of Virginia and the District of Maryland.

• • • • • • •

My career with the FBI was over at the end of 2014. The effort against the Hizballah criminal enterprise lived on, but as a shadow of the decade long interagency full court press that resulted in so many prosecutions and sanctions. It was mixed bag. Many of the major players like Ali Kharroubi and Mohammed Bazzi were temporarily taken off the playing field but have managed to find a way back by circumventing the sanctions in spite of the demise of LCB and the preeminent exchange houses. I was able to convict several Virginia-based auto dealers whom we proved, I believe, were supporting Hizballah. Philadelphia division knocked it out of the park, but I would leave it up to them to present their case to the public. I don't want to steal their thunder if they have any thunder left.

Other shipping businesses and freight forwarders were, along the way, subjected to Treasury sanctions. The domestic effort against the used auto exporters, clearly in league with Hizballah, are still in business. The bureau's efforts have lost steam. The bad guys have not. Some few younger agents in places like Detroit and Newark are still carrying the torch as far as I know, but are like Sisyfus, rolling a rock up a hill. Hizballah still operates in the US, and over the past few years, several Hizballah operators have been identified and arrested, and a few operations targeting the US have been neutralized. Two Hizballah operators of the secretive Islamic Jihad organization were arrested in New York; Ali Kourani and Samer Eldebek, for providing material support to Hizballah. Both had admitted to receiving military training in Lebanon and had attempted to funnel arms to Hizballah from the US to Lebanon. My very small part in that effort was to develop some interview questions for their debriefings. The case agents in those cases were certainly outstanding agents.

As for the remaining auto exporters in the DC area, I left behind reams of intelligence and several outstanding CHSs, but there seems to be no interest in pursuing them. These subjects continue to support Hizballah and most Likely Hamas, and who knows who else, using their businesses and bank accounts to launder funds for those organizations and engage in providing materiel clandestinely.

Hizballah still has lots of money to be invested and laundered. They are as an organization, extremely adept at making money through illicit activity such as the procurement and deployment of aerial drones, arms, missile technology, illegal drugs, sophisticated frauds, money laundering for profit, and counterfeiting, and finding ways to invest it. Hizballah thrives as a shadow government in Lebanon, maintains a well-equipped army, supported by and funded by the Iranian IRGC, has a massive arsenal of anywhere between 10,000 and 100,000 rockets and missiles, and operates an intelligence operation that spans the globe.

I tried to stay positive. As for the few folks who were unsupportive, risk averse, passive aggressive, or just asleep at the wheel, well, I had to highlight what oftentimes caused us to lose heart, and how we got the job done in spite of it all.

I give so much credit to the agents of FBI, DEA, Commerce OEE, and USSS, and especially the many people I've named here for hanging in there as long as we all did. I worked with some outstanding investigators over the year, a few who remain friends today, and some who I wish were still in my circle of friends. I hope if any lost ones actually read this book, that is, the ones I said positive things about, will reach out and reconnect. Mike and Rich are still in touch, although life always get in the way. I recently reconnected with Joe Simon, Mike Lipsner, Dave Rodski and more recently JD Taylor who just called me out of the blue. It was like we hadn't missed a beat. That was why I could include their full names in this book.

I hope the next generation of agents will be just plain stubborn in pursuing their bad guys. Stubbornness is the one thing that defines a good agent more than anything else, and it takes a willingness to get things done more often than not, "in spite of", as opposed to "because of". I wish for those agents that they can go forward Because Of.

Disclaimer

It really only took me about six months to write this book. Or yet perhaps it took 40 years, depending on how you look at it. Either way I consider it a labor of love. As a former FBI "employee", I was required to submit the original manuscript to the FBI's Prepublication Review Office. That was the most painful part of the whole process. It presented a pitched battle that lasted almost two years. In the end I had to appeal massive, arbitrary redactions, and in the end, I was able to restore a significant portion and maintain the integrity of the book. Small victories. Nevertheless, I am required to add the following caveat:

In accordance with my obligation as a former FBI employee and pursuant to my employment agreement, this book has undergone a prepublication review for the purpose of identifying classified information or prohibited disclosures, but it has not been reviewed for editorial content or accuracy. The FBI does not endorse or validate any information that I have described in this book. The opinions expressed in this book are mine and not those of the FBI or any other government agency. Enough said.

References

https://govinfo.library.edu/911/staff/911TerrTravch2.pdf

Washington Post: "A Willing Witness, a Painful Price", (Alrababah) May 5, 2002

Washington Post: "Grand Jury Indicts Man on ID Fraud Charges, (Alrababah) December 18, 2001

NJ Star Ledger: NJ Man Supplied Fake IDs to Hijackers

Washington Post: Powell Seeks Top Consular Officials Resignation, July 2002

Washington Post: Man Charged in ID Scam to Aid Hijackers, (Alrababah) 2/28/2002

FINDLAW (https://LP.FINDLAW.COM) UNITED STATES v. ABUELHAWA; United States Court of Appeals, Fourth Circuit. United States of America, Plaintiff-Appellee, v. Salman Khade Abuelhawa, Defendant-Appellant. No.07-4693. Decided April 25,2008.

9/11 Commission Report: Page 450, "thousands of interviews conducted by FBI"; page 230/ footnotes 74-78, page 523, multiple FBI interviews (FD302s) of Eyad Alrababah (6/10/2002, 10/10/2003, 11/06/2003); Ahmad Ahmad (10/04/2002), Derar Saleh (1/16/2003); Various FBI communications related to "Hijackers Timeline" serial 1859.

CNN.com/U.S.; "NJ Man charged with helping hijackers get IDs" (Abdel Rahman Omar Alfauru)

New York Daily News; "FBI-2 Aided Hijackers", (Arababah) 2/28/2002 Washington Post; "Witness Recounts Time with Hijackers" (Alrababah), May 7, 2002

Letter from US House of Representatives Committee on Homeland Security, Washington, DC to Secretary of Homeland Security and US Attorney General, regarding Daoud Chehazeh, Eyad Alrababah, and Anwar Awlaki (Wikipedia). October 25, 2011

Fox News on-line; "Exclusive: Syrian with ties to 9/11 hijackers still in US, virtually immune from deportation (Authors, Catherine Herridge, Pamela K. Brown), https://wwwfoxnews.com/ politics/ exclusivesyrian-with-tiesto-9-11)

9/11 Research Wiki, "Facts as stated in Chehazeh's removal hearing" New Herald News: "Jordanians Nabbed on Bank Fraud Rap", 7/18/1994

The Record-New Jersey: "Bakery Owners Ready for Trial in Check Scam", 2/18/1998

Washingtonian Magazine: "The Terrorists Next Door" (Harry Jaffe, author), January 2010

United States Attorney's Office, Eastern District of Virginia, WWW.JUSTICE.GOV/USOA/VAE/ press release; "Vienna Man Pleads Guilty to

Attempted Money Laundering" (Mufid Mark Mrad). July 31, 2012

Washington Examiner; "Fairfax man accused of trying to smuggle cash for terrorists", https://www.washingtonexaminer.com/fairfax, June 5, 2012

The Investigative Project on Terrorism; "Va. Man Charged With Smuggling Cash to Hizballah (Mrad); https://www.investigativeproject.org/3618/vaman-charged-), June 7, 2012

Washington Post: "FBI, 'Cash Cab' Investigators Tested D.C. Council Member" (Jim Graham, Ted Loza)

United States Attorney's Office Southern District of New York press release; "Manhattan US Attorney's Office Files Civil Money Laundering and Forfeiture Suit Seeking More Than $480 Million Dollars From Entities Including Lebanese Financial Institutions That Facilitated a Hizballah-Related Money Luandering Scheme"; (Lebanese Canadian Bank, Hassan Ayash Exchange, Ellissa Holdings, https://www.justice.gov/usao/nys December 14, 2011

US Treasury Public Affairs press release, "Treasury Identifies Kassem Rmeity and Company for Exchange and Halawi Holding SAL as Financial Institutions of "Primary Money Laundering Concern"; April 2013

USAO Southern District of New York press release; "Bronx Man and Michigan Man Arrested For Terrorist Activities on Behalf of Hizballah's Islamic Jihad Organization" (Ali Khourani, Samer

Eldebek), https://www.justice.gov/usaosdny/pr/bronx-man-); June 8, 2017

Index

A

Abdul Kamus, 128

Ahmed Ahmed, 50

Akram Saleh, 142

Al-Qaeda, 40, 60, 119, 120, 122, 151, 153, 161, 165

Ali Kharroubi, 170, 197, 214, 227

Amjad Hamed, 122, 150

Anwar Al-Awlaki, 29

ASAC (FBI Assistant Special Agent in Charge), 21, 22, 34, 64, 83, 133, 134, 166

AUSA (Assistant US Attorney-federal prosecutor), 37, 40, 50, 78, 79, 112, 113, 115, 146, 160, 202,

Ayash Exchange, 164, 169, 197, 213, 234

Ayman Joumaa, 163, 196, 197, 218

C

car parc, 169, 170, 213

CENTCOM (US Central Command), 180, 181, 205, 219

CHS (Confidential Human Source), 62, 68, 69, 70, 71, 72 73, 76, 78,. 80. 83, 84, 86, 87, 88, 89, 90, 91, 92, 93, 94, 95, 107, 109, 121, 159, 168, 175, 178, 179, 191, 192, 196, 201, 203, 221, 222, 224

D

Dar Al Hizra Mosque,

Daoud Chehazeh-Doaud Souliman, 24

DEA (Drug Enforcement Administration), 63, 71, 113, 119, 156, 161, 163, 165, 169, 170, 179, 181, 182, 184, 189, 190, 196, 197, 199, 212, 213, 214, 229

Department of Commerce BIS-OEE, 125, 156

Derar Saleh, 38 42, 43, 44, 46, 50, 57, 59, 233

DL-51, 12, 15, 16

drug trafficking, vii, 1, 64, 65, 71, 79. 84, 97, 106, 156, 161, 163, 182, 212, 214, 218, 221

DSS (Diplomatice Security Service-US State Department), 47, 48, 49, 59, 124, 126, 145, 146, 196

E

EDVA (Eastern District of Virginia), 40, 41, 50, 51, 61, 63, 79, 85, 147

Ellissa Exchange 164, 169, 197, 198

ERT (Evidence Response Team), vii, 8

Eyad Alrababah, 12, 16, 25, 36, 50, 233, 234

F

FD-302, 15, 124

FinCEN (US Treasury Financial Crimes Enforcement Network), 167, 196, 198, 211

FISA (foreign surveillance wiretap), 64, 95

Flight 77, 2, 3, 7, 8, 11, 12, 16, 21, 24, 59, 60, 61, 63

Fraud, 11, 12, 35, 45, 47, 48, 49, 52, 57, 61, 63, 71, 72, 74, 76, 122, 123, 124, 126, 139, 143, 144, 145, 146, 150, 164, 202, 233, 234

G

Garret Mountain Resident Agency/West Paterson NJ RA, vi, 71

George Noufal, 167, 170

H

Halawi Exchange, 156 164, 169, 197, 211, 213

Hamas (Palestinian terrorist organization), 78, 93, 119, 120, 121, 122, 123, 127, 133, 135, 151, 153, 154, 156, 159, 160, 161, 165, 168, 188, 189, 190, 209, 228

Hani Hanjour, 21, 25, 31, 50, 53, 54, 71, 78

Hizballah (Lebanese terrorist organization), 93, 119, 120, 122, 127, 128, 132, 133, 134, 135, 136, 138, 139, 146, 151, 153, 154, 155, 156, 157, 160, 161, 163, 165, 167, 168, 169, 170, 171, 172, 173, 139, 180, 181, 182, 183, 187, 188, 190, 191, 193, 194,

196, 197, 198, 199, 201, 202, 203, 209, 211, 212, 213, 214, 215, 217, 218, 219, 222, 224, 227, 228, 234, 235

I

Ibrahim Hamed, 138, 142, 150

ICE (Immigration and Customs Enforcement), 103, 143, 144, 145, 146, 159, 160, 179, 202, 225

INS-Immigration and Naturalization Service (See ICE), vi, 28, 29, 30, 35, 37, 39, 50, 52, 67, 72, 103

IRGC (Iranian Islamic Revolutionary Guard Corps), 120, 155, 163, 179 180, 183, 218, 228

Issam Khatib, 80, 81, 83, 84, 89, 93, 94

J

Jim Graham, 128, 209, 234, 241

Jordan, 23, 24, 44, 46, 47, 51, 58, 76, 89, 122, 127, 140, 141, 143, 172, 178, 191, 195, 205, 237

JTTF (FBI Joint Terrorism Task Force), 177, 179, 180, 184

K

Khalid M. A. Almidhar, 9

L

LCB (Lebanese Canadian Bank), 164, 167, 196, 197, 198, 214, 215, 218, 227

M

Mahmoud Al-Labadi, Majed M.GH.

Moqed, 9

Middle East, 28, 32, 45, 72, 123, 124, 140, 157, 169, 177, 178, 190, 191, 197, 205, 215, 218

Mohammed Abdelaziz, 140, 160

Mohammed Bazzi, 169, 170, 197, 215, 217, 227

Mohammed Said, 80, 81, 82, 83, 85, 89, 98, 106

money laundering, 35, 65, 71, 74, 76, 77, 79, 122, 140, 156, 159, 160, 161, 165, 171, 178, 180, 182, 184, 187, 196, 197, 198, 201, 202, 203, 206, 208m, 209, 212, 213, 214, 215, 218, 221, 228, 234, 235

Mufid "Mark" Mrad, 168 Musa Quidisat, 50

N

Nawaf Al-Hazmi, 9

O

OFAC (Treasury Office of Foreign Assets Control), 156, 167, 181, 184, 189, 196, 197, 211, 212, 214, 218

Omar Tawfiq Alfauru, 12, 18, 28

Operation Eagle Strike,

P

Passaic County Prosecutor's Office, vi, 29, 35, 67

Pentagon, 2, 3, 4, 5, 7, 8, 9, 137

PENTTBOM, 11, 35, 60, 91

R

Rafiq "Sam" Ghanem, 221

Rasmi Shannaq, 45, 46, 48, 49, 57, 58

RA (Resident Agency), vi, vii, 1, 13, 14, 21, 71

Rmeity Exchange, 164, 197, 211

S

SAC (Special Agent in Charge), 21, 34, 59, 133, 202

Said Abdelreheem, 93, 96, 99

Salem Al Hazmi, 9

Salman Abuelhawa, 82, 85, 90, 100

Sami Said, 51, 81, 82, 83, 97, 98, 157

Saudi, 23, 26, 35, 36, 40, 53, 54, 56, 58, 63, 90, 93, 120, 124, 140, 156, 158, 159, 160, 192

Skyline Butcher, 51, 61, 63, 79, 80, 84

Skyline Grill, 61, 80, 84

SOCOM (US Special Operations Command), 180, 181, 205, 219

SOG (Special Operations Group), 97

Southern District of New York, 39, 198, 234, 235

T

Ted Loza, 128, 234

The Secrets of 9/11, 25, 60

The Terrorists Next Door, iii, 117, 234

Title III (criminal wiretap authorization), 61

U

US Marshals Service, 21

US Secret Service, 156, 167, 179

US Supreme Court, 85, 100, 106

USAO (US Atorney's Office), 48, 51, 53, 131, 235

W

Washingtonian Magazine, 62, 117, 234

World Trade Center, 1, 9, 12, 71

Y

Yasmin Trading, 164, 169, 172